SHERLOCK HOLMES
AND A SCANDAL
IN BATAVIA

SHERLOCK HOLMES

AND A SCANDAL
IN BATAVIA

A deposition by John H. Watson, M.D.,
not to be published during the lifetime
of certain persons named herein.

But now published as edited by

Jeremy Kingston

ROBERT HALE · LONDON

© Jeremy Kingston 2015
First published in Great Britain 2015

ISBN 978-0-7198-1611-6

Robert Hale Limited
Clerkenwell House
Clerkenwell Green
London EC1R 0HT

www.halebooks.com

The right of Jeremy Kingston to be identified as author
of this work has been asserted by him in accordance with
the Copyright, Designs and Patents Act 1988

2 4 6 8 10 9 7 5 3

Typeset in Palatino
Printed in Great Britain by Berforts Information Press Ltd

For an Eastbourne beekeeper

CONTENTS

EDITOR'S FOREWORD

THIS REMARKABLE DOCUMENT came my way by the strangest chance.

On Monday 5 January 1981 my father, W.H. Kingston, bee-keeper and sometime Treasurer of the Crowborough (Sussex) Agricultural Society, answered a knock at his door. Outside stood a total stranger who introduced himself as a partner in a firm of solicitors practising in the town.

My father invited him into the house. The man entered but came no further than the hall, where he asked two questions. Did my father keep bees?

'I have done so for more than forty years,' came the reply.

'Are you about to retire to Eastbourne?'

'Yes.'

'Then this is for you,' said the stranger, handing him a packet wrapped in oilskin covers, and additionally enclosed within a transparent plastic bag through which could be seen a sheet of paper pinned to the oilskin and bearing, in faded ink, the inscription: 'For an Eastbourne beekeeper'.

'There must be some mistake,' said my father, relying upon cliché to help him out of an unexpected situation.

'No mistake,' said the solicitor, 'if you are an Eastbourne beekeeper.'

'Well, I will be,' agreed my father.

The solicitor nodded, and after the usual exchange of farewell courtesies departed into the night.

My father now wondered if he had been handed a bomb. Irish letter bombs were finding their way to a number of people at the time. Accordingly, he drew the packet out of the plastic bag with a pair of fire tongs. Further assisted by the poker and a dressing-table mirror, and keeping in the cover of his armchair, he endeavoured to unwrap the oilskin.

This proved more difficult than he expected and eventually he gave up the attempt and opened the packet with his bare hands. It contained eighty-two foolscap pages closely covered with writing in the hand of John H. Watson, M.D., the indefatigable chronicler of the work of Sherlock Holmes. A glance at the opening pages showed it to be a hitherto unrecorded adventure, set in the early years of the famous partnership.

Yet in one sense my father's fears were well grounded. The manuscript was a bombshell, and would have caused a very great scandal indeed had it been published during the lifetime of Queen Victoria.

Knowing my interest in the subject, my father handed over the manuscript to me and retired, like Sherlock Holmes before him, to keep bees in Eastbourne. This coincidence of course explains how my father happened to be given the packet. Dr Watson presumably sent the manuscript to Holmes in his Eastbourne retirement (where he wrote *The Practical Handbook of Bee Culture*, a book so rare that it has never appeared in a bookseller's catalogue), and by some oversight the inscription remained pinned to the packet. Solicitors are a pettifogging breed at the best of times and this particular Crowborough firm, which I shall not name, are said to pride themselves upon always adhering to the letter of their instructions. I could not persuade them to reveal how the manuscript came into their possession, but I suspect the hand of Sir Arthur Conan Doyle, the well-known doctor and novelist, who owned a house in Crowborough and set one of his Professor Challenger tales in the neighbourhood.

As to why the manuscript took so long to reach the light of day, this is easily answered. Behind the first sheet of paper was pinned a second, headed with the most famous address in the world, upon which Watson had written the names of five royal persons:

Helen, Duchess of Albany
Princess Alice of Albany
Prince Charles of Albany
Queen Emma of the Netherlands
Princess Wilhelmina of the Netherlands

As stated in the first page of the manuscript, Watson left instructions that his deposition was not to be made public until the death had occurred of all five of these eminent persons. Alongside the names sundry other hands have added the dates of their deaths. The last entry, written in green biro, is against the name of Princess Alice (Countess of Athlone), last surviving grandchild of Queen Victoria, who died a few weeks before her 98th birthday, on Saturday, 3 January 1981.

It is evident that at intervals over the years, the packet was inspected and the names of these royal persons crossed, so to speak, off the list. Upon the death of Princess Alice, the list was complete and the manuscript could at last make its way into the public domain.

Dr Watson can hardly have expected it to lie in the dark so long, even though Prince Charles of Albany was but a newly christened babe in arms when the narrative ends. Only the extraordinary longevity of his elder sister Alice kept *A Scandal in Batavia* unknown for nearly a century. Personal concerns of my own delayed its publication until now. Yet perhaps that delay is no bad thing. In spite of Watson's confident hopes for the contrary, the Irish troubles of the nineteenth century led to the Irish Troubles of the twentieth. Soviet Russia's fateful ambitions in

Afghanistan and elsewhere were prefigured in those of Tsarist Russia a century before. What Holmes discovered of a connection between Ireland, Russia and the United States might have agitated that movement towards Irish peace which now at last appears to have reached its objective.

Ingenious admirers of Holmes have often fished for the reality behind the false names Watson felt obliged to use for his published version of the cases. Who was the true King of Bohemia who strides dramatically into the first of the short stories? In *The Red-Headed League* why is the treasure coveted by John Clay, whose 'grandfather was a royal duke', to be reached from Saxe-Coburg Square, the name borne at the time by the British Royal Family? It is good to find the answers to such questions suggested here. On two occasions the published cases hint that Holmes rendered invaluable but unmentionable service to the reigning family of Holland. Here, perhaps, are the facts. Here, also, is the explanation for Watson's seeming uncertainty as to which part of his body was struck by a Jezail bullet at the fatal Battle of Maiwand. Was it the shoulder, as he records in *A Study in Scarlet*? Or, as he subsequently tells us, in his leg?

The style seems pretty much at Watson's usual level, and he makes the occasional chronological slip. During his flight with the Prince of Orange along the Kentish coast, the two of them go to sleep on a Saturday and wake up on a Monday. Twenty-four hours is only a modest warp in Watson's sense of time. In *The Sign of Four* Holmes opens a letter in July and a few hours later drives out into a foggy September night.

As for my own contribution to what follows, I must confess that I suggested the title. Watson gives no headings to his chapters but headings have been pencilled in, evidently after the publication of the first stories in the *Strand Magazine* since they refer punningly to them. I like to think that they were put there by Holmes himself. I have retained these examples of his humorous spirit and taken one for the title of the whole. Batavia, I am given to understand, is the old Roman name for the Netherlands.

Without more ado, explanation or comment, let the following passages now speak for themselves.

Jeremy Kingston

1

A SCANDAL IN BATAVIA

WHEN THESE PAGES come to be read by other eyes than mine, I shall have been dead many years. After compiling this memoir of the most distressing case that my friend Mr Sherlock Holmes was ever required to solve, I shall entrust the document to the safe-keeping of my lawyers with instructions that it is not to see the light of day until the five exalted persons who are most intimately affected by these tragic happenings shall all have crossed that bourn from which no mortal traveller returns. Since, as I write these words, the youngest is barely one year old, the twentieth century will be far advanced before the last is called to the fate which is that of all mankind.

It is therefore to readers yet unborn that I address these pages. Readers who inhabit, I dare to hope, an easier and a kindlier world, in which the desperate passions of the year 1884 must seem unimaginably remote. The vexed Irish Question will surely be a conflict of the past; Russian ambitions no longer threaten the security of Europe and the Dutch succession crisis lies forgotten by all save students of the history of that stout-hearted people.

For three years, I had been sharing rooms in Baker Street with my remarkable friend Mr Sherlock Holmes. During this time I was privileged to observe him conclude several cases that had exhausted the resources of Scotland Yard, or which were brought directly to him as the fame of his ability and successes continued to spread. I never tired of witnessing him apply his extraordinary mental processes to draw together facts that had seemed unconnected, and make clear what was previously entirely obscured.

Things in Baker Street had been quiet for several weeks. The case of O'Donnell, the Leitrim murderer, no longer agitated the press, and there had settled over the country one of those uneasy lulls that invariably presage storms to come. General Gordon had set off for Egypt with the hopes of the country pinned upon him. The world awaited news of the outcome, and till the news came, the world held its breath. Vivid sunsets night after night painted half the sky with crimson, acid green and murky orange. These unprecedented evening shows, outside the experience even of those who had witnessed the splendours of a Tropic night, were interpreted by many as the mute herald of approaching doom.[1]

Sherlock Holmes was engaged in pasting cuttings into his commonplace book, an occupation that he never commenced save in periods of enforced idleness, and which normally brought a sort of ease to his restless spirit. On this occasion, his labours were producing the very opposite effect. From where I sat beside the fire, turning over the pages of an old *Blackwood's*, I could hear a succession of muttered imprecations as he searched among the mass of papers for one that eluded him. At length, and greatly unlike himself, he let out a muffled oath, occasioned by an impatient gesture that had overturned the paste-pot.

'It calls for no great powers of deduction, Holmes,' I said, 'to guess that you are in want of a case.'

My observation was intended as a tribute to the intellectual system, which he had originated, and refined through years of patient study, but my clumsy choice of words brought down upon me a full measure of my friend's displeasure.

'You pay me a poor compliment to bracket the science of deduction with guesswork,' he remarked coldly. 'The two activities stand as far from each other as a Horace from a Hottentot. The mind that hazards a guess has noted the superficies of a problem, and through laziness or want of strict attention, or from innate feebleness of brain, does not extend its knowledge by precise analysis of the data. It jumps to a conclusion. You have watched me at work for long enough to know that this is not my method.'

'What of the inspired guess?' I interjected.

Holmes smiled sardonically. 'The inspired guess, as you poetically term it, is merely a longer jump than usual. A jump which, by the random workings of chance, happens to fall close enough to the truth to astonish the ignorant. But ask your inspired guesser to repeat his feat and he will fail, because he arrived at his conclusion athletically, if I may so put it, and not scientifically.'

'Be that as it may,' I replied. 'These are anxious times, and they trouble you as they do us.'

'I think not,' he said, walking to the window, where he stood looking out at the houses across the street. The upper windows formed a double rank of crimson rectangles, reflecting that most unnatural of winter sunsets, and chimney stacks the length of Baker Street were flushed with a murky red. When Holmes spoke again it was in a tone of the utmost seriousness. 'Last weekend the Turcomans submitted to the Russians at Merv. The British Government does not act, the press remains silent, the public are unmoved. But Merv brings the Russian bear only twelve days march from the heart of Afghanistan. The gateway to India is within his grasp.'[2]

'You take a pessimistic view of the prospect?' I inquired.

'I observe the facts,' he said sternly. 'In international affairs, as in the least domestic crimes, the majority of people fix their eyes upon the obvious features and blind themselves to everything else. Today it is all Egypt and the Soudan. Islam is resurgent, and the people gaze at Khartoum as though one faded soldier and his army could cure all.'

'My dear Holmes!' I protested. 'General Gordon carries with him the confidence of every Briton.'

'He does not carry mine,' Holmes answered shortly and pointed to the coloured lithograph of the General in that week's *Illustrated*. 'Even this official portrait, abominably tinted though it is, reveals a character that must assuredly bring the Soudan expedition to disaster. The jutting lower lip denotes a pugnacity ungoverned by the urges of reason. The engraver has endeavoured to soften the petulant lines beside the cheeks but he cannot remove them altogether, nor alter the mad and visionary gleam in the left eye. Here is a man who believes himself inspired by Providence alone. He will listen to no counsel but his own inner voice, and what that has to say to him will take his men to their deaths.'[3]

'But this is terrible, Holmes!' I cried. 'What can be done?'

For answer, he pulled the coloured print from the magazine and pinned it to the wall. 'Let us see how swiftly events confirm my deductions. This portrait shall remain here as a warning against men who are inspired by guesses and blind themselves to facts.[4] As to your anxiety for a case, you may not have to wait much longer. I hear a cab at the door.'

As he spoke there had come the sharp sound of horses' hooves and grating wheels against the kerb.

'Strange,' remarked Holmes. 'Our visitor appears reluctant to emerge.'

I joined him at the window in time to see the driver jump down from the brougham and step to our door, where he pulled the bell so violently that its clanging resounded through the house. Only when the boy had answered the door did there come any sign of movement within the brougham. A long and unnaturally pale face appeared at the window; its owner glanced to right and left, and after a further delay, during which he retired to the other side of the carriage, the door was abruptly flung open. Still no one emerged. For another minute, we waited until there happened to come an interval in the throng of passers-by, where-upon, and with the suddenness of a rabbit bolting from a trap to its hole, the figure of a man sprang from the interior of the cab, shot across the pavement and was inside the house before we had time to see more than a glimpse of him.

'Curiouser and curiouser,' said my friend. 'Our client may have need of your services, Watson, as well as mine. Enter.'

The man who entered our room was by no means old, some thirty-three at the outside, and yet the tall hat which he wore was of a style that had not been seen on the streets of London for a quarter of a century, very high and wider at the crown than at its curly brim. That part of the face visible above the astrakhan collar, which he kept turned up, was intensely pale and haggard, like that of a man whose every moment is dogged by some great fear. The only splashes of colour in that waxen countenance were the feverishly bright blue eyes and the long fair beard that strag-gled past the extremity of his chin.

'You had my note?' he asked, with a light nervous voice. He looked from one to the other of us, as if uncertain who to address.

'Pray take a seat,' said Holmes. 'This is my friend and col-league, Dr Watson, who is occasionally good enough to assist me. We received fewer communications today than usual and none that could lead us to expect so august a visitor.'

'Then it is as I feared,' muttered our strange visitor. 'He has followed me to London. He or one of his minions. And if he has stolen my note, he will know of my visit to you. Stand clear of the window, I beg you! He is a ruthless and a deadly shot.' He had put down his curious hat upon the side-table, but now he placed it upon his knees, gazing down at the crown as if for reassurance. 'Yet how did he suspect that I was leaving? I took every precau-tion necessary to keep my departure secret!'

'Not every precaution, evidently,' said Holmes drily.

'He is a wizard, and I am powerless to resist him!' cried our visitor with a gesture of despair.

'You may feel powerless but I do not,' said Holmes, leaning back in his chair, with his fingertips together, and gazing sideways into the fire. 'Have you not found the smoke of London injurious to the health of Java sparrows?'

'Indeed, I have,' he answered, 'for one of my birds died this morning.' Then, suddenly realizing the full import of Holmes's words, he gave a violent start, and looked up with fear and dismay upon his blanched face. 'You were told about me!' he cried. 'You have been bought by my enemies and ranged against me!'

He sprang from his chair and was halfway to the door when Holmes remarked, with a touch of asperity, 'I am bought by no man. My employers are Truth and Justice. They stand alone, as do I.'

An expression of terrible weariness passed across our visitor's features and he gazed at the floor with an air of indescribable melancholy. 'You are right. Truth is its own standard. Yet how can you have known of my sparrows?'

'Never mind,' said Holmes, taking his arm and persuading him to resume his seat. 'It is my business to know things. Perhaps I have trained myself to see what others overlook. If not, why should Your Royal Highness have come to consult me?'

Again, our visitor stared at Holmes with a startled look. He glanced apprehensively at the door through which he had entered, and then at the other doors of the room.

Holmes said immediately: 'I have no wish to be the cause of further alarm. Let me assure Your Royal Highness that it is by the powers of observation and deduction that I know I am addressing Alexander Willem Karel Hendrik Frederik of Orange-Nassau, Prince of Orange, heir to the king of Holland and the grand Duchy of Luxembourg.'

Our visitor was silent a moment, turning the stovepipe in his hands. 'You must understand,' he said finally, 'that my face is scarcely known even in my native country, where I have lived as a recluse for many years. If I should chance to walk the boulevards of The Hague, I would pass unrecognized. In this country not even my name is known to the great mass of the people. I have heard of your brilliance in solving the most baffling mysteries, and yet in recognizing me you have given birth to as great a mystery as the one which has brought me to you.'

Holmes smiled. 'Let us hope that the one proves to be as straightforward as the other.'

I had been taking a good look at our visitor, endeavouring, after the habit of my companion, to interpret the data presented by his dress and appearance. It was easy to recognize him as a person of delicacy and refinement, but beyond the features above noted, and his boots, which were fitted with high heels, I could discover nothing that might have enabled me to make the identification so boldly and correctly deduced by Sherlock Holmes.

Holmes gazed at the Prince with the compassionate air that came so naturally to him in the presence of someone in distress.

'It is not my practice,' said he, 'to trace the steps of my deductions. But so as to secure your confidence in the all-sufficiency of my methods, I draw your attention to the astrakhan collar and cuffs of your overcoat. The material is ideally suited for retaining hairs, dust, and in this instance, birdseed, which you are evidently in the habit of sprinkling upon your shoulder for your birds to feed there.'

'You are perfectly right, but how did you know that I had brought them with me to London?'

'The seeds are only lightly attached to the fibres of the wool. Last week's gales have abated, but even yesterday's milder winds would have dislodged them. Clearly, the birds have been fed today.'

'Admirably reasoned, but what of the species of bird?'

'The vinaceous breast-feather adhering to the inside of your right cuff has an iridescence characteristic of many pan-tropical birds. But the feet of scarcely a dozen are capable of leaving the narrowly spaced marks on the fingers of your gloves. Only the Java sparrow has the habit of disgorging the hard seed of the jujube berry, one of which is visible on the brim of your hat.'

'So it is. My nationality, then, and identity, in a population of five million Dutchmen?'

'The flakes of ash on your left cuff are from a Bolnak cigar, a cheap Dutch brand of torpedo shape that is never sold in this country. When it is smoked by a man of your evident financial standing, it suggests a dissatisfaction with the position he occupies in society. The pallor of your complexion indicates that you shun the open air, preferring the satisfactions and discipline of a life of study. Philosophy and ornithology are known to be Your Royal Highness's preferred pursuits.[5] These facts are quite sufficient to provide an accurate identification without the confirmation presented by the device of a lion rampant upon a field of billets which is engraved on your signet ring. After the spate of deaths that your house has had the misfortune to suffer in recent years, only two men are entitled to bear the arms of Orange-Nassau without quartering: the reigning King of Holland, who is in his sixties, and his third and only surviving son, the Prince of Orange.'

'Wonderful!' the Prince ejaculated. 'You have removed all my doubts and confirmed the best reports I have heard of your achievements. I even dare to hope that you can rid me of the horror that dogs my life, although I question whether, even in your experience, you have listened to a more cruel chain of events than that which has afflicted me.'

'You fill me with interest,' said Holmes. 'If you will kindly lay before me all the details, from the earliest particular, I will afterwards question you on those points where I require further elucidation.'

2

THE LAST ORANGE PIP

'I AM THE last representative,' Prince Alexander began 'of the ancient house of Orange. Princes of Orange have ruled in Holland for many centuries. A Prince of Orange became your King William III. A Prince of Orange fought alongside the Duke of Wellington at Waterloo. Until that time, there had never been kings in Holland, but that Prince of Orange became King William I. His son succeeded him as king, and was in turn succeeded by my father, King William III. My father was one of three sons, and himself had three sons. Now all of them are dead, brothers, cousins, uncles, save only the King my father and myself.'

The Prince paused in his narrative, as if the recollection of the next stage of his recital caused him pain.

'My father married, against the wishes of his parents, a princess of Wurtemberg, a positive angel, Mr Holmes, a woman of exceptional beauty and rare intelligence, holding liberal views of the best sort and a superb linguist. As the years passed, she grew ever more angelic, more dignified in the face of suffering, more beloved by the people, even as my father was becoming more intolerant and brutish. At length, my mother could no longer endure his profligacy and insults, and moved from the Royal

Palace into a residence of her own, within a wooded garden ringed with moats, about a mile outside The Hague.

'Seven years ago my mother died, and the House in the Wood, for that was its name, was shut up. My father made every public demonstration of grief at the funeral, but six years later he married a girl forty years younger than himself from the pettiest state in all Germany.[6] He was sixty-two, she barely twenty. Neither I nor my elder brother attended the wedding. Six months later, my brother was dead.'

'What year was this?' asked Holmes.

'June 1879.'

'Did you then become heir to the throne?'

'Yes.'

'Pray continue.'

'The following year, the new queen gave birth to a daughter, Wilhelmina. As is frequently the case when a girl is born to a man of advanced years, she became the apple of his eye. Every day she brings him a bunch of flowers. He kisses her upon the forehead and places the flowers on his desk.'

'A charming picture.'

'So I have been told.'

'You have not witnessed it?'

'I have seen neither the child nor her mother. I have not set eyes upon my father since his second marriage.'

'I understand perfectly.'

'There will be no more children of that marriage. When my father dies, I shall be King of Holland and Grand Duke of Luxembourg. Should I die unmarried, Princess Wilhelmina will become Queen. But though a woman can reign in Holland she cannot do so in Luxembourg, where the Salic Law prevails.[7] Should she ever become Queen, the Grand Duchy of Luxembourg will pass to a distant cousin of the house of Nassau. Not that my father would care a fig for that. Twenty years ago he tried to sell Luxembourg to the French, to clear his debts.'

'I remember the incident,' said Holmes. 'Prince Bismarck was opposed to the sale and threatened war.'

'It was fortunate for Holland and the cause of peace that he did so,' answered the Prince. 'A strong Germany is a strong Europe.'

Holmes nodded approvingly. 'There is Russian blood in Your Royal Highness's ancestry, yet you see clearly where the danger to Europe always lies. Why is it that you require my advice?'

'During the Easter festivities last year, a deputation of Luxemburgers urged me to take a wife in order to secure the continuation of the male line. Their visit threw my father into a towering rage. In his view, I inherited the nervous weakness of my mother and will soon be dead – although she lived to be sixty, Mr Holmes, and I am only thirty-three! He boasted of the excellent health which his daughter enjoys, and added that, should she suffer an accident, his sister in Weimar is still a vigorous woman with healthy and energetic sons and daughters. He attacked me in the vilest language for contemplating a marriage that was entirely unnecessary, although until the visit of the Luxemburgers I had never considered myself strong enough to contemplate the responsibility of matrimony.'

'How did the king convey these observations to you?'

'By letter.'

'Do you have the letter?'

'There were two. I destroyed them immediately.'

'That is a pity. Can you recall whether the handwriting reflected the passion of the contents?'

'My father did not write the letters himself.'

'That is interesting. Who wrote them?'

'He dictated them to one of his secretaries, and signed them with his initial: W.'

'Do you know this secretary?'

'I have nothing to do with what occurs at the Palace. I keep to my residence at the Kneuterdijk, which I leave as seldom as possible.'

'I understand. Did the letters put an end to your thoughts of marriage?'

'Quite the reverse. Almost at once fortune smiled upon me, with the arrival at The Hague of my cousin Elizabeth Sibylla von Saxe-Weimar. We had met as children, when I had not cared for her, but now she bravely called upon me and I discovered that she had grown into a beautiful young woman. Plumper than the accepted ideal of womanly perfection, but intelligent and vivacious, yet with a well-developed sense of dignity. Her request that I should escort her to the House in the Wood strangely touched me, and it became the place where we always met, and walked together in the shade of the great beech trees, where once *she* had walked.' The Prince was silent for a moment as he recalled the sufferings of his unhappy mother. 'Elsi was staying at her mother's residence, and we were obliged to meet secretly. She was required to attend functions at the palace, but whenever it was possible for her to escape, she would send a message to arrange our meeting for that evening.'

'Only in the evening?'

'She had recently recovered from the measles and preferred not to walk in the daylight. For the same reason, she wore tinted glasses against the glare. I did not mind. On our first walk I knew that she would make an agreeable wife and an admirable queen. When at last I declared my love for her, she was apprehensive of my father's opposition. I explained that he had married without his parents' consent, and it was only fitting that I should do the same. So it was agreed. Elsi was due to accompany the King and Queen on the annual ten-day state visit to Amsterdam. I wanted the matter settled by then. Accordingly, I arranged for the announcement of our engagement to be sent to the newspapers at midday on the day that we were to be married.[8] By the time that my father learned of the matter, Elsi and I would be husband and wife and on our way to Thuringia.'

'An ingenious plan,' said Holmes. 'I take it that something

went wrong.'

'The worst that could have happened. She vanished on the day of our wedding.'

'Ha!' said Holmes, sitting up his chair. 'You interest me extremely. Before the ceremony?'

'On the way to the church.'

'Oh, excellent!' cried Holmes.

'It was not excellent for me,' said the Prince reproachfully. 'Everything appeared to be running smoothly. My equerry Vanderbanck met Elsi and her attendant at a pre-arranged spot. Vanderbanck and I went on ahead, and the two women followed in a four-wheeler. We got to the church first, and when the four-wheeler drew up we waited for them to step out, but they never did, and when the cabman got down from his box and looked, there was no one there! The cabman said he could not imagine what had become of them, for he had seen them get in with his own eyes. Since that day, I have neither seen nor heard one word from her. Nor do I expect to do so, although I soon learned that she was alive and well and living in Weimar. The make-believe, for that is what it was, Mr Holmes, the walks in my mother's garden, the tender exchange of tokens, all had been prepared by my father to punish me for thinking of marriage.'[9]

'There is certainly evidence of a cruel charade.'

'I wrote letter after letter to Elsi but received no reply. I became very ill, and even when I had regained some of my former health I no longer had any wish to leave my house. Vanderbanck explained that one effect of the affair had been to publicly embarrass me. The announcement of the engagement had been published, you see, and Elsi's father issued a statement denying there was any truth in it.'

'How did the king react to the announcement?'

'He sent me another letter.'

'Was this also dictated to his secretary?'

'No. He wrote it himself.'

'Do you still have this letter?'

The Prince shook his head. 'I kept it no longer than I kept the others. To the best of my recollection, my father said that one man's jam is not the next man's honey. With a coarseness that is wholly typical of him, he added that each must plough his own furrow in the mud.'

'Did he sign this letter with his initial?'

'No. He signed his full name. But below his name he placed the word "Papa", which is how I addressed him when I was a child. You see that he wishes to treat me as a child today.'

'And your stepmother? Did she communicate with you after the incident?'

'It is interesting that you should ask this. She did write to me – and I would have preferred her to keep her silence than spoon out hypocritical effusions of sympathy.'

Holmes fixed his gaze upon the Prince until the Prince smiled sadly and turned his head away.

Holmes said, 'It seems to me that you have been very shame-fully treated.'

'Oh, the treatment achieved its purpose. I dismissed all thought of marriage from my mind. After all, it had only recently entered in there. If they had left matters at that, I would not have been forced to escape by night and make my way across four countries to you. Events have taken an altogether more sinister turn. It is not enough that I remain a bachelor. Now they must try to kill me! You may raise your eyebrows, Mr Holmes, but they have already killed poor Vanderbanck, and I believe that he died in mistake for me.'

Holmes had sat up in his chair at the news of the equerry's death. A steely look entered into his eye and his mouth set in a firm line. 'How did he die?' he asked.

'He was poisoned, Mr Holmes.'

'I know the symptoms of eighty-four separate poisons. What course did the poison take?'

The Prince shuddered. 'It was horrible. You must understand that I possess a large collection of rare birds. In the past few years, explorers in our East Indian colonies have discovered vast numbers of new and remarkable species, several of which have been sent to me and now occupy an honoured place in my aviaries. Three months ago, I received word that a previously unknown species of bristle-bird had been captured near Tapanuli[10] in North Sumatra and that a pair was being despatched to me. Last week the ship docked at Rotterdam, and on the following day the birds were delivered to my door. I realized at once that they had been shamefully neglected during the voyage. Bristle-birds feed exclusively upon berries and fruit, yet the dishes in their cages contained only seeds. The birds were in very poor health. The spiny wattles which give the bristle-bird its name were unusually scaly, and several appeared to be disintegrating.

'The training of birds requires patience on the part of the trainer, and good health and spirits from the bird. Clearly no training programme could be considered until my new arrivals had recovered, and so I concentrated my endeavours to that end. I fed them grapes and other pulpy fruits similar to those which flourish in their mountainous homeland. All to no avail. The birds were suffering from an affliction far more grievous than a deficiency in diet; they were mortally sick. In the hope of alleviating their sufferings I carefully took the hen from the cage and carried her to the window where I proceeded to examine her minutely.'

'What conclusion did you form?'

'I could arrive at none! The symptoms were beyond anything in my experience.'

'But possibly not in mine. Proceed.'

'At the base of all the feathers, the flesh supporting the quill was inflamed and covered with greenish pustules. At the base of the wing coverts, the inflammation had reached a more advanced stage, resulting in the loss of nearly all the primaries. The nails on both hind toes had become detached, and one dropped out as I placed the bird on the table. The iris was contracted.'

Sherlock Holmes broke in upon this catalogue of horrors. 'I trust that you wore a mask during this examination?'

'No, but I protected my hands with gloves.'

'You have been very fortunate.'

'Indeed I think so, as you may judge from the sequel. I had taken the examination as far as my knowledge extends when my equerry Vanderbanck entered the room. Jacob Vanderbanck had been a friend, and more than a friend, since we were students together at Leyden. His abrupt entry alarmed the bird who, confused in its attempts to escape, slid over the edge of the table and fell to the floor. It lay there as if dead until Vanderbanck bent over it, when the wretched creature lifted up its bill and pecked him beside the eye. Vanderbanck let out a terrible shriek and fled from the room. My servants tell me that he ran through the house and onto the street like a man pursued by all the demons in hell. Within the hour, a cab drove up and a certain Dr Ranke, expert in oriental diseases, asked if he might take the birds away with him. He explained that my unhappy friend had arrived at his house fainting with pain, and that unless he analyzed the bird's saliva he could not hope to treat his injury with the necessary expedition. I naturally consented, warning him to take the greatest care when handling them. It was no use. Both the birds soon died, and Vanderbanck expired yesterday.'

'Were his symptoms similar to those of the bird you examined?'

'To a surprising extent they seemed to echo them. I never saw my friend again but I was informed that his hair dropped out with alarming rapidity, and his teeth also. His face became leprous and his hands swelled to a monstrous size and were covered with the same greenish pustules. A crust formed around his mouth, the nails loosened – in short, all the extremities of his body decomposed into running ulcers.'[11]

I shuddered that so hideous a death should be visited upon a loyal servant, but Sherlock Holmes said casually, 'Did this Dr Ranke claim to have diagnosed the disease?'

The Prince shook his head. 'Nor could either of us identify it. I have searched through all my books of ornithology without success.'

'You will find nothing about it there. It is an alkaloid poison extracted from the sap of an Amazonian shrub. The natives make use of it to settle inter-tribal conflicts in the forests of northern Brazil and Curaçao, which is a Dutch possession, I believe.'

'But how could a South American poison infect an East Indian bird?'

'That is one of the problems which we have to solve. Your Royal Highness is fortunate to be alive. Poisons of this sort take effect when brought into contact with the mucous membrane, the eyes, nose, mouth, and so forth. Whoever planned this devilish crime undoubtedly knew that you follow the practice of many trainers of birds, and encourage them to press their beaks into the corners of your mouth.'

'Yes, of course,' said the Prince. 'It is the simplest trick. I will show you.'

He took up his hat and held it carefully upright in one hand while inserting the other into the interior and drawing out a small cylindrical cage, ingeniously made to fit into the swollen crown.

'Ah, your hat,' said Holmes with a smile. 'I have been hoping that you did not carry too many birds within it.'

'Just the one, now that her mate has died,' said the Prince, opening the door of the cage where a small bundle of brilliantly-coloured feathers could be seen in a corner.

'Drop it!' cried Holmes urgently, and with a sudden gesture he lunged forward and struck the birdcage from the Prince's hands. It fell to the floor, where it bounced and rolled across the room, scattering seeds and crimson feathers, to come to rest against the leg of Holmes's chair. The little inhabitant of the cage had been hurled from it and lay weakly fluttering on the carpet. Holmes seized the meat-safe from the sideboard, where it had been shielding our joint of beef, and dropped it over the struggling bird.

'What a fool I have been!' he cried. 'You say that one bird died this morning? Even a bird as small as this, and accustomed to the maritime climate of The Hague, would not expire with such rapidity upon exposure to the denser atmosphere of London. Pass me that copy of the *Daily News*, Watson. It will do to slide under this meat-safe. Excellent. Now I will put on my gloves and cautiously examine this poor creature. Do those patches of green at the base of the feathers strike you as familiar?'

'Oh, dear God!' exclaimed the Prince.

'I shall collect this bubble of saliva from the side of its bill for analysis, but there is no doubt in my mind that in your journey to England you have carried death in your hat. It will be a kindness to put this wight out of its misery.'

The Prince nodded. And with a swift blow from a knife Holmes severed the bird's neck.

'I never thought ...' the Prince murmured, nervously brushing the seeds from his collar. 'I never connected the death of the other Java sparrow this morning with that of the Tapanuli bristle-birds.'

'You are in greater peril even than I feared. Someone who knows your most intimate habits, watches your every move. Where are you staying?'

'At the Langham.'

'I could have wished for somewhere less open, but we may be able to use that to our advantage. Your Royal Highness, if your life is to be saved, you must do exactly as I say.'

'I place myself entirely in your hands.'

'You have undoubtedly been followed to this house and will undoubtedly be followed when you leave. For that reason it will be useless to change to another hotel today. When you return to the Langham you must take a different room. Insist that it is upon a different floor from the room where you slept last night. You will retain the first room but do not on any account enter it. Your enemies may have tampered with the contents of your luggage. What did you bring with you?'

'Two valises and a portmanteau.'

'Give orders that they are to remain in your present room. You can say that you propose to return there shortly and wish everything to be in its original place.'

'I understand.'

'On leaving here, buy new valises and whatever articles you require. At the hotel go straight to your new room and do not leave it. Allow no one to enter it. If a message is sent up to you do not open the door but insist that the message is passed under it. I will call upon you myself this evening.'

'You will need a password,' I interjected.

'I think not, Watson.'

'Then at least a special knock.' I rapped out the opening notes of a song popular at that time.

'Passwords and rhythmic knocks are easily overheard. Let me see. Ha. I have it!' He picked an orange from the sideboard and tossed it into the air. 'This fruit will serve our purpose. It is both simple and apt.'

'I cannot think of anything less practical,' I objected. 'Or do you intend to peel it, write a message upon the inside of the peel, and push it beneath the door?'

Sherlock Holmes chuckled. 'It is always a sign that things are looking up when you are waggish, Watson. No, we shall not need to carry the whole orange.'

He tore the fruit in half and squeezed out five orange pips.

'Here is our sign,' he told the Prince. 'I shall knock on your door and roll these pips beneath it, out of sight and hearing of anyone passing in the corridor. Only when you see those pips will you know that it is safe to unfasten the door.'

'I understand.'

'This is all that we can do for the present. I have a wire to send and then I will call you a cab. By tomorrow morning we shall be ready to act – but we have our web to weave, while theirs is woven already. Our first consideration must be to remove you to a place of safety. The second is to clear up the mystery, and identify your persecutor.'

'I thank you,' said the Prince, rising and taking up his hat. 'You have given me fresh life and hope. I shall certainly do as you advise.'

Holmes and I stood in the window recess as the cab bore our troubled visitor away down Baker Street.

'I hope that I have acted wisely in letting him go alone,' said Holmes.[12] 'I do not expect the enemy to attack him in the open street, but who is the enemy?'

'Can there be a father so vile,' I exclaimed, 'as to wish to visit so terrible a death upon his only surviving son!'

'These are high stakes, Watson. Thrones, grand duchies, palaces. Men will sin greatly, aye, and women too, to secure their hold upon them. What's this? Ah, I suspected as much. You see the elegant brougham that is approaching our door? It was waiting at the corner as our visitor departed. Since it is making no attempt to follow him, it must be we who are the object of interest.'

As the cab slowly passed the house I became aware of a pair of upturned moustaches against a sallow face peering from the windows of the cab. The cab did not stop, nor did the owner of the face look up us, but, having ascertained the number of the house, sank back out of sight.

'But this is terrible,' I said in a hushed voice, when the brougham had passed.

'Did the rather Germanic moustaches dismay you, Watson? Or was it the coat of arms upon the panel?'

'They were the *royal* arms, Holmes!' I cried. 'The lion and the unicorn were plainly visible.'

'We are indeed fortunate to have a street lamp so close to our door.'

'But how can a member of our own Royal Family be involved in so loathsome a business?'

'I confess I had not expected it,' said my friend, 'but we should be grateful, since it may give us our way into the case. Come. Let us discover which member of the Royal Family is so interested in the heir to the throne of Holland.'

3

THE ROYAL CORONET

'ONE OF OUR lawmakers has remarked,' said Holmes, 'that all knowledge has some use, except heraldry.[13] Hand me the latest *Almanack*, Watson, and we shall put his maxim to the test.'

He opened the scarlet-backed volume and turned the pages rapidly.

'To the man who reads their language, Watson, these leaping harts and lions, bars and bends and crosses, are the pictograms of a syllabary as precise as that used to dedicate the monuments of dynastic Egypt. A man's arms will generally descend unchanged to his son, will they not?'

'Certainly,' I replied.

'But what if he has more than one son? All members of an armorial house are entitled to bear arms, yet the laws of heraldry state that no man may bear the same arms as any other.'[14]

'Perhaps the charges could be reversed?' I suggested. 'Or the colours changed?'

'Both these practices have been employed in the past,' said Holmes. 'That is the origin of the double border around the Scottish lion. But the result of such bold changes is that, within a few generations, the coat of arms of the cadet branches alters beyond recognition. No, the science of heraldry demands clarity and exactness, and so the principles of differencing, or cadency, were evolved. Her Majesty, of course, as the head of her house, bears the royal arms undifferenced – that is to say, a shield quartered with the lions of England twice, the rampant lion of Scotland, and the Irish harp. But the arms on the door panel of the brougham included an additional shield, or inescutcheon in the centre.'

'Striped black and gold,' I answered, 'with a green branch curving across it.'

'Exactly. The Rautencranz or garland of rue, the arms of Saxe-Coburg borne by all Her Majesty's children in right of their father, the late Prince Consort, who was a prince of that duchy. Let me see. We have a choice of four royal sons and five living daughters – hum. We need not consider the daughters, because those who are married will have impaled their arms with those of their husbands, while the arms of Princess Beatrice, who is not yet married, are enclosed within a spinster's lozenge instead of a shield. This leaves us with the four princes – well, that is not so many. What else did you observe of the coat of arms on the panel?'

I shut my eyes and endeavoured to recall any remarkable details of the familiar shield. 'It could not be seen in its entirety,' I answered lamely. 'A splash of mud had been thrown up on the door.'

'Although we have had no rain for a week? Well, then, where was this fortuitous splash of mud?'

'Across the top of the shield, almost parallel with the upper edge.'

'Exactly parallel, I think, Watson, and limited to the width of the shield. What does that fact suggest to you?'

I shook my head.

'Possibly you observed certain protuberances beneath the splash – drips, you would perhaps term them?'

'You are right,' I agreed. 'Two, or maybe three, rectangular drips had formed below the smear.'

'Three,' said Holmes, 'and evenly spaced. What you have lightly dismissed as a splash of mud is nothing less than a label of difference, the heraldic indication that the bearer of the arms is not the head of his family. To distinguish further between several sons, individual charges are placed on the drips, or points as we will properly call them.'

'Red!' I cried, clapping my hand on the table. 'At the centre of each of the three points there was painted a red emblem. But too small for me to recognize it,' I finished.

'The colour may be sufficient for us,' Holmes said, smiling. 'The Prince of Wales, as the eldest son, bears no charge upon his label. It was not he who took so keen an interest in our front door.'

'I am thankful for it,' I said.

'Let us see what the *Almanack* tells us of Her Majesty's second son. Prince Alfred, Duke of Edinburgh, bears on his arms a label charged at the centre point with a cross gules, and on each of the other points an anchor azure. That is one red and two blue. We can eliminate the Duke of Edinburgh. The Duke of Connaught likewise bears a red cross at the centre, but the two outer charges are blue fleurs-de-lis. Red and blue again. You are sure that all three charges were red?'

'Quite certain.'

'Then our hopes are pinned, like those of the fabulist, upon the youngest son.' He turned a page and ran his finger lightly down the columns of close print. 'Royal arms ... inescutcheon for Saxony ... ha! "A label of three points charged at the centre point with a cross gules and on each of the others with a heart gules."' He looked up at me with a wry smile. 'Your three red devices, Watson. Our street door has been honoured with the attentive scrutiny of His Royal Highness Prince Leopold George Duncan Albert, Duke of Albany.'

'But why?' I expostulated.

38

'Well, let us see what else we can discover. Born in 1853 ... hum. Educated at Oxford ... ha. Tour of Canada and America ... quite so. Married – ah, my dear Watson, listen to this! – married in April 1882 to Princess Hélène of Waldeck-Pyrmont, youngest sister to the present Queen of Holland!' He shut the book with a slam. 'So much for the uselessness of heraldry, eh? What do you think of that?'

'I do not know what to think,' I confessed. 'Her Majesty's youngest son is by all accounts a studious and amiable prince. How he could stoop to further the criminal ambitions of his wife's family is past my comprehension.'

'Well, it may not be as bad as you suppose,' said my friend cheerfully. 'He may be on a watching brief. However, there is no doubt that the young[15] Prince of Orange is being closely watched, and some of those who do so plot his death. Come in.'

The boy entered with a telegram, which Holmes read with evident satisfaction.

'Capital,' he said. 'Watson, our paths must separate for a time. I must see to the safety and well-being of our illustrious client. Are you ready to assist me?'

'You know that I am always at your service,' I answered.

'I knew that I could rely upon you, although my request may strike you as an unusual one. A young acquaintance of mine is visiting London with her aunt, but would greatly prefer a personable fellow such as yourself to introduce her to the sights of our brave city. Her name is Mary Sutherland. She is from your part of the world. Can you meet her in the Burlington Arcade in one hour's time?'

I was more than put out to learn that the best use that Holmes could make of my services was to act as *chaperon* to a young Highland Mary. I am not averse to the charms of the fair sex, and the monkish tenor of our life in Baker Street had more than once prompted my thoughts to dwell wistfully upon the attractions of a very different sort of establishment. But wherever my soul in dreamier moments may have strayed, it was with a rude shock to be allotted the easeful rôle of warden, while my friend set off alone to pit himself against a dark and ruthless force emanating from the very throne-rooms of Europe.

I consented with as good a grace as I could muster, and at the appointed time made my way down Bond Street to the graceful line of arches that announced the entrance to the Burlington Arcade. It was the fashionable hour, and the pretty thoroughfare was thronged with an endless stream of shoppers intent upon purchasing the latest hats, fans, silks, and other necessities of life. Passing to and fro between the double line of bow windows came a succession of the most renowned beauties of England, and my step took on an added bounce as I sought the name of the tiny boutique which was to be the place of rendezvous.

Holmes had instructed me to enter the shop and ask to see a pair of French gloves. But no sooner had I pushed open the door when a young lady rose from a chair beside the counter and addressed me.

'Dr Watson, I presume? My name is Mary Sutherland. It is good of you to come.'

Miss Sutherland was a slim young lady, above the common height, with dark hair and eyes, and dressed in the most perfect taste. There was a simple elegance about her costume which betokened a due regard for fashion and yet a wise resistance to its wilder dictates. The dress was a dark coffee brown, trimmed with jet, with edgings of black braid, and she wore a small straw hat of the same brown hue, relieved by a feather of a brickish red. Her face had the clear, fresh beauty that spoke of a childhood passed far from the vanities and grime of city life, and there was a brightness in her dark and steadfast eye which, when she smiled, lit up the interior of the little shop like a diamond in a jewel-case.

'My friend, Mr Holmes,' she said, 'assured me that you would not fail him. I see that he was right to place his faith in you.'

She spoke with such fervour and directness of feeling that I instantly forgave my friend for not asking me to accompany him. I assured her that I would do my level best to make her stay in London a pleasant one, and asked her to name any special field in which her inclinations lay. She confessed with a blush, that, as a child, she had always longed to visit the lion-house in the Zoological Gardens, whereupon I declared that not another day should pass without her having satisfied her youthful desire. In a matter of moments we were in a cab bowling along in the direction of the Regent's Park.

Few other visitors were in the Gardens, for the afternoon, though sunny, was cold and the wind was returning to the east. There were some idlers who appeared to have nothing better to do than follow us around gawping at my companion. I shook my stick at the most persistent of them, a stocky young man with a white mark upon his forehead, whereupon the group moved away and pestered us no more.

In the lion-house, my fair companion studied the great tawny beasts with a close attention. The tiger's roar did not alarm her, and I found myself telling her of my experience in Afghanistan when a tiger cub invaded my tent at dead of night. Her reception of this anecdote encouraged me to recount others, and throughout the protracted and, I fear, egotistic discourse that followed, she listened with the most flattering attention. Her occasional questions were of a pertinence that I had never before encountered in a woman, and her grasp of military and even medical detail made the afternoon in her company one of the white days of my life, never to be forgotten.

The antics of the sea-lion and chimpanzee delighted her.[16] In the reptile-house, we gazed with fascinated awe at the assembled serpents, some motionless in slumber while others had coiled around the bare stump of a tree, whence they subjected the onlooker to the merciless stare of their cold, glittering eyes. The name of one particularly loathsome snake, the Sumatran *koa*, caught my attention, and I recalled the sensational story of poison and cruelty recounted by the Prince of Orange only a few hours before. If Holmes failed him, was he destined to finish his days like the small mouse lying still in a corner of the venomous creature's cage?

These thoughts recurred as I escorted Miss Sutherland to her hotel. 'At the Langham,' she had answered, when I asked her where she and her aunt were staying.

'That is strange,' I remarked, and as we approached the marble and bronze doorway of the hotel I glanced up at the soaring cliff-face of windows and cornices. One of its rooms sheltered the last scion of an ancient house. Would my friend succeed in exposing his assailants before the wave of their enmity broke over his temporary refuge?

I wished my charming new acquaintance a good night and strolled back to Baker Street, where I found Holmes in the position that I had left him, seated by the fire with his black pipe clamped to his teeth and the blue smoke curling in a wavering column to the ceiling.

He glanced at me sardonically as I took my accustomed place at the fireside. 'I trust that your afternoon was not too fatiguing?' he remarked.

'Miss Sutherland is a most accomplished young lady,' I replied, 'and I am most grateful to you for the task which you have laid upon me.'

'I am glad to hear it,' said he, and, turning his face, gazed once more into the glowing fire.

I saw little of Holmes during the next few days. He was out of the house before I descended for breakfast, and did not return until after I had retired to my room. The greater part of my time was passed in the company of Miss Sutherland, who proved to be an indefatigable explorer of London's lesser-known monuments. Not for her the resorts of fashion, but those treasures that are to be found where history lingers, in the aisles of City churches or quaint corners of the Inns of Court. She declined my suggestion that she might care for a drive in the Park.

'I know it is where all of Society goes to see and be seen,' she said. 'But I think I neither wish to scrutinize nor be the object of scrutiny. Unless you would especially care to go?' she added, smiling.

I assured her that the to-ing and fro-ing of duchesses meant nothing to me, and privately set down her decision as a further mark of her sobriety and good sense.

On our second afternoon we were joined by her aunt, Mrs Allindale, a dumpy, overdressed woman with an eczematous flush, whose chief topic of conversation was her nightly dreams. Otherwise we had the day to ourselves. Together we stood beneath the great dome which soars above the office roofs at the heart of the metropolis; together we paced the grim wards of the Tower, where the hopes and enterprises of so many have been ended on the axeman's block.

On the morning of 22 February I presented myself at the Langham Hotel as usual. My thoughts strayed over the pleasant prospect of the hours ahead, little suspecting that before the day was out I should be embarked upon a dangerous and horrifying adventure that would take me half across Europe and jar the destiny of nations.

I was accustomed to wait in the entrance hall, between the newspaper-stands and the theatre and railway ticket offices. Scarcely had I taken up my position there when, to my stupefaction, I saw the young man who had pestered us at the Zoo walking from a corridor towards me. There was no mistaking the short white scar above the left eye. He recognized me immediately, and, as he passed, cast me an impudent smile. For a moment, I stood there rigid, dumbfounded by this unexpected apparition. He must have followed Miss Sutherland to the hotel on that first day, with the purpose of forcing his attentions upon her. Then a more alarming possibility occurred to me. Suppose that it was I who had been followed, and, through my attachment to Miss Sutherland, was placing her at risk?

I scribbled her a note, urging her to remain in her room, or in the company of her aunt, until I communicated with her again, and returned rapidly to Baker Street.

Here another shock awaited me. I entered the sitting room to find a cabman's large cape flung over one of the chairs, and the cabman himself, a swarthy, red-faced man with ginger whiskers, standing at the table poring over a large street map.

'What the devil are you doing in this room?' I demanded.

The cabman stared insolently at me but said nothing until I moved to pick up the poker from the hearth. To my amazement a familiar voice issued from that ruddy countenance. 'Why, what brings you back so early from the Langham, Watson?'

'Holmes!' I cried. 'Can it be you?'

I was familiar with his prowess in the adoption of disguise, yet so skilfully had he increased the thickness of his neck and coloured his cheeks that it was only when I had stepped closer and taken a hard look that I could discern the lean, bird-like features of my friend beneath the coarse and weather-beaten face of a London jarvey.

'The Prince of Orange's adversary is aware that I have been consulted,' he explained briskly. 'This gives him the advantage for as long as the identity of his agents remains unknown to me. I can achieve nothing by pacing the streets as Sherlock Holmes. At this moment, therefore, Sherlock Holmes is in a private room at the British Museum studying the *Liber Apium*. A neglected work, but the foundation of British bee-farming.'

'But why go to the Museum,' I asked. 'Why not remain here?'

'This house is watched, front and back, and the Museum is ideal for my purpose. Since I was able to render the Keeper of Manuscripts a small service in the troublesome matter of the Wurzburg Codex, he has occasionally placed the facilities of the building at my disposal.[17] Its two principal entrances and seven minor ones allow me to use it as a convenient, if over-large, changing room. But what of your news?'

When I told him of the appearance of the young man with the scar his expression became grave.

'Our opponents grow audacious. The time approaches when we must act or they will play their hand. The man you speak of is one of the most ingenious and daring young criminals in Europe. His name is John Klee, or that is the name under which he passes at the moment. He is part English, part Canadian, and his mother – well, no matter who his mother was. Enough that his grandfather was a Royal Duke. You see that this case is taking us into high places.'

'John Klee,' said I. 'I do not recall the name.'[18]

'He takes a fresh one for each enterprise, as freely as a woman puts on new gloves. His aptitude for the criminal life showed itself at an early age. He is believed to have killed a groom in a fit of rage while still at Eton. He was expelled from Oxford before the end of his first year, afterwards studying physical and organic chemistry at the Universities of Paris and Marburg. He could have been a brilliant scientist, but laboratory life promised insufficient excitement. The bad blood that was his inheritance took the upper hand and he placed his gifts at the service of the highest bidder.

'Political allegiances mean nothing to him. The scar on his temple is the result of an acid burn, received three years ago while preparing the bomb that killed the Czar of Russia. Yet last year he was working for Soudekin, head of the Russian secret police.[19] He will chop and change as his taste for gold dictates, and he takes a sardonic pleasure in plotting against men he has formerly served. If we made him an offer to betray his present master for ten thousand pounds, he might do it. But that would place us in the power of an unscrupulous villain. If the solution of this case can put John Klee behind bars, the world will be an easier place to live in. Here is the boy with the post. Ha, what do you make of this, Watson?'

He tossed over an envelope with a familiar crest upon the back.

'It is from the Duke of Albany!' I cried.

'I confess that I had not foreseen this development. This is what he says in his letter:

"My dear Mr Sherlock Holmes, – I must speak to you upon a matter of the very deepest moment. I shall esteem it a great kindness if you call here at three o'clock in the afternoon. Should you have any other engagement at that time, I hope you will postpone it, as this is a matter of paramount importance. Yours faithfully,
                    ALBANY."

It is dated from Claremont House, written with a quill pen, and His Royal Highness has had the misfortune to get a smear of ink upon the outer side of his right little finger,' remarked Holmes, as he folded up the epistle.

'What can this mean?' I asked.

'It may be that they intend to strike this afternoon and need to ensure my absence. Well, we can take care of that. I think I shall be visiting Claremont House. It is two miles the other side of Esher, and I should be greatly obliged, Watson, if you would accompany me. Write a letter to Miss Sutherland saying that urgent business has called you out of town. I have some telegrams to send, after which I will drive you to the Museum in my cab. The Byzantine Physiologus is worth a glance. You will find it in the Manuscript Saloon, at the back of Case O. When Sherlock Holmes has joined you there, we can be on our way to Waterloo.'

4

THE NOVEL ENTREATY

IN THE TRAIN to Esher, Sherlock Holmes, once again in his own garb and style, sank into one of the profound silences that always indicated intense mental effort. I knew better than to interrupt him before the ratiocinative process had reached a conclusion. As the train carried us through the spreading suburbs of south London, I knew that his mind reviewed all the details of the case, estimating the degree of probability in each and inexorably becoming master of their underlying form.

We had reached the open countryside beyond Kingston when he gave a quick shrug and regarded me quizzically.

'I fear that I have taken you from Miss Sutherland,' he said. 'You will find it hard to forgive.'

'Nonsense,' I exclaimed. 'She is a most understanding woman.'

'And you a most understanding man. Well, we shall see. While you have been assisting me so gallantly, my own inquiries have been proceeding satisfactorily.'

'I am glad to hear it,' said I. 'How is the Prince of Orange?'

'He has fortunately long been accustomed to a sequestered existence and is bearing up well. Our signal of the five orange pips has worked excellently. Twice a day his rations are brought to him by a pageboy, who puts the tray down on the floor outside the Prince's door. This places him easily and naturally in a position to roll the pips beneath the door. I have satisfied myself that a man standing nine inches behind him would not observe him doing so.'

'But do you think it wise,' I asked, 'to entrust so responsible a task to a pageboy?'

'A different boy brings the tray each time.'

'Surely that can only increase the risk? Among so many there is bound to be one whose loyalty can be bought.'

Holmes smiled as he shook his head. 'I think the allegiance of this band is beyond question. One feature of the more luxurious kind of hotel is its prodigality in the matter of pageboys. Such numbers are employed in running errands or summoning cabs, or merely positioned against the wall as a sort of smirking statuette, that one or two more pass unnoticed. You remember the unofficial detective force of street Arabs which I employed in the Jefferson Hope case?'

'Your Baker Street Irregulars? What of them?'

'Remove their grubby clothes and insert them into a brass-buttoned suit, and you have the perfect means of communication with our royal prisoner.'

I could not help laughing at the brilliant simplicity of his scheme. 'I hope that you made the little ragamuffins clean themselves up beforehand,' I remarked.

'Yes,' he agreed, chuckling. 'Convincing them of the necessity of that was quite the hardest part of the exercise. As for our adversary, I have confirmed that he does not lack for funds. Two of his men are lodged at the Langham itself, and another two at establishments nearby. If he has not wealth of his own, he can call upon the riches of others.'

'Is the Duke of Albany a wealthy man?' I asked.

'He is a pauper compared with many princes. But Parliament grants him twenty-five thousand pounds a year. Claremont

House stands in five hundred acres of rich farmland and valuable timber. I daresay His Royal Highness has enough to rub along with, and perhaps a bob or two to spare.'

I was silent for a moment. 'Why do you suppose he wishes to see you,' I asked at last.

'I suppose nothing,' answered Holmes. 'It is the depth of folly to stitch a pattern before you have studied the design.'

'But I have heard you say that theorizing is the essence of the scientific method.'

'Theorizing is a different process absolutely,' he replied, 'for it does not rest upon supposition but on a substratum of facts. When the facts are few, the theories that accommodate them are numerous. As the facts accumulate, the number of permissible theories diminishes until at last only one remains that satisfies every detail. When that point is reached the case is done. And so, I see, is our journey. Those are the stands of the Sandown Park racecourse, and here is the station.'

We hired a trap at the inn, and were soon driving through the pleasant village of Esher. The coppices beyond the gardens were dusted with a brimstone-yellow mist of catkins, but those early harbingers of spring brought little relief to my mind. I dreaded the encounter that lay ahead, lest it might bring disclosures of shameful deeds in high places. The yellow haze seemed rather a sulphurous miasma drifting towards us from the smokes of hell.

We turned off the road between two neat lodging-houses and drove for some time through a heavily timbered park. Everything that we saw bore the sign of unstinted expenditure of great wealth. Four superb chestnut horses were being led back to the stable block where several carriages had been drawn out and polished to a mirror brightness. Above high garden walls of mellow brick jutted the glass and iron roofs of palm-houses and vineries. Suddenly my companion tapped me on the shoulder and pointed.

'Look there,' said he.

Ahead of us, at the highest point of a sharp eminence, stood a massive square mansion of grey brick with stone dressings. Four colossal columns rose above a steep flight of steps to support a heavy pediment bearing an imposing coat of arms.

'Claremont House,' said Holmes.[20]

The sun was already sinking and the western sky beyond the house was aflame with another of the terrible sunsets. Lurid bands of orange, murky greens and crimson suggested the banners of some infernal army massed upon the distant Surrey hills.

In silence we mounted the steps to the house, where a footman ushered us through a succession of magnificent halls to the Duke's sitting room. There was little time to take in the character of the room, with its many bookcases and displays of foreign guns, before the Duke joined us.

He was surprisingly small in stature, not more than five-foot six inches, and very slender. His movements were animated, and yet his general appearance gave an undue impression of age, for he had a slight forward stoop, and a little bend of the knees as he walked. His hair, too, was thin upon the top. He had a thoughtful, cultured face, high-nosed and pale, with something perhaps of petulance about the mouth, and with the steady, well-opened eye of a man whose pleasant lot it has ever been to command and be obeyed. His blond moustache and little beard were carefully waxed. As to his dress, it was careful to the point of foppishness, with high collar, lavender small-checked suit, the coat a double-breasted jacket, buttoned high, with a button-hole bouquet in the lapel; his necktie a polka-dotted maroon ornamented with a gold pin. He limped slightly and held in his right hand a slender cane, while on the fingers of both hands he wore a large number of gold rings.[21]

'Good day, Mr Holmes,' said the Duke, extending his hand, and turning a puzzled glance in my direction.

'Your Royal Highness,' said Holmes, bowing, 'may I introduce my friend and colleague, Dr Watson.'

'To be sure. Dr Watson,' the Duke remarked. 'You have been in Afghanistan, I perceive.'

'How on earth did Your Royal Highness know that?' I asked in astonishment.

'It is not so very difficult,' he explained, smiling. 'I saw you start just now upon seeing the Jezail rifle above the Winterhalter. It was presented to me by my medical attendant, Dr Roylott, who obtained it in India. It is not an Indian weapon, however, but village-made beyond the Khyber, and employed to deadly effect by the Afghans. You clearly recognized it for what it was, and the only other visitor to do so was General Roberts, who relieved Candahar in '80 and brought something of a dignified conclusion to that unhappy conflict. I saw your hand move impulsively towards your left shoulder, which I had already noticed that you hold stiffly. It is not so difficult to surmise that you have been wounded by a Jezail bullet, a misfortune that can only have occurred in Afghanistan.'[22]

'But this is most remarkable!' I exclaimed. The grim clouds of suspicion that for days had weighed upon my spirits melted before this demonstration of deductive skill so strangely akin to that which had been displayed by Sherlock Holmes on the afternoon of our first meeting. 'What do you say, Holmes?'

'I think His Royal Highness has talents above the ordinary,' said Holmes, gravely. 'I wonder that I can be of service to him.'

The smile faded from the young duke's face. He glanced down at the head of his stick, which for some time he had been playing with in a nervous fashion, and when he looked up there was an expression of something like entreaty in his eyes.

'You can help me,' he said earnestly, 'by helping another.' He seated himself and indicated with a wave of the hand that we should do the same. 'I will come directly to the point. I mean the Prince of Orange, heir to the throne of Holland. He was observed to call at your rooms last Monday. I have reason to believe that he travelled to England in the hope, indeed the expectation, that you would relieve his fears that a curse lies upon his ancient house.'

He cocked his head at Holmes, as though to invite the confirmation of his statement. When none came, he coloured slightly and continued. 'I will not inquire what passed between you, but I believe I may confidently suggest two alternatives. One, that you relieved his mind; the second, that you did not. If the first alternative were correct, however, the Prince would have felt able to return to his native country to take up again the duties of his exalted position. Since he has not done so – since he refuses to leave his hotel room and allows no one to enter it – I must draw one of two conclusions. Either, that you have failed: which is unthinkable.'

Sherlock Holmes allowed a thin smile to flicker around the corners of his mouth.

'Or else his case does not interest you.'

'Many cases call for my attention at the present time,' remarked Holmes.

'Then I ask you to drop them. I join my appeal to his. Take on this case, Mr Holmes. Give Prince Alexander the strength to return to Holland.'

'I wish that I could do so,' said Holmes, pushing out his lips and weaving his hands together in a most uncharacteristic manner. 'But the apicultural research on which I am currently engaged is absorbing all my energies. I would not be here now if Dr Watson had not observed Your Royal Highness's crest upon the envelope and, loyal friend and colleague that he is, crossed London to winkle me from my folios.'

'But surely your researches can wait a little,' the duke exclaimed. 'The British Museum will not go away.'

'True, very true,' Holmes murmured. 'I take it that Your Royal Highness has tried to communicate with the Prince of Orange?'

'Several times. On behalf of my wife, you understand, who, as you may know, is sister to the present Queen of Holland.'

'There has been consultation between your wife and her sister in this matter?'

'The Prince was traced to London by a loyal officer of the Dutch Crown, who duly reported his whereabouts to The Hague. Their Majesties are naturally anxious that no harm should befall the heir to the throne.'

'Naturally.'

'He has led a secluded life for so many years, Mr Holmes. Unaccustomed to the ways of the world, here, in a foreign land. You will know the perils that he runs.'

'The assassin's knife?' said Holmes.

'Why, no!'

'The bullet? The poison arrow?'

'Good heavens, nothing of that nature. We are living in the 1880s.'

'It was in 1881 that Czar Alexander of Russia was killed by a bomb thrown into his carriage. In that same fateful year President Garfield of the United States was shot down in Washington.'

'Such things may happen abroad,' observed the duke, sententiously, 'but we are in England. No, Mr Holmes, I mean that the hubbub of London, the strangeness, the very energy in our streets, must have a disturbing influence upon a man whose nature has always inclined him towards the morbid.'

Holmes shook his head and gave utterance to a long sigh. 'The affair is not without its appealing elements. My own researches, however....'

'Damn your researches, Sir!' cried the duke. He reached for his stick, and took a turn about the room before resuming, in a bitter tone. 'Can you imagine what it is like, Mr Holmes, to have been born an invalid? To have endured bad health from the day of your birth, with no hope of respite, no possibility of cure? I tell you that has been my lot. "Prince Leopold is not strong." "His Royal Highness's health will not permit." For thirty years I have been surrounded by watching eyes, hands outstretched to catch me lest I fall, or bruise myself against a table or a door. My recreations are restricted, my preferred choice of work is closed to me. And why is this? Because I am diseased.'

He had come to stand by my chair, and now brought his hand, with a sudden movement, down forcefully upon mine. Too late I saw the flash of steel in the air. The point of a paper-knife penetrated the skin of my left forefinger, just below the knuckle, and I gave a cry of pain. Holmes jumped to his feet, but too late to forestall the attack. The duke smiled thinly and gazed at the speck of blood upon the knife-blade.

'Sir, may I ask the meaning of this assault?' I gasped.

'A scientific experiment, Doctor,' he replied, pressing at the ruby drop with the tip of his finger. 'What physical change will now occur within this spot of blood?'

'Sir, really I must ask for an explanation....'

'It will coagulate,' said Holmes, quietly.'

'It will coagulate,' the duke repeated. 'And how is that process effected?'

Holmes turned to me. 'This is your field, Watson.'

I rubbed the cut on my hand irritably. 'Upon exposure to the air a meshwork of fibres will form, to entangle the corpuscles within its threads, forming the clot.'

'You can see that it has done so already. A useful property, you will agree, should you cut your skin with a razor, or strike your leg against a chair. If blood did not clot, Dr Watson, what would then happen? Would it pour from the wound like wine from a broken butt until there was no more!'

I stared at him in some alarm. A kind of fever seemed to have taken possession of him. A fire glittered in the depths of his pale eyes, his voice was unnaturally high, and his limbs trembled. I could see that Holmes was watching his every movement with the closest attention.

'I have cut you; you rub your hand, and think no more of it.

But if I were to cut my hand,' and here he twisted the point of the paper-knife upon the back of his thumb, 'I should have to summon Dr Roylott at once; the nurses would carry me to bed, and cover my hand with paste, and bandages, and more paste, and more bandages, but still the blood would flow. For hours, possibly. When I was eight years old a cut on my neck bled for three days. Do you understand me now?'

I gazed at him in a kind of awe. 'Your Royal Highness is haemophiliac.'

The duke bowed ironically. 'It is my mother's natal gift to her children.[23] Where it sprang from, we do not know, but the family is rotted with the disease, and we are spreading it throughout Europe with our marriages. One of my nephews has already bled to death. One day the same fate will be mine. I long to ride, shoot, campaign like my brothers, tumble whore – yes, gentlemen, live the normal active life of a healthy man, but I am denied this by my lymphatic blood. I asked to follow my brother-in-law[24] as Governor-General of Canada but no! oh, no! "His Royal Highness's health will not permit." Instead, I am President of the Windsor Tapestry Works. Well, perhaps it is not too late.' He smiled grimly. 'A man born to poor health can either fight his weakness, or surrender to it. I fight its power, and will always fight. But Alexander of Holland is the other side of the coin. He locks himself away with his animals and birds. A few trusted associates keep him company. Now that his closest friend is dead, I fear lest his wits become unhinged.'

Sherlock Holmes sat silent for some time, with his brows knitted and his eyes fixed upon the carpet.

'Before the Prince could be persuaded to return,' said he at length, 'it should be established what incident caused him to leave.'

'I understand that it was grief at the sudden death of his equerry, Vanderbanck.'

'Then a return to his residence in The Hague is likely to arouse poignant memories of that incident.'

'But he is a philosopher, Mr Holmes. The consolations of philosophy are true comforts – remind him of this. It is not every prince who is genuinely scholastic. Here at Claremont we do our best. Mr Ruskin is a friend. Sarah Bernhardt—'

'Your Royal Highness's interest in philosophical speculation is well-known,' said Holmes suavely. 'Prince Alexander led, as you have observed, a more secluded life. Why should the death of his equerry cause him to leave the country, for the first time in many years?'

'I understand they were deeply attached.'

'That may have played its part. Nothing is more calculated to agitate the soul of man than an interruption in the course of love. To pay court to someone who at the eleventh hour vanishes without a word inflicts a wound upon even the most robust suitor.'

At these words, the duke glanced about the room and gripped his stick in an agitated manner.

'Your Royal Highness must know,' Holmes remarked quietly, 'that I cannot render any assistance while significant facts are withheld from me. Perhaps if Her Royal Highness could be persuaded to join us?'

For the first time I observed that the door at the far end of the room stood slightly ajar. A moment passed, and then a young lady appeared in the doorway. She was a little below the middle height, with pretty features, although a little plump, beneath a mass of fine, golden hair.

'He is right, Leo,' she said, entering the room. 'Mr Holmes must be told.' Her serious expression was in keeping with the gravity of our business, but in the upturned corners of her mouth there was a certain indication that, upon happier occasions, the duke's young wife might be a spirited and merry companion.

'Gentlemen,' said the duke, after presenting us, 'you have heard Her Royal Highness's decision.'

'May I assure Your Royal Highnesses that it is a wise one,' said Holmes. Gone now was the hesitation of his earlier manner. 'This is perhaps the gravest and most alarming case that has ever been brought to my notice. Only swift, decisive action can prevent a tragic outcome. I have brought with me in this packet two photographs. I should like Her Royal Highness's opinion of them. Here is the first.'

He handed the duchess a small studio photograph, which she glanced at briefly.

'It is a photograph of my sister, Emma, the Queen of Holland,' she said. 'Though not a good one.'

'And this?'

The second photograph was the portrait of a conventionally pretty, dark-haired young woman with a triple row of pearls around her slender throat. As the duchess took the photograph from him and turned it round in her fingers, the colour drained from her face.

'Can you identify this lady?' Holmes repeated.

'It is Elsi,' she replied in a trembling voice. That is, Princess Elizabeth Sibylla of Saxe-Weimar.'

'Whose engagement to the Prince of Orange was announced last year?'

There was silence in the room as we waited for the young duchess to answer. But it was her husband who spoke for her. 'The very same,' he said. 'Though how the deuce you hit upon it beats me.'

'Perhaps it is my business to hit upon things,' observed Holmes, holding out his hand for the photograph.

'It is proper that you should know,' the duchess murmured. 'The matter has weighed upon my conscience, and upon my sister's, but I must confess that I do not see that it bears closely upon the present case.'

'I hope to show that the incident bears upon it directly,' my friend replied. 'Let me first run over the details of what occurred.

Here is the face of one charming young lady, with dark hair, whom the Prince of Orange has not seen for so many years that he retains only the vaguest recollection of her appearance. All that a second charming young lady would need to do is cover her hair.' Holmes whipped out a pencil and drew a number of thick black strokes across the photograph of the Queen of Holland, 'and obscure those keen eyes behind tinted glasses.' He added two shaded circles across the eye, 'And behave in a relaxed and happy manner – which must have come as welcome relief after the stodgy etiquette of the Dutch court. The result is a love-sick Prince.'

'It was begun as a joke,' murmured the duchess.

'I am glad to hear of it. But in time the joke became serious, upon the gentleman's part. He precipitated the crisis by insisting upon marriage. Aided by the egregious Vanderbanck, your sister conveniently vanishes away by the old trick of stepping in at one door of a four-wheeler, and out at the other. The letters the Prince wrote to the real Princess Elsi were returned with indignant denials. He was confirmed in his misogyny, and has remained unmarried.'

'That was an unforeseen consequence.'

'On the contrary. It was a consequence foreseen and prepared for, down to the last detail.'

'I do not know by whom!' replied the duchess with some heat. 'Certainly not by my sister. I have the letters which she addressed to me during the episode. They bubble with gaiety and happiness. You should know – perhaps you do know – that my sister's marriage to the King of Holland was not a love-match. How could it be! She a girl of one-and-twenty and he a drunkard of sixty-two. He is also a profligate, and a brute. Mamma arranged the match, and my sister acquiesced. But the circumstance in which she found herself placed was hardly one to be envied. Her curiosity was naturally aroused by the Prince who would not meet her, and whom no one permitted her to meet.

'The pretence enabled her to meet him. And he captivated her. Oh, yes, Mr Holmes, his seriousness, and his sensitivity, and his situation – all this moved her deeply. She confessed to me that she sincerely wished that she had been allowed to marry the son instead of the father. The termination of the episode greatly distressed her. Most wounding of all, the letter that she wrote to him – as Queen, you understand – was returned to her cut into pieces and marked unread.'

There were tears in the duchess' eyes, and a special gentleness in Holmes's voice when he spoke again, for he was always alert to the sensibilities of women who spoke freely and honestly to him.

'Your Royal Highness has been exceedingly helpful, and your statement has cleared up several points I wished to be certain about. I have only two further questions to put to you. Who conceived the plan that enabled your sister to meet the Prince?'

'Well, I cannot say. My sister has always enjoyed playing charades. She had quite a talent for it when we were children. The plan may have been hers from the start.'

'I see. My second question concerns the future of Luxembourg. In the event of the Prince of Orange dying without a male heir, a distant relative of the House will become the Grand Duke. May I ask you to give me his name?'

'Yes, of course. He is Duke Adolphe, the former reigning Duke of Nassau. His duchy was taken away from him by the victorious Prussians in '66, and since then he has lived in retirement in Vienna.'[25]

'Are you and your sister acquainted with him?'

'Certainly. We have known him all our lives. He is my uncle. Mamma, who was a Princess of Nassau, is his elder sister.'

'Thank you,' said Holmes.

5

THE PATIENT RESIDENT

'IT WAS PLAIN to me from the start,' said Sherlock Holmes as
we travelled back to London, 'that the disappearing bride of
the Prince of Orange was a straightforward case of personation.
The fact that she would only meet the Prince in the evenings,
and then preferred to walk in the diffused light of the wood-
lands, was suggestive. So were the tinted glasses, and the closely
covered hair. You will find a parallel case, if you consult my
index, in Andover in '77.[26] Familiar as is the idea, however, there
were one or two details which were new to me. The personation
had to be of a young lady of royal birth, who could be considered
a suitable match by the young man. Yet, no particular effort was
made to resemble the Princess Elsi. The Prince had not seen her
for many years, but in that case why go to the inconvenience of
a disguise at all? Evidently it was more important to conceal the
young actress' own features than to counterfeit those of another.'

'But the Prince of Orange had never met the Queen,' I
observed.

'There was always the possibility that he had studied her
picture in one of the journals. It is an unusual man who can
entirely suppress his curiosity concerning the object of his father's

remarriage. The Prince is an uncommon man, but he was devoted to his mother's memory, and would almost certainly wish to acquaint himself with the appearance of the woman who had succeeded her. Let that be as it may, it was a natural precaution for the conspirators to take. My suspicions had already centred upon Queen Emma when I learned that the Prince's meetings with his young affianced were linked absolutely with Court functions. You remember that the episode reached its bizarre climax because the King was about to leave The Hague on his official visit to Amsterdam. While the Queen was certainly expected to accompany him, there was no reason for the more remote members of the royal family to do so.'

'But why should the Queen have played so cruel a joke?' I asked.

'I do not think that we need to look further than the reason suggested by her sister, the Duchess of Albany. Curiosity, Watson. The mystery of the unknown prince in his tower. At the start, the adventure must have possessed the compelling allure of a fairy tale. When she discovered the strength of his feelings, she behaved foolishly, but I believe that, almost to the end, her actions were dictated by a reluctance to cause pain to a man of whom she had grown fond.'

'Yet she was ready to lend herself to that last heartless masquerade.'

'She may have had no choice. A family that is prepared to sacrifice a young girl in marriage to a man old enough to be her grandfather is unlikely to be moved by ordinary scruples. She had placed herself in a false position, and to extricate herself she did what she was told.'

'Then you think that it was some member of her ambitious family who devised this foul plot?'

'I do not say so, although it is undoubtedly they who will gain most if the Prince of Orange remains a bachelor.'

'What of poor Vanderbanck, whose terrible end was designed

for his master?'

'Poor Vanderbanck betrayed his master's trust in the most calculating and pitiless manner.'

'My dear Holmes!' I protested. 'They were childhood friends.'

'Childhood fiddlesticks! An innocent man, if he is bitten by a savage bird, washes the injured part in hot water and summons medical aid. Only a guilty heart will flee from the house as though the hounds of hell were upon his track. The wretched Vanderbanck knew full well that a deadly poison coursed through his veins. His only hope lay in reaching this Dr Ranke, who, I have little doubt, was also privy to the devilish plan. Well, Vanderbanck's speed did not save him, and he has paid the full price for his treachery.'

'It is a horrible retribution,' I said with a shudder.

'The evidence suggests that he was implicated in the personation plot as well. But that is not the end of it. There are elements in this case which lead us far beyond the fate of the Prince of Orange. At Claremont, this afternoon, I caught the scent for an instant. You observed that his Royal Highness was aware that I had been visiting the Museum?'

'How could he have known that?'

'Precisely. Did it also strike you as curious that he is particularly anxious that the Prince should return to Holland, while his wife, in whose name he professes to act, did not mention it at all.'

'You are right.'

'Furthermore, following His Royal Highness's passionate account of the frustrations consequent upon his ill-health, he remarked, to employ his own words, that perhaps it was not too late. What do you suppose provoked in him that flash of hope?'

'I cannot say. Could he have in mind some enterprise to make the Canadian appointment come his way?'

'It may well be. A number of different strands come together at Claremont House. There is much here that is uncertain. I do not remember when we last tackled a case so rich in possibilities.'

'Perhaps the "Speckled Band."'

'Perhaps that. And yet the Prince of Orange seems to me to be walking along a darker valley than did Miss Stoner. In the shadows, fantastic dangers dog his footsteps. How and where will they strike next?'

We were not destined to wait long for an answer. As we alighted from our cab in Baker Street, a ragged and grubby street Arab disengaged himself from the bustling evening throng and accompanied us up the steps to the door. It was the youthful leader of Holmes's auxiliary detective force, the Baker Street Irregulars.

'Ah, Wiggins,' said my friend. 'You have something to report?'

'Yes, Sir. There's been a hexplosion at the 'otel, and Roper's got hisself pinched.'

'That was very remiss of Roper. Was the explosion a loud one?'

'No, Sir, but it was on the same floor as the *certain person*.'

'Tut. You had better come upstairs. Watson, your anxiety to go at once to ascertain Miss Sutherland's safety is evident from your expression and does you credit. However, we shall be better advised to hear the remainder of what Wiggins has to tell us. Fortunately, no bomb appears to have discommoded our rooms. It is only the clock ticking upon the mantelpiece. Well, Wiggins?'

The urchin brought his boots smartly together in a comical imitation of military deportment.

'The hexplosion occurred at ten minutes past four, Sir.'

'That is nearly two hours ago. Well, it cannot be helped. Proceed.'

'I was waiting in the 'Ive when Armsworth come running up to tell me. Roper 'ad been on the *certain floor*, and was nabbed at the top of the stairs by the manager.'

'Is Roper injured?'

'Oh, no, Sir. The door was not even shook off its 'inges. And Roper won't say nuffink, except what I told all of 'em to say if took, that they was there on the hinstructions of Mister Sherlock

'Olmes.'

'That was well done. Armsworth did not wait to discover the extent of the damage? No, well, we shall learn that soon enough. I hear Lestrade's step upon the stair. Return to the Hive, and I will join you as soon as the Inspector is gone. The Hive, Watson, is the headquarters I have established for the Irregulars. It is in a mews behind the Langham. Good evening, Lestrade. Dr Watson and I have only just returned, and the fire is low, but you are welcome to a seat beside it.'

It was indeed the heavy-footed detective, who came bustling into the room, without a knock, and stood glaring at Holmes, with a sour expression in his beady eyes.

'I can't afford the time for fireside chats, Mr Holmes,' he snorted. 'I leave that to the amateurs like yourself. I have come straight from the Langham, where we have taken a boy who has no business to be there, but will say nothing except that he is there by your orders. If I'm not mistaken, that was another of them I passed on the stair. What's your game, Mr Holmes?'

'I have been out of town for much of the day,' Holmes replied, in the mildest of tones. 'Pray tell me what has occurred in my absence.'

'Now that won't do,' the detective snarled. 'You may be able to pull the wool over Toby Gregson's eyes, but you'll have to get up early in the day to run circles around Gwylim Lestrade.'

'It is true that I rise early,' murmured Holmes. 'But I hear that there has been a disturbance at the Langham. Did Mr Gosden, the manager, call you in?'

'He did not. And I don't mind telling you that he looked pretty sore when I walked into his office. "This was no Fenian explosion," he kept repeating. "There is no call to alarm the visitors." Scared stiff that I'd frighten them off to another hotel, d'you see. I wouldn't be surprised if somebody won't lose his position for reporting the matter to us instead of taking it to Mr Gosden. Between ourselves, Mr Holmes, there are some people at the Yard who have a bit of a bee in their bonnets where the Fenians are concerned. You and I know that all that business belongs in the past, but certain gentlemen won't have it so. They see Irish dynamite inside every parcel, and an armed Invincible lurking down every alley.[27] There are going to be some red faces when I tell them the explosion was no more than an unfortunate accident.'

The detective let out a cackle of laughter at the prospect of his rivals' discomfiture.

Holmes regarded him thoughtfully. 'Perhaps the Yard may take a more serious view of the matter than you suppose. Or do they encourage foreigners to conduct chemical experiments in their hotel suites?'

Lestrade's mouth fell open and he goggled at Holmes without, for a moment, managing to utter a sound. When he regained his voice, he slapped his hand upon the table and said, 'It seems to me that you know a sight more about this business than you should.'

'On the contrary,' replied Holmes coolly. 'I believe that I now know everything that I require. The suite in question was taken last Monday by a certain John Klee, described on his cards as a Doctor of Chemistry at the Universities of Paris and Marburg. Yesterday afternoon, he purchased from Garrett and Frere, of High Holborn, a consignment of chemical apparatus. Here is a list of the apparatus he obtained, together with a separate list of the chemicals that he ordered at the same time. You will observe that the apparatus consists of a retort, pipette, set of beakers, a tripod and stand with clamps, and a Bunsen burner.'

'Well, there's none of that left in one piece now,' said Lestrade. 'Smashed to smithereens – and several windows too. The gentleman was evidently preparing a chemistry lecture.'

'Do you think so?' said Holmes.

'You may depend upon it. Study the names of the forthcoming lecturers at the scientific institutions and you are sure to find Dr Klee's name amongst them. Paris, you say, and where else?'

'Marburg. It is an ancient seat of learning in the German province of Hesse-Nassau.'

'Ah – another foreign place. And his name is decidedly German.'

'Or Swiss,' suggested Holmes.

'I favour Germany, and for this reason: his description mentions a scar upon his forehead. That is almost certainly a duelling scar, caused in his student days.'

Holmes's face was inscrutable. 'I marvel at you, Lestrade.'

'That is the sort of clue that one must train oneself to look out for. The whole accident came about because, as a foreigner, he was unused to dealing with English chemical apparatus. He set up the retort upon the washstand, and lit the flame beneath. He must then have left the room, on some business or other, and while he was away, the liquid in the retort boiled dry, and exploded. He has not been seen since. Too embarrassed to show his face, if you ask my opinion. But when he does show up, Mr Gosden wants no publicity, and will not press charges. Therefore, so far as I am concerned, the matter is concluded. Except for the boy. Now, Mr Holmes, you cannot go around planting page boys where you fancy. What's it all about? Come clean.'

Holmes pressed his lips and took a moment before replying. 'My account of Klee's chemical purchases does not exhaust my information about him. But the remainder trespasses upon an area which I am not yet at liberty to divulge. However, I can tell you that a certain lady is also staying at the Langham, and that the boy whom I have introduced there enables me to communicate with her frequently but discreetly. I must go to make my peace with Mr Gosden, but when desperate matters are afoot, desperate measures must sometimes be taken.'

'I should have guessed there would be a woman in it somewhere,' said Lestrade, shaking his head and chuckling in a knowing fashion. 'Well, I wish that all my cases proved to be so simple. A woman in distress and a chemist rehearsing a lecture

– the world of the criminal investigator throws up strange bed-fellows.' He picked up his hat and started chuckling to himself again. '"This was no Fenian explosion." Oh, dear, oh, dear.'

'Of course it may be a coincidence,' Holmes remarked as the detective reached for the door, 'but the word "Klee" is pronounced "Clay" in German, where it means "shamrock", the creeping weed that has become the emblem of the Irish separatists. Good day, Lestrade.'

'Wait a moment,' said the ferrety detective, turning to Holmes and staring up at him, with a glitter in his little eyes. 'What is that supposed to mean? Is he a Fenian after all? Was he manufacturing dynamite in his room?'

'It would be a strange dynamite that is made without glycerine, without diatomite,' said Holmes.

'That is true. Of course it could not be. But for a moment you had me thinking.'

'Well, that would have been something achieved,' laughed Holmes, when Lestrade had departed. 'Did you ever have to listen to such a mish-mash of guesswork and conceit! It was as much as I could do to keep my countenance while he sketched his portrait of the duelling chemist. I confess that the challenge to pull the wool over his eyes was one that I could not resist. Yet I took care to say nothing that was not the truth. It is no business of mine if he believes that a man is likely to set up a chemical demonstration without bothering to purchase a test tube.'

'Were none listed among his purchases?'

'Only the items I have named.'

'Then what was he trying to do?'

'To create an explosion.'

'But you have said that there were not the necessary ingredients.'

'The chemical ingredients of dynamite were not present. Why construct a sledgehammer to open a nut? Sodium nitrite titrated with caustic soda will make a modest explosion with a sufficiently audible report. I shall be surprised if this was not the method employed by our resourceful chemist.'

'They are trying to frighten the Prince from the hotel!' I cried, in sudden comprehension.

'Exactly so. Once outside the protective hedge which I have set about him, the Prince is at the mercy of his enemies. They will spirit him out of the country, and back to the isolation of the Kneuterdijk, where his death can shortly afterwards be announced to an unastonished world. I have hedged him around so impenetrably that they were certain to resort to some desperate measure. I had merely to wait to see what form it would take. Yesterday afternoon Klee entered the premises of Garrett and Frere, and two minutes afterwards he was followed into the shop by a flustered laboratory assistant cursed with a stammer but gifted with remarkably good sight. A modest explosion was always the most likely eventuality, and Klee's scientific knowledge enabled him to calculate the proportions to a nicety.'

'Has the Prince left his room?' I asked.

'I warned him to be on his guard against just such a stratagem as this. You see now, Watson, why it was essential to lead the Prince's enemies to suppose that Sherlock Holmes was not interested in the case, and that the Prince was alone in London, friendless and unadvised. But I am concerned about the effect of the explosion upon Miss Sutherland, for her rooms are directly above the Prince's.'

'I did not know that! That is very alarming.'

'She and Mrs Allindale might prefer to move to another hotel. Claridge's would be suitable. What is your opinion?'

'I think it highly desirable that they should leave at once. If a first assault has failed to dislodge the Prince, his enemies are likely to attempt another.'

Holmes nodded. 'May I ask you to make the necessary arrangements, Watson. You have the art of inspiring the gentler sex with confidence, and I must remain here for the answer to a telegram, which I expect to bear crucially upon the case.'

'I shall be happy to go.'

'And yet there is the question of the boy Roper. Hum. It will be better if that business were disposed of first. Can I ask you to await the telegram while I proceed to the Langham?'

'You know that I am at your service, Holmes. Do you expect the telegram shortly?'

'Within half an hour.'

'If you wish, I can bring it with me to the Langham, for I would like to escort Miss Sutherland and her aunt to their new hotel.'

'An excellent proposal. Leave the wire for me under the name of Sigerson.' He darted into his room, and returned in a few moments wearing a dress suit of distinctly foreign cut and a gold breast-pin set with a large green stone. Across his arm he carried a heavy coat of dark blue cloth thickly lined with fur, which, when he had put it on, gave him the appearance of a continental virtuoso. With his lean, almost skeletal, and intense face, he lacked only the Stradivarius to pass as a living portrait of Paganini. 'I shall advise the so-good ladies to expect you shortly,' he said, in a rhythmic lilt which I recognized to be Norwegian. 'Good luck, Watson.'

With this conventional phrase of encouragement, which I had never before heard pass his lips, he was gone, and a moment later I heard him on the street, hailing a cab in the same remarkable accent, one of many in which he was a passed-master.

I am reckoned to be a man of sanguine temperament, by nature disposed to let the future open her secrets to me in her own due time, but in the half-hour that ensued, dragging past on leaden feet, my mind was assailed by the most terrifying alarms and fears. Holmes's revelation that Miss Sutherland's rooms lay above those of the beleaguered Prince had been a distinct shock to me. I burned to snatch her to safety, for further assaults must assuredly come. In every noise from the street I heard the roar of a new detonation and several times I strode to the door, moved by a sudden resolution to go at once to the hotel, whither the boy could follow me when the telegram came. But at each occasion my promise to Holmes held me back. I turned from the door and resumed my restless pacing, until at last I heard the blessed sound of the lad's step upon the stairs. I tore the telegram from his hand and bounded down to the street four steps at a time.

At the Langham I hastened to the writing room, where I enclosed the telegram in an envelope superscribed as Holmes had requested. Returning to the hall I heard my name called and, turning in the direction of the voice, observed the plump person of Mrs Allindale hobbling towards me through the crowd.

'You are here on the dot, Doctor,' she greeted me in her piercing voice, clutching my arm and bobbing her head so that the heavy plumes upon her bonnet kept up a continuous dance. 'Our departure is no surprise to me, I can assure you. My dreams last night relate to it exactly.'

'Remarkable,' said I. 'Has Miss Sutherland descended?'

'I was standing in a large room, not like this hall at all, but undoubtedly the entrance to a hotel because the people were moving up and down the steps all the time – and carrying their own luggage! You are not taking us to any place so far down the scale, I can be confident of that, can I not?'

'I understand that Claridge's employ sufficient servants to carry out that duty,' I answered.

'Claridge's? Well, that will do very nicely. One's sight of the future cannot be expected to be precise in every detail. It is a privilege to pierce the veil at all.'

She rattled on, glancing at the lift whenever the door was opened, and then looking away with a frown.

'I am afraid that Mary has not been well this evening,' she said, as loudly as before.

'What has happened to her?' I asked, in some anxiety.

'Oh, it is not serious, although of course it is uncomfortable while it persists. We drove in the Park this afternoon, and the wind brought on her neuralgia.'

'I did not know she was a sufferer.'

'Always when the wind is from the east, but she was insistent that we go there. Young girls become so riveted to the doings of society, do they not! I have given her valerian drops and made sure that she rested upon her bed in the dark.'

'Tincture of camphor is a surer remedy,' said I. 'I will procure her some. Dear me. I trust the motion of the cab will not be too distressing.'

'She is eager to leave. Tincture of camphor, well, now! When I was a girl we were made to chew roots of horseradish. I remember the taste to this day. Here is Mary.'

The door to the lift had opened and Miss Sutherland stepped out from it, wearing that same dark coffee-brown dress that she had worn upon the day that we met. I felt the blood rise to my face as I dared to interpret the sentiment that she wished to impart by this sign. Was it possible, then, that my own emotions were requited? I dared to hope so, and resolved to make my feelings known to her that very night.

In deference to the lateness of the hour, and the gathering chill of the evening, she wore over her dress a long coffee-coloured cape, and beneath her close-fitting hat with the demure red feather she had attached a dark veil, which covered the greater part of her face. She walked towards us, looking neither to right nor left, as though the very slightest sideways motion of her head would cause her pain.

'Don't try to talk, dear,' Mrs Allindale urged her, in her usual high pitch, as though the veil were impenetrable to sound as well as to light. 'The doctor has suggested a remedy of his own to relieve the pain.'

Miss Sutherland turned her head slowly in my direction and lowered it slightly, but at once she uttered a low moan and put a hand up to one side of her eyes.

'Take her arm, Doctor,' said her aunt. 'Now the first thing we shall do when we reach Claridge's is put you straight to bed, my dear, and Dr Watson will give you his camphor stick.'

While talking in this fashion, Mrs Allindale had begun walking towards the doors to the street, and Miss Sutherland, holding herself very erect, and I followed. I was aware of several grim-faced men standing upon the steps, who subjected us to more than casual scrutiny. They glanced uncertainly from Miss Sutherland to myself, but after a word from one who stood at their rear they stepped aside and allowed us to pass. Within a few moments we were inside a growler, with the ladies' luggage above us, rattling south towards the Regent Circus.

Almost immediately Mrs Allindale turned to her niece. 'I think that we are safe now,' she confided.

'Quite safe,' I assured them. 'It would take a full ton of dynamite to reach you here.'

Mrs Allindale touched the veil that Miss Sutherland had not yet raised. 'Do not be alarmed by our companion's appearance,' she said to me, and as she ran the veil up to the brim the face below it was not that of the girl whom I had hoped to call 'my Mary' but the Prince of Orange, without his beard.

I had barely time to express my consternation and dismay when the cab rattled to a halt, and the door on the Prince's side was pulled open. The Prince tried frantically to cover his face, and I reached for my stick, but before I could wield it, the intruder sprang into the cab and took the seat beside me. Throwing open his blue fur-lined cloak, and unpeeling his imperial, Sherlock Holmes said,

'I owe you an explanation, Watson.'

6

THE NUBILE BACHELOR

'WHERE IS MISS SUTHERLAND?' I cried, greatly alarmed. 'Why is she not with us?'

'Because the Prince of Orange is with us instead,' answered Holmes, with a chuckle. 'A most gratifying outcome. May I be the first to congratulate Your Royal Highness.' He rubbed his hands together in a very ecstasy of satisfaction.

'I became nervous as we approached the steps,' said the Prince.

'He could not have managed it better,' broke in Mrs Allindale. 'You looked the very image of a lady,' she told the Prince. 'If I may say so, you were like a princess! It was as much as I could do to stop myself dropping a curtsey, and that would never have helped us.'

'But Holmes,' I protested, 'you have surely not left Miss Sutherland in the Prince's room, at the mercy of his enemies!'

'Your chivalrous spirit comes to the fore as always, Watson.' He rapped on the roof of the cab and we set off again. 'The talented Miss Sutherland is still in her own room. Before our departure for Claremont this afternoon, I sent a telegram to Mrs Allindale and Miss Sutherland, and a message to His Royal Highness by way of the boy Roper. Preparations for the Prince's escape wanted only that signal to be set in motion. Once darkness had fallen, Mrs Allindale and her niece lowered a rope ladder from one of the windows of their suite to the Prince's window below.'

'When I was a student at Leyden,' said the Prince with a smile, 'I climbed to the roof of the University, to win a wager.'

'Once safely admitted to Miss Sutherland's room,' continued Holmes, 'her dress awaited him. His Royal Highness's build is slim, and she, as you know, is taller than the average woman.'

'You chose her for that purpose,' I said in a trembling voice.

'I confess that I did.'

'You calculated that my feelings would be drawn towards her, and the closer they became the better pleased you were. All so that when I left the hotel no one would doubt that she was my companion still!'

I spoke with bitterness, because my heart was sore. For the past four days I had fashioned an estate of dreams, where, hand in hand, I wandered with one whom I dared to call 'Beloved'. Now that paradise had vanished, and she was gone as if she had never been.

'What a fool I have been, what a blind fool!' I cried. 'And what must you think of me, Holmes, to trust you so abjectly! Stop the cab! I will make my own way home.'

'One moment, Watson, my dear friend,' Holmes said gently. 'You must know that I have always had the completest confidence in your ability to assist me in any affair that calls for courage and endurance. Yet the rescue of the Prince required a further skill – which is, deceit. Your nature is so straight that deception is repugnant to you.'

'I thank heaven for it,' I interjected.

'It is your tower of strength. But if the escape from the hotel was to succeed, it was necessary for you to take Miss Sutherland's arm, and to escort her with all the chivalrous concern that a gentleman would naturally extend to an ailing companion. Tell me, Watson, do you think that you would have persuaded the watchers on the steps so completely had you known that you were holding the arm of the Crown Prince of Holland?'

In my heart I knew that he was right, and yet this could not lessen the pain that gripped me.

'As for Miss Sutherland,' continued Holmes, 'I have it from her own lips that the past days have been among the happiest in her life. Here is a letter which she asked me to deliver to you.'

'And here is another,' said Mrs Allindale. 'With a bunch of violets which she picked for you in the Park.'

I am not easily moved to tears, but as I took the letters, and breathed again the fragrance of the young woman whom I had hoped to call my own, turning over in my hands the fragile blooms which she herself had gathered, the emotions that rose within me threatened to prove greater than I could bear with manly dignity.

'I will read them later,' I said gruffly.

Holmes placed his hand upon my arm. 'I can honestly say, that without the part you have played in this drama, the Prince of Orange would not be a free man today.'

'Dr Watson, I thank you,' said the Prince, holding out his hand.

'Very well,' I said. 'Can you assure me that Miss Sutherland will be able to leave the Langham in safety?'

'She will do so by one of the rear doors, whence she will make her way to Claridge's Hotel, before returning to her residence in Maida Vale.'

'I see. She is an actress?'

'She has been upon the stage,' said Mrs Allindale, 'but is now retired.'

'Well. That is done. There is no more to be said.'[28]

'I knew that I could count upon you,' said Holmes. He looked out of the window. 'We are in Brook Street and approaching our first stage-post. Here is Grosvenor Square. You will observe that we are being followed by two hansom cabs. Do not be alarmed. They will take you for the next stage. I took the liberty of including your old service revolver, along with other necessaries, in a valise which is in the second cab. Here is Doyle's Yard.'

Our cab turned suddenly into the narrow entrance of a spacious mews, closely followed by the two hansoms, and all three came to a halt in an otherwise empty corner of the yard. By the time that we had stepped out, the three drivers under Holmes's direction were transferring the luggage of Mrs Allindale and Miss Sutherland from the roof of the four-wheeler to the first hansom.

'Thank you, Mr Holmes,' Mrs Allindale said, taking her seat in the hansom. 'It has been a pleasure to work with you again. Your Royal Highness. Dr Watson.' With a last nod from her long feathers she subsided into the cab and was driven away.

The driver of the second hansom came up to Holmes and saluted respectfully. 'Cab ready, Sir.'

'Thank you, Simpson.' He consulted his watch. 'The Paris train leaves in thirty-two minutes. Can you make it?'

'Do it easy, Sir.'

'Are these men to be trusted?' I asked Holmes in a low voice. 'What if they are traced here, or volunteer information? They are not like your Baker Street Irregulars.'

Holmes laughed aloud. 'There you are wrong, my dear Watson. They are very like them indeed. Not so long ago the three drivers whom I have employed this evening *were* the Baker Street Irregulars. The original three, I believe.'

'That's so, Sir,' said the one who had driven our growler, a young man with a cheery face and, like his colleagues, a pair of the brightest eyes imaginable.

'It was the Vamberry Case that began it all, Mr Holmes,' said the one named Simpson.[29] 'You had us tracking they wine barrels all around Stepney for more than a week.'

'I believe you are right,' said Holmes, smiling. 'You see, Watson, the ineluctable laws of life that allow my auxiliaries to perform such useful work at a young age, prevent them from doing so when they pass beyond it. Doyle was in need of a set of reliable cabmen, and so I recommended these three stout lads. So it has gone on. Leave London for ten years, and, when you return, Wiggins or Roper will hail you at the station from the top of a cab. But time presses. We have freed the Prince. Next to secure the men who would have abducted him. That is a task which must fall to me.'

'You shall not go alone,' I expostulated.

'I thank you, Watson, but I shall be watched and followed by my band of minuscule desperadoes. May I, however, in spite of my scurvy treatment of you, still count upon your assistance?'

'Holmes, you may.'

'Until his enemies are outwitted, the Prince must stay in a place of refuge, where he will need a bodyguard. I leave the choice of place to you, provided that it is not a large metropolis or one of the greater entrepôts.'

'I shall await you at Orange,' the Prince declared. 'It is the cradle of our house, but since the territory was ceded to France no member of my family has visited it.'

'An excellent choice,' agreed Holmes. 'The town is on the main route to Marseilles, yet few travellers think it worth their while to linger there. Until you reach Paris, Your Royal Highness had better remain *en travestie*. Did you bring with you any of your own clothes?'

'None.'

'Here is the name of an establishment in the Rue de la Harpe where such exigencies are familiar to them. In eight hours you will be in Paris. *Tot ziens.*'

The Prince lowered his veil and climbed into the hansom. The graceful tipples of the coffee-coloured cape as it fell across that familiar dress brought a stab of pain to my heart. Holmes called me to the head of the horse, where he addressed me in a grave and subdued voice.

'We have saved the Prince from his visible enemies, but I fear lest they have an ally working from within. Months of inaction followed by a burst of unusual stimulation cannot but take their toll of a constitution that has never been vigorous.'

'You are concerned about the balance of his mind?'

'We have had dealings before with the *epigone* of an ancient line, who fell a prey to melancholy. *Aetas parentum peior avis tulit nos nequiores.*[30] You know the conclusion.'

With the sombre words of the poet echoing in my ears, we took our leave. I looked back as the cab left the yard, and saw my friend standing in the pale light from a wheezing lamp, gazing after us with a pensive look upon his gaunt, austere features.

An omnibus had overturned in Piccadilly, and this brought about a greater congestion than was usual at that hour. Our driver was resourceful, and seized every chance to advance our progress, but the station clock was standing upon the stroke of eight when the Prince and I hurried onto the Continental plat-form. We walked swiftly down the line of carriages, glancing in at the windows to find one that was unoccupied, when a guard overtook us.

'Now then, Sir, look sharp, the train's going,' said he.

'First class,' I answered.

The guard turned the handle of the nearest door. In the car-riage sat a young man with a cigar in his mouth who glanced up as the door was opened. I paused with a foot upon the step, unable to move a limb nor tear my eyes away from that cold young face, with its tell-tale scar above the right eye.[31]

It is a mystery to me that I was able to keep my presence of mind when I heard the guard behind us urging me to enter. 'This is a smoking compartment,' I said. 'The lady dislikes smoke.'

The guard slammed the door of the carriage, opened that of the next one, which was empty, and thrust us in. At the same moment, he sounded his whistle, and the wheels of the train began to turn. There was still time for us to jump from the train, but the Prince was already seated at his ease, supposing that we had successfully completed another stage of our journey.[32]

One thought ran backward and forward in my brain, as I stood undecided with my hand upon the door. How had we been discovered? Klee could not have tracked us, because he was seated in his compartment before we arrived. Holmes would have obtained our tickets with the utmost circumspection, and spoken of our departure to no one. It could only be Chance, the wilful demon rigorously excluded from Holmes's philosophy, that had brought hunter and prey into such dangerous proximity.

'We are undone!' I cried, flinging myself upon the seat. 'John Klee, chief of your enemies, the man who blew up his room to drive you from the hotel, is travelling in the next compartment!'

The Prince turned pale. From the handbag beside him on the seat he took a small ivory-handled pistol. 'I am not unarmed,' said he.

'I do not think that the villain will shoot,' I replied. 'But he will follow us aboard the boat, and he can call upon others, whom we shall not recognize, to dog our every step.'

'Does the train stop before Dover?'

'No.'

'Then we are safe until then.'

I did not immediately reply. Holmes's practice, when preparing to outwit an adversary, was to place himself, in imagination, in the other man's position. He would then proceed to plan, in the minutest detail, all possible attacks upon himself, and by this means become aware of weaknesses in his own defences that might otherwise have been passed over. I set about following my friend's example, and considered our present situation as Klee might see it.

I did not think that he would willingly wait until we reached Dover before taking action. But the several schemes that I imagined for passing a message from the train were so doubtful of success, or required the sure-footedness of a Blondin, that I discarded each of them in turn. However, while the speed of the train might make it impossible for him to communicate with the outside world, only the thickness of the wall between our compartments prevented him listening to every word that we uttered. I sprang to my feet and swiftly examined the panels for cracks in the wood or empty bolt-holes.

'What is Klee doing?' asked the Prince.

'I wish that I knew,' I cried.

He picked up the handbag, unfastened it and fastidiously lifted out and placed upon the seat a green filigree purse, a card-case, a vinaigrette, a booklet of powder-paper, and a hand-mirror set in tortoiseshell.

'Tie this to your cane,' he said, handing the mirror to me. 'If you can succeed in holding it out of the window, you may be able to see into his compartment.'

'That is an excellent suggestion, Sir,' I replied, enthusiastically. A length of bandage soon secured the handle of the mirror to one end of my cane, and a careful adjustment of its position provided us with a rough but ready periscope. I lowered the window, took a firm grip of the cane and began to push it along the outside of the carriage towards the neighbouring compartment. Although my shoulders acted as a partial shield against the wind rushing like a hurricane past the sides of the train, the cane still rocked violently in my hands. Not until the train was upon the long outward bend at Chislehurst was I able to hold the cane relatively still. Steadily I inched it further away from me until it was against the nearest window of our neighbour's carriage. By holding the cane six inches from the glass, and tilting it this way and that, I found that I could obtain a view of the complete interior of the compartment.

'What is he doing?' demanded the Prince again.

I withdrew my cane and looked at him gravely. 'There is no one there,' I said. 'The compartment is empty.'

'But where can he have gone? Surely he has not leaped from the moving train?'

'I suppose that he must have jumped off at Victoria, before the train gathered speed. This is very unfortunate. He will have ample time to telegraph a confederate at Dover.'

For the remainder of our journey, my thoughts were preoccupied with fears of what awaited us at journey's end. The Prince, however, appeared singularly untroubled by the future. Nor did it seem that the dress, which it had been necessary for him to adopt, disconcerted him to any degree. With his hands clasped upon his lap, where his fingers occasionally played with a jet bead, he discoursed in a most animated fashion upon a broad variety of subjects. He was deeply conversant with Hebrew funerary art, and the works of Mrs Molesworth,[33] and he produced for my inspection a small lens, one inch in diameter, which had been ground and polished by Spinoza. In accordance with the teaching of his race, the humble philosopher had made himself master of a mechanical craft, and earned his living by it. The Prince told me that he regarded this small piece of glass as the most valuable of his possessions, from which he would never be willingly parted.

All too soon we emerged from the Lydden tunnel, and Dover lay before us, dark and glittering in the frosty moonlight. A few moments more and the train came to a halt at the quayside. Cautiously we descended to the platform. The bustling procession of fellow-travellers, wrapped tightly against the sea-wind in ulsters and fur-lined hoods, paid us no heed as they hurried across to the great steamboat that lay alongside. Nearer to us a small group of officials waited expectantly at the door of a first-class carriage. At the apex of the group stood the station-master and the harbour-master, wearing full-dress uniforms, and as we approached them, the door opened and a man in middle age, red-faced and heavily built, stepped quickly down and took up a position beside the step. At a sign from the station-master the officials came to the salute, and a familiar figure, wearing a heavy overcoat covered and lined with rich fur, appeared in the doorway of the compartment.

'It is the Duke of Albany!' I gasped to my companion. 'Confound it! What is he doing here?'

'Dr Watson!' called the duke, in his clear, piercing voice. 'Thank you, gentlemen. Shall we enjoy a good crossing?'

The harbour-master made answer. 'There is every indication of it, Sir, with no wind to mention.'

'I am glad to hear it. Help me down these damned steps, Roylott. You two brothers of the knife should be acquainted. Only this afternoon Dr Watson was admiring that old Jezail rifle.'

The duke's gaze lingered curiously upon the veiled Prince at my side. I knew what I must do, although the words tore at my heart.

'Your Royal Highness,' I murmured, 'may I present Miss Mary Sutherland.'

The Prince of Orange, to whom the situation cannot have been a familiar one, managed a modest bob and curtsey.

'Miss Sutherland has been visited by a violent migraine,' I added, to explain the discourtesy of the unraised veil.

'My sympathies to the lady,' remarked the duke.

At this moment, one of the junior officials held out to him a round silver tray, upon the brilliantly polished surface of which lay a telegram. The duke took it up, and read the contents, and folded it away in a pocket.

'You are travelling far?' he inquired, addressing himself to me again.

'To Paris, Sir.'

'Where else would gentleman take fair lady! Then I suppose that Mr Holmes is not accompanying you? No? Well, I hope to have the pleasure of your company upon the boat. Do you play whist, Miss Sutherland?'

I had been undecided whether or not to proceed upon our journey, but the duke's invitation put an end to my uncertainty.

'I am afraid that Miss Sutherland will not be strong enough to undertake the crossing tonight,' I replied.

'Come, come,' answered the duke. 'You have heard what the harbour-master has said. It will be a perfect crossing.'

'Nonetheless, I fear that it would not be in my patient's best interest.'

'Ha, your patient, is she? Well, we cannot break that redoubtable bond, eh, Roylott? Try though we may. The Lord Warden Hotel is much patronized by invalids. I have stayed there myself. Will the Prince of Orange be returning to his own country?'

The bluntness of this unexpected inquiry stopped the blood in my veins. I could feel the Prince's arm trembling in mine as a nameless dread seized me. All my suspicions of the duke's concern for the Prince of Orange returned, along with the further fear that, in some manner scarcely conceivable, he and John Klee were associates. In an unsteady voice I made reply.

'The Prince has greatly improved in health, but is not yet himself.'

The duke turned and, leaning heavily upon his stick, limped towards the boat. His ruddy-complexioned medical attendant, who had said not a word, nodded briefly and followed his royal master.[34] The Prince of Orange and I walked away in the opposite direction. Above the town the rolling wall of cliffs that is England's foremost bastion against attack soared against the night sky. Against these natural bulwarks foreign tyrants have spent their force in vain.

We had just quitted the jetty when the man who had handed the duke his telegram overtook us, walking at speed. I called him back.

'Can you direct me to the nearest telegraph office?'

'I am going there myself,' came the reply. 'I have just been given a wire to despatch, and I will convey yours there, if the lady is not well.'

'Did the Duke of Albany give you the telegram?'

'Yes.'

'A telegram for London?'

'I believe so. Do you wish to send a wire?'

'I may do so later.'

'Then you will excuse me. The Northallerton-street office is your closest in the main part of the town. But if you are staying at the Lord Warden you will find the usual telegraphic facilities there.'

He tipped his cap and strode away past the square, white block of the hotel, which marked the commencement of the town.

'Is that where we shall pass the night?' asked the Prince.

'It is the one place in England where we shall not do so,' I replied. 'Our arrival has been observed. The night train will bring down all your enemies from London. A multitude of fishing smacks rides in the harbour, any one of which can be the means of conveying you secretly from these shores. We shall not be safe tonight save at the obscurest inn in Dover. We will take this cab. To the nearest telegraph office, cabby.'

The cabman looked closely at us, chewing upon his moustache. 'You'll be wanting the Golden Lion after?' he said.

'We are not familiar with the hotels in Dover,' I replied. 'Is it out of the way? The lady is of a retiring disposition.'

'The Golden Lion is very out of the way, Sir. And if you was disposed to retire early, I don't suppose any person there will raise an objection.'

'Very good.'

He whipped up the horse and we rattled off along the foot of the cliff, and had soon plunged into a maze of twisted streets, set close together in the shabbiest area of the town.

7

THE DOVER QUEERS[35]

IN AN EXPERIENCE of dockside hostelries which extends over many nations and four continents, I have learned that few are of a character to which one would wish to introduce a lady. In Dover the military garrison above the town intrudes its own rough element. But since the cabman had himself suggested the Golden Lion, I decided that I would place my trust in his knowledge of the town.

The cab stopped at last, at the bottom of a steep, sharply curving street, drawing up behind a second cab from which stepped a grey-haired man of upright carriage and military bearing. He helped down a young lady who looked, in the uncertain light of the street, to be no more than eighteen years old. She wore a dress of garishly contrasting checks, in scarlet and electric blue, of a character no longer worn in London, and I reflected that, while a new fashion is slow to reach the provinces, so a longer time elapses before it departs.

The presence of the young lady, and of the man whom I took to be her guardian, removed what doubts I had reserved of the propriety of our destination.

'We will almost certainly be asked to share a room, Sir,' I

explained to the Prince. 'But tomorrow an early cab will take us to Folkestone, or Newhaven, where we will resume our journey.'

'My father and my brother repaired to low places,' observed the Prince, stepping down to the studded door through which the previous couple had already passed. 'It runs in the family after all.'[36]

The front aspect of the building, which was low and square-windowed, gave no inkling of the labyrinthine interior. The walls of two, or possibly more, adjacent houses had been pierced with doors and curtained arches to form a succession of rooms on many different levels. From somewhere to the rear of the building came the voice of a woman singing, in what I judged to be a large room from the number of answering voices which sang out the choruses. Those men who passed us in the anteroom were, for the most part, elegantly dressed, but the styles of their companions ranged across an uncommonly broad spectrum of the feminine type. Some were positively mannish, and the upper lip of one, who may have been Belgian, was remarkably hirsute for so young a person. The variety of the dresses, both in style and quality, covered almost as great a range, though none that I saw could compare for refinement of taste with the dress worn by my companion. When he removed his travelling cape, the full elegance of the dark-coffee-coloured robe was visible again, and the delicacy and profusion of the trimmings excited considerable comment from those who passed by.

While we stood waiting for attention, the elderly man and his ward, whom we had seen earlier, emerged from one of the side rooms. The young girl ran boldly up to the Prince, who was of course still veiled, and conveyed her admiration of the dress in the most profuse terms. In doing so, she took him by the hands and commenced to draw him away towards the stairs.

I stepped after them, but at the foot of the staircase my way was barred by a dark-eyed young woman, who stepped out from a curtained recess, and whose close resemblance to the unfortunate Empress Eugenie was so lifelike, even to the mole upon her cheek, that I fell back in astonishment. With a peal of gay laughter, she turned and followed the others up the staircase.

'Permit me to introduce myself,' said the military veteran. 'I am Colonel Warburton, formerly of the 53rd Foot. I think you have seen service?'

Since I felt confident that for the time being the safety of the Prince was assured, I accompanied the Colonel into a galleried room where suppers were being served. As the minutes passed, however, without the return either of the Prince or of the Colonel's young companion, whose name, he informed me, was Miss Paula Bell, I found myself glancing with ever more anxious frequency at the door which led from the hall. Nearly half an hour passed before the Prince reappeared, without his veil, but wearing upon his face the light additions with which fair women are wont to gild the lily. His skin looked whiter, his lips more red, the blue eyes sparkled, and, most remarkable of all, Miss Bell had from somewhere procured a cluster of golden ringlets which fell in a festoon from beneath the rim of his hat.

'They know my secret,' the Prince murmured in a low voice, as he took his place beside me at the table. 'But I have been discreet. Do not fear.'

'What have you told them?'

'That I am from Holland.'

'What else?'

'They may call me Sophie.'

'Was not Sophie the name of your mother?'

'It was.'

'Your choice was a fine one.'

I reflected that our encounter with Colonel Warburton and Miss Bell was fortunate. In a place so thronged as the Golden Lion had proved to be, a veiled woman would have been as conspicuous as a Mrs Grundy in a *bal turque*.

'With some powder and paint,' I said jovially, 'what wonders could be done with all the men in this room!'

General laughter greeted this sally, and the four of us proceeded to our supper of sole and Chablis.

I did not expect the Prince to take a full part in our conversation. He ate and drank abstemiously, and I observed that he cast frequent glances at the unfamiliar image of himself that was reflected in a glass upon the opposite wall. Gone was the animation that he had exhibited on the train, and in its place had come a mood of grave reserve. Miss Bell, on the other hand, was the life and soul of the party, keeping up an almost constant stream of good-natured banter, frequently capping my remarks with a droll pun, and engaging in contests of raillery with friends, of whom she appeared to possess a great number, at the surrounding tables.

'I had not expected to find such gaiety outside London,' said I, laughing.[37]

'I know of several couples who have come down from London expressly for the occasion,' replied the Colonel.

'Why, what occasion is that?' I asked.

'Our special occasion,' cried Miss Bell, resting her hand upon my arm. 'Once in every four years it is the ladies' privilege to propose to you!'

'Of course!' I exclaimed. 'February the 29th! It is Leap Year!'

The Colonel glanced at me with an expression of surprise. 'Then you have come here by chance?'

'Entirely. We are travelling to Paris and have been obliged to leave the train.'

The Colonel asked no further questions and the conversation drifted off into other topics. We had both served in India, though he more gloriously than I, for he had marched with Campbell to relieve Lucknow, and could have told many a tale of bravery and horror from that grim campaign. He spoke of those experiences almost curtly, as if he wished to share no part of the glory of them. He had lived hard and achieved great things, but I formed the impression that he had also seen more than he had wished, so that the milder alarums of Shorncliff Camp presented a not unwelcome coda to his career.[38] His mention of Shorncliff, which lies two miles from Folkestone, suggested to me a plan whereby the Prince and I might leave England in a simple and inconspicuous manner.

'It is my friend's misfortune,' I began, 'to have mislaid his luggage, containing all his clothes and necessaries, save the dress which you see him wearing.'

'I wish that I had such a dress,' sighed Miss Bell, gazing fondly at it and stroking the sleeve with a light touch. 'It is in the latest style, I know it.'

'I do not know what we shall do until the missing trunks are found,' I continued.

As I had hoped, my remark brought an immediate response from Miss Bell.

'But surely,' she implored the Colonel, 'you can spare some clothes for poor Sophie to wear? You are nearly the same height. The grey check, now, when did you last wear that? Confess that you have not put it on this past year. Is it settled?' She took the Colonel's hands impulsively in hers and gazed into his eyes. 'Oh, say that it is.'

'Would it be taxing your generosity too far,' I continued, 'if we left the dress with you until our return to England? It is the property of a friend – and yet I do not think that she expects it to be returned. No, I am certain that she does not.'

So the bargain was struck. Several hours later, when the Colonel's carriage arrived at the door, four wearied revellers made the journey along the crest of the Downs to Shorncliff Camp. The sky was still dark when we arrived at the Colonel's villa. While the others stepped upstairs, I waited in the sitting room, where I must instantly have fallen asleep, for when I next took note of my surroundings, a grey light was filtering between the shutters, and the Prince of Orange was standing before me, wearing a grey checked suit and holding a brown billycock in his hand.

'Good morning, Doctor,' said he. 'Colonel Warburton asks me to inform you that we must leave the house in half an hour if we are to take the morning boat.'

I washed and shaved briskly, and had done justice to the greater part of my breakfast when the Colonel entered the room to announce that his fly was at the door. His servant, who was to drive us to Folkestone, so closely resembled Miss Bell in build and feature that I ventured to comment upon the likeness.

'Oh, we are cousins,' the young man said, with a cheery grin. 'Many people have said how alike we are.'

'It is truly remarkable. Do you not think so?' I asked the Prince.

'Nature teems with curious sports,' he replied succinctly.

The drive to Folkestone was a short one, and the packet was in. Travellers who had slept the night at local hotels were already on board, and a straggling procession from the London train was moving slowly towards the gangway. The usual sort of loafer that gathers about a boat in harbour gazed with curiosity at the faces of the travellers. The Prince and I turned up our collars and joined the end of the shuffling line.

'We are not safe yet,' I warned him. 'Keep a good look-out at your side, and I will do the same at mine.'

We had almost reached the gangway, without the occurrence of anything untoward, when a bystander suddenly flung up his arms, clawed wildly at the air like one who is slipping from a cliff, and sank, moaning to the ground. A woman cried, 'A doctor! Bring a doctor!' and I hastened forward to discover what relief I could give to the poor wretch, who was now writhing violently upon the ground.

His colour was normal but his eyes were fixed, and a small quantity of foam had issued from his mouth. In epileptic cases, medical attention is best confined to rendering the sufferer as comfortable as possible, allowing time to bring its own remedy. I eased the fellow onto his left side, and in happening to glance behind me, observed a small knot of men retreating rapidly towards a stationary cab some distance away. I looked around for the Prince, and a cry of horror escaped me. My Dutch companion was nowhere to be seen.

I sprang to my feet, but as I did so the man upon the ground twisted his arm around my ankles and held me fast. Some time elapsed before I could shake myself free of the imposter's grip and set off in pursuit of the men. In their midst I now made out a desperately struggling figure. Thankful that the Jezail bullet, which had put paid to my military career, had entered my shoulder and not a leg, I covered the ground swiftly. But the sham fit had given the Prince's assailants a head start, and well before I had halved the distance between us the ruffians were bundling him unceremoniously into the cab.

I ran on, blinded with self-reproach. Not only had I betrayed the prince's trust, I had betrayed the trust of the friend who had thought me worthy to fight at his side. Oppressed by the bitterest thoughts I scarcely took in the laden fish-cart which had been drawn up in front of the cab. As the horses set off, the cart abruptly collapsed, and splintering crates, baskets and loose fish cascaded over the cobbles directly in the path of the advancing horses. The leading horse slipped and fell, bringing the second down with it. The puzzled face of one of the ruffians appeared at the window of the cab, at the same time as a local fisherman sprang forward and opened the door. He pulled the ruffian out, plucked the Prince out after him, and came dashing towards me.

'Come on, Watson! There is not a moment to lose!'

It was Holmes, in the loose black trousers and sacking shawl of an inshore fisherman. A thousand questions crowded into my mind but this was neither the time nor the place to put them. Holmes led me to a stationary hansom facing the way into town. He put the Prince inside, and, when I had followed, himself mounted to the seat and called to the horse. Next moment we were rattling up the High Street towards the station.

'We have seven minutes to make the London train!' he cried.

'But shall we not be followed?' I exclaimed in alarm. The narrowness of our escape had dawned upon me, and also upon the Prince, who was pressed against the corner of the cab, shaking like a man with an ague.

'For certain we shall be followed,' Holmes answered, as the cab swung up to the station. 'Hurry. The train is in.' He strode down the platform, peering into the compartments but passing by every one, even those that were empty, until we had reached the front of the train. Here he turned and led us back the way that we had come, at last opening and entering one of the first carriages that we had passed. 'We shall be followed by a man named Burton, sallow complexion, pug nose, wearing a long brown overcoat with buttons of imitation quartz; and a shorter man, passing by the name of Daley, bony fingers, excitable in his movements, smoking American cigars. They are occupying the first compartment in the next coach.'

'Don't let them see you!' I cried, as he thrust his head out of the window.

'They have already seen me. They have seen all of us. Why else should we have twice walked the length of the train? There is the whistle. Good. Our friends at the harbour have not caught up with us, so that we have only Burton and his animated companion to reckon with.'

'But why was anyone waiting for us at the harbour?' I exclaimed. 'What brought you to Folkestone, when we have come here only because of a chance encounter late last night?'

Sherlock Holmes settled himself into his seat and brought out his cigar case. 'A long journey lies ahead of us, gentlemen, with several changes. I suggest that you tell me of your experiences, after which I shall give you an account of what has occurred in London during your absence.'

8

THE MOLE VALLEY TWISTERS

THE SUN HAD cleared the hills, and as our train bore us through the rich, tree-shrouded valleys of Kent, the Prince and I gave Holmes an account of our abortive journey. Several times he stopped us with a request to clarify a detail, although I was seldom able to grasp the reasoning behind his questions.

'You are certain that Klee recognized you, Watson, at Victoria station?' he asked.

'Quite certain.'

'Did he observe His Royal Highness?'

'Possibly not. But he heard me speak of a lady.'

'So we do not know that he recognized the Prince?'

'The proof that he did so is that he left the train!' I protested. 'On his own he was no match for the two of us. He went to marshal his forces and plan his attack, which came close to success, as we have seen this morning. Why else should he leave the train?'

'We will come to that,' said Holmes. 'Proceed with your narrative.'

'Nothing eventful occurred until we reached Dover, where the Duke of Albany received a telegram, probably from London, since it was to London that he sent his reply.'

'A plausible deduction, Watson,' agreed Holmes, 'although by no means conclusive without further data. The first might have been a bon voyage from the duchess, the second a last reminder to his bootmaker to despatch the Waukenphasts.[39] However, other data support your assumption of a link between the two.' He rubbed the tips of his fingers together in a sudden access of good humour. 'I could not have foreseen that the Duke of Albany would be travelling abroad, but you see how it accounts for the presence of Klee upon the train.'

'It does not do so for me, Holmes, although I fear the worst.'

'The case certainly presents a tangled appearance. I might say that its unique feature lies in the multifariousness of the strands which compose it. Think back upon the problems that are generally presented to me to solve. A missing document. A purloined tiara. A poisoned amanuensis. Such little puzzles provide moments of intense interest, and in some of them we have caught a whiff of that evil which coils itself about men's hearts. Consider the first case we ever worked upon together – that memorable *Study in Scarlet*. Puzzling, I grant you. Bizarre, without a question. But very simple.'

'It did not seem so at the time.'

'Yet you will agree that it does so today? A crime was committed; I deduced the identity of the criminal; we waited for him to step into our trap.'

'When you put it like that, the case does appear straightforward.'

'It is the same with all the others. They may cut deep but they are narrow. How different this case proves to be! Isolate one strand, and it draws up a second. Identify that, and a third is seen to exist, linked in some mysterious manner to the other two. How many more are we to uncover before the whole mass is resting in our hands, and the villains under lock and key! When this case is done, we shall not call it simple.'

'But surely, Holmes,' I remonstrated, 'is not the case what it has always been? The threat to the life of His Royal Highness.'

'Which Royal Highness?' Holmes inquired, blandly.

'Why, the Prince of Orange!' I exclaimed.

'And what of the other Royal Highness, the Duke of Albany?'

'Is his life in danger?'

'I greatly fear that it will be, unless he chooses better company. And there is yet a further threat, even more widespread and destructive in its effect, which may shortly burst upon us.'

'In God's name, what is this!' I cried.

'I have brought you nothing but trouble!' lamented the Prince of Orange, turning to face us once more. His pale cheeks were wet with tears. 'It is the same wherever I go. Nothing but disasters.[40] I should have stayed at home, awaiting death like a philosopher. We cannot escape the fate of all men. Why should we dodge and hide as though we could fend it off!'

'We can elude it,' said Holmes, sternly. 'Not for ever, but until we reach the Psalmist's term. Even beyond. A man's name may live long beyond the grave. Is William the Silent dead, though struck down by a Burgundian fortune-hunter? Your Royal Highness is barely thirty. A reign of many years lies ahead of you. Years of revived greatness for your people under their first Alexander. But resign yourself to the treacherous solace of despondency, and you risk becoming *de vergeten kroonprins*.'[41]

'*De vergeten kroonprins ...*' the Prince mused, half to himself, nodding his head thoughtfully. 'Yes, Mr Holmes, I believe that you are right.'

'Now, Watson,' Holmes continued briskly. 'In the wire that you sent from Dover you gave some account of your conversation with the duke. I would like to be clear about certain points. You are positive that he had received his telegram before asking if I was travelling with you?'

'I am.'

'And before he asked your destination?'

'Yes.'

'His last question was whether the Prince of Orange would be returning to his own country?'

'I am afraid it was. It was this question that made me fear that his connection with the Prince was less innocent than he had pretended.'

'You did not feel rather that it suggested his innocence? Well, we shall see. This is Ashford Junction. Our wait here is a short one. Burton and Daley will alight when they see us do so, and will follow us when we board the Hastings train.'

'But we have only to remain on this train, and it will take us direct to Victoria.'

'You are perfectly right, Watson, and that is where we are bound. But why pass by the opportunity to admire the beauties of the Sussex coast. The train skirts Romney Marsh, where the terrain should put Your Royal Highness in mind of his native land. A peculiarly hardy breed of sheep survives there. Burton is Klee's principal henchman. I have been keeping him under observation since the beginning of the case. He has rented a room in Langham Mews, twenty yards from the Hive. I must explain to Your Royal Highness that this is the name I give to the nomadic headquarters of my small company of irregulars. It is at present situated in the secluded corner of a grocer's warehouse, chosen because it overlooks the entrance to the lodging-house where Burton has taken a room.

'Scarcely had I returned to the Hive yesterday after your departure from Doyle's Yard, than a cab drew up and Klee emerged from it. The gang uses Burton's room as a sort of office, and shortly after Klee entered it, Burton set off in a great hurry for a cab. "Claridge's Hotel, and double-quick!" he shouted. I sent Roper after him, but Burton was in and out of the hotel so fast that as Roper arrived at the door Burton was climbing back into his cab. Fortunately, the lad is of the brightest and he marched into the hotel to ask if a Miss Sutherland or a Mrs Allindale had arrived there. "You are the second in as many minutes to ask that question," came the reply. "They are in the dining room." Evidently Klee's suspicions had been aroused, although I had no means of knowing what had alerted him.

'Daley, if that is his name, hurried off to despatch a telegram. I could see the paper fluttering between his bony fingers. After his return nothing occurred for an hour. At half-past-ten a telegraph boy walked up to their door.

'Ah, boys, I said, if only we could learn the contents of that wire. "Shall us knock 'im dahn?" suggested Wiggins. "Snatch it orf of 'im?" piped up another. No, no, I told them. We will endeavour to deduce the contents by observing the consequences.

'Well, the consequences were immediate. Burton and Daley positively ran from the Mews, and shortly afterwards returned with every one of the fellows who had been loitering at the Langham. By this time, I was becoming seriously concerned for your wellbeing, and had determined to send a wire to Calais to ascertain your situation, when your welcome telegram was brought to me from Baker Street by the page. This clarified the situation, and from that moment Klee's plans and mine ran parallel courses.'

I gave voice to the dread that had seized hold of me at Dover.

'Do you think that the telegram the duke received was from Klee?'

'I do.'

'Then it may have requested him to ask just the questions which he did ask.'

'The duke was certainly called upon to furnish one piece of information. You must remember that your appearance in the train must have been a considerable shock to Klee. I had given him no inkling that I was interested in the case. For reasons of his own he set off for Paris, leaving the matter of extracting the Prince of Orange from the hotel to Burton and the others. Then you appeared at his compartment door. He has no wish to have us upon his trail, and so he jumps the train. He returns to Burton's room, where he learns that you, Watson, have left the Langham with two ladies bound for Claridge's. Who, then, were you taking to Paris? The duke's reply from Dover presents him with two Miss Sutherlands, eighty miles apart. One is clearly a pretender. A trip to Claridge's confirmed which is which, and his men are given their orders.'

I shuddered as I recalled how narrowly the Prince had escaped the consequence of those orders at Folkestone harbour. As if in confirmation of my fears the Prince turned his head from the window to address Holmes.

'This creature Klee,' said he. 'You speak of reasons of his own that required him to leave London. Do you suspect that he intended to approach the Duke of Albany aboard the boat?'

'I think it highly probable. Nor would this have been their first encounter.'

'Dear God!' I exclaimed.

'The duke has been dangerously unwise in permitting so hazardous an association.'

'But should we not alert His Royal Highness to the peril he is in?'

'That course should certainly be considered if an opportunity presents itself. However, a telegram that I received from Claremont House, in reply to one that I sent to Her Royal Highness, informed me that the duke is journeying to Cannes. Klee may attempt to visit him there but for the present he remains in London, possibly in pursuit of another of his dastardly enterprises.'

'And what may that be?'

Holmes did not elaborate upon his remark, and now a further question presented itself to my mind.

'What took you to Folkestone,' I asked, 'when we could as easily have planned to sail from Newhaven, or Southampton, or even tried again at Dover?'

'Ah, Watson, I am afraid that you will not consider it so astonishing when I tell you. Why should I trouble to go to Southampton when no steamer leaves there until tomorrow? At Newhaven there is not a steamer until midnight. The Royal Mail will sail from Dover at midday, but the first boat to leave the English shore today was the packet that you tried to board this morning at Folkestone. A moment's perusal of Bradshaw gave me this information, and I have no doubt that it was also consulted by Klee. He was still in Langham Mews when I left there early this morning, but wherever he goes today a member of my little force will shadow him. They will stick like burrs to his heels, observing all, but indistinguishable amid the crowd.'

'But what of the Duke of Albany? What part does he play in this complex affair?'

'A dangerous part. I see that we are approaching Brighton, which closes the second stage of our journey.'

At Brighton, as at Ashford, and again at Chichester, we left the train, and the two men travelling in the next coach stepped onto the platform immediately after us; without attempting to conceal their proximity, they stood close by us until our next train drew in. Having assured themselves that we intended to travel onward in that train, they took their seats in a neighbouring compartment.

'Will they follow us all the way back to London?' asked the Prince.

'It is undoubtedly their intention. The train will take us to Waterloo if we remain upon it.'

'You intend to leave at one of the intermediate stations?'

'At Leatherhead. This is Dorking, which is the previous station. The train waits here for two minutes. The first minute is gone. I will now open the door and step onto the platform. Do not follow me, although you observe that Burton has left his compartment and is on the platform watching this door. His companion will almost certainly be at the opposite side of the train, ensuring that you do not leave by the other door and cross the rails. So much for Dorking. At Leatherhead we will again make no move until the first minute has elapsed. I shall then step out of the train, followed immediately by Your Royal Highness, and with you, Watson, bringing up the rear. It is imperative that we are swift. A trap awaits us in the station yard. The train is slowing. Here is the station. Make no move until I give the signal. Now!'

Holmes flung open the door and leapt down onto the platform. An instant later and the Dutch prince followed. Another instant and I had joined them, racing towards the barrier as though an Afghan horde was at my heels. In the yard, a trap was drawn up immediately outside the station doors.

'Well done, Phipps!' Holmes cried to the driver. 'Off and away!'

Our driver was the bright-eyed cabby who had driven us from the Langham. We took our places in the trap, he whipped up the horse, and we shot out of the yard in a cloud of yellow dust. As we came onto the London Road, I looked back and saw our two pursuers climbing into a second trap and making agitated gestures in our direction to the driver.

'If only the second coach had not been there!' cried the Prince.

Holmes gave an enigmatic smile.

'How else could our two bloodhounds resume their pursuit of us?' said he.

'Can you be serious, Holmes?' I exclaimed. 'Do you wish them to follow us, and have placed a trap at the station for that purpose?'

'Did you not recognize young Cartwright on the box?[42] He will give them a good run for our money, I daresay. On, Phipps.'

Our carriage hurtled through the narrow roads of Leatherhead and was soon in the open countryside. As we entered the Epsom Road the Prince, who had been gazing back along the way that we had come with an intent and troubled expression, gave a cry of alarm, and pointed to a cloud of dust a quarter of a mile

100

behind us. It was the following trap, and as we began to climb the hill, the distance between us steadily diminished.

Holmes gazed alternately behind and ahead. Beads of perspiration stood out upon his fiercely knitted brow, and his hands rapidly struck the sides of the carriage as if to urge it forward. 'We must be a clear two hundred yards ahead of them at the crest of the hill!' he cried.

'Never fear, Sir,' came the confident reply. 'Cartwright will slow down, just as we have had to.'

'Of course Cartwright will slow down,' Holmes replied impatiently. 'But the hill must do it and not the snaffle. They are Irishmen following us, Phipps, who know every sly trick that you can play with a horse.'

We crested the hill and at once picked up speed, racing past bare hedges and dead oaks gloved with ivy.

'We are now out of sight of our pursuers,' said Holmes, 'and have forty seconds before we come into their view again. May I trouble Your Royal Highness to give me your travelling-cape. Thank you. This is the Sun, Phipps. Turn in!'

Phipps pulled the horse hard round, the trap veered to the right, and with the wheels uttering a protesting scream at such abuse, we swerved off the road into the yard of the old inn. But we had not come to a halt behind the stable wall before another trap, seemingly identical to our own, and which had been waiting there, shot past us and onto the highway. As it did so, Holmes stood up and flung the Prince's cape to one of the three passengers, who caught it nimbly and draped it around his shoulders. The leaner of the two other passengers wore a cape and cap similar to those worn by Holmes, and the third was clad in an ulster like my own.

'I could not know what Your Royal Highness might be wearing,' explained Holmes, as he leapt down from the trap and made his way stealthily to the corner of the stable, from which point he could command a view of the road while remaining unseen. The rattle of the departing trap had scarcely faded when the wheels of the second trap could be heard rapidly approaching. In an agony of suspense we waited to learn if Holmes's ruse had succeeded. The desperate grinding of the wheels, the pounding hooves of the horses, grew louder until the sound was a thunderous roar in our ears. At its greatest volume, the sound was abruptly cut off by the inn buildings, which intervened between us and the road. When we followed Holmes across the yard, our pursuers were already invisible within a cloud of dust receding rapidly along the road in the direction of Epsom.

Holmes gathered up from the bench a neatly folded cape and passed it to the Prince. 'Cartwright will lead them a merry dance,' said he, with a laugh. 'We offered them the picturesque beauties of Sussex, and now they will be taken through the more homely delights of Surrey.'

'Sooner or later the second trap will catch up with the first,' said I. 'What then?'

'I expect the encounter to occur on the outskirts of Croydon. Perhaps it will not be until they reach Beulah Hill. Wherever it occurs, Messrs Burton and Daley will find a trio of London jarveys enjoying a cabman's holiday. I hope that the Irish couple can take their disappointment mildly, for cabmen are not, on the whole, a breed to be abused with impunity. Now, Phipps, you may drive back along the road to Leatherhead, and I will direct you to our destination.'

Our journey now took a more leisurely and circuitous course, through several of the charming, small villages and hamlets of West Surrey. Darkness had fallen when we turned off the road by a red brick gatehouse and drove along an avenue of recently planted chestnuts. Some minutes later, the ground began to rise and I observed ahead of us a large house standing four-square upon the crest of a hill.

'Surely this is Claremont House?' I exclaimed.[43]

'Your memory is not at fault, Watson, although it is fully two days since last you were here.'

'Is it not the residence of the Duke of Albany?' asked the Prince.

'And of his charming duchess. She is a lady of noble character and delicate sensitivity. Her sister, as you may know, is the present Queen of Holland.'

The effect of this statement upon the Prince was electrifying. He sprang to his feet, and with a cry of despair threw himself over the side of the moving vehicle. Holmes had anticipated this outburst, and in an instant had seized the Prince about the waist; I grasped the Dutchman's shoulders, and together we pulled him back into the trap.

'How dare you bring me to this place!' he shrieked. 'Let go of me at once! Take your hands off me, I say!'

'Your Royal Highness—' Holmes spoke sternly, '—where does Spinoza ask, "Is the pear tree harmful because of the berries that grow upon the yew?"[44] It is natural, though unfortunate, that you should wish to avoid your father's second wife. But no blame for that match can be attached to her younger sister. She, too, is a stranger in a strange land, and agreed at once to my suggestion that she offer her home as a place of refuge.'

'I cannot do it!'

'I think that you can,' persisted Holmes. 'I know that you must. England is still dangerous for you.'

'Cannot I stay with you?' the Prince implored.

Holmes shook his head. 'We have shaken off the hounds for a while, but tomorrow they will be upon my trail once more. Here we are at the house. The flight of steps is a mountain that we must climb, but I believe that a Beatrice will be found upon the corniche.'

The duchess received us in her boudoir, which was a charmingly furnished room, where ranks of photographs in silver frames stood upon every table. It was a moving spectacle to see with what tenderness the young duchess took the Prince into her motherly protection. Normally so shy in the presence of the fair sex, his troubled spirit found in her generous heart a sheltered harbour in which to lie at rest. The hour was late when Holmes and I left Claremont House, but we did so in the confident knowledge that the Prince was in safe hands.

'When it became clear that Klee had learned of your arrival at Dover,' said Holmes, 'I knew that I must go down to Kent to seek you out. But what was I to do with the Prince when I had found him? Klee's men would certainly be covering every escape-road from Folkestone. Clearly, our opportunity lay in accepting that we must be followed from there, and to make preparations for an escape somewhere along the line. Leatherhead presented itself as a suitable place. We were there last year, and I am tolerably well acquainted with the environs. It also suggested to me where the Prince might ingeniously be concealed – in the lion's den.'

'The lion's den,' I repeated. 'Then my fears are justified! Oh, Holmes, what is to be done! It will break his royal mother's heart.'

'We can do nothing more tonight. Our journey back to London has been roundabout, but I see Victoria station ahead. Set us down here, Phipps. It will not do for you to be seen in Baker Street. Let us look for a late hansom. The gondola of London will be especially welcome on so raw a night. The station yard is quite deserted.'

We walked towards the glass-roofed portico, under which, for twenty out of the twenty-four hours of the day, cabs are discharging passengers and luggage; we were no farther than a dozen yards from it when a brilliant red flash lit up the interior of the booking-hall beyond, instantly followed by a dull thud of extraordinary amplitude. Slates, masonry, and metal fragments shot into the air as from a volcanic crater, while the glass portico disintegrated before our eyes.

The silence that eerily followed was broken by the clamour of a thousand dogs, each voicing its individual protest. And I became aware of other sounds, of the cries of frightened horses, cab-wheels crunching over broken glass, and men's voices raised in pain and fear.

'What is it, Holmes?' I gasped. 'Is it an explosive bomb?

'Worse than that,' answered my friend, gravely. 'It is the declaration of war.'

9

THE IRISH INTERPOLATOR

INSIDE THE BOOKING-HALL, a scene of utter destruction met our eyes. The cloakroom and a neighbouring waiting room had been reduced to heaps of splintered boards, glass, slates and twisted ironwork, to which the torn and battered remnants of passengers' luggage added the culminating, poignant touch. Blue flames rippled over the debris, but above the smell of gas escaping from the ruptured pipes, there hung in the air the pungent odour, impossible for any man to forget who has once been brought into contact with it amidst the smoke and carnage of the battlefield.

'Dynamite,' said Holmes, 'or one of its cognate compounds. And a considerable quantity of it, to bring about such general destruction. Take care where you walk, Watson. There is still broken glass above you, which may fall at any moment.'[45]

Even as he spoke a fragment of glass broke free of the iron ribs above us, and fell like a dagger, narrowly missing a station porter, already dust-covered and bleeding from a cut above the eye, who was dragging a hose across the floor.

'Does any poor wretch lie buried beneath the rubble?' my friend asked him.

'No, Sir,' came the reply. 'The cloakroom was closed an hour

106

ago at midnight. Only the night-inspector and two porters remain on duty after the last train is in.'

'Let me take that hose from you,' Holmes said, 'while you connect another to the hydrant.'

'Thank you, Sir. Mr Manning has sent for the fire engine, but in the meantime we must prevent the flames reaching the main building at any price.'

'Take the second hose, Watson. It is not the station alone that we must work to save. The container which held the dynamite will have been blown to smithereens, but any fragment which remains may afford invaluable data.'

We stood shoulder to shoulder with the porter, directing our hoses upon the snaking flames, which ever sprang up afresh when we turned our streams of water elsewhere, until a cab was driven into the station yard at a furious speed, and Inspector Lestrade jumped out. His consternation upon seeing Holmes and myself was comical to behold.

'This beats everything!' he exclaimed. 'I set off upon the instant that the news reached the Yard, yet you are here before me!'

We handed over our hoses and withdrew with the detective to the other side of the booking-hall where, after a moment during which he contemplated the scene, he addressed himself to Holmes.

'Do you consider the gas to be the immediate cause of the explosion?'

'No,' Holmes replied.

'Nor do I. In fact, I had discarded the possibility before arriving at the station.'

'It is a confident mind who will form conclusions in advance of his data.'

'You are right, Mr Holmes. I am confident. Beneath that heap of rubble lies the evidence that will point without a doubt to the perpetrators of this outrage.'

'You mean the Fenians?' said Holmes.

The lean detective laughed shortly. 'Ah, Mr Holmes, we know your theories about the Irish unrest. No, Sir, not the Fenians, who as I remarked the other day, are a spent force. This desperate act is the work of the Anarchists.'

Holmes nodded. 'There is certainly a peripheral connection with that misguided movement,' he remarked.

'Peripheral?' answered Lestrade, with a sneer. 'The Anarchists proclaim their intention to spread alarm, and terror throughout the civilized world. What is this outrage calculated to do, if not that!'

'Perhaps something less,' said Holmes.

The detective looked puzzled.

'To spread alarm and terror throughout England,' Holmes continued. 'The Irish have no quarrel with the rest of the world.'

'You are a proper terrier, Mr Holmes, the way you never give up a theory,' said the detective, shaking his head in a patronizing manner.

'On the contrary,' Holmes replied crisply. 'It is the mark of the truly inquiring mind to be ready to abandon a theory when the facts are ranged against it. But that is far from being the present situation. I have read no reports of explosions in Berlin or St Petersburg, although the governments in those places are particularly detested by the Anarchist societies. You would be well-advised to alert the other London termini.'

'Just a moment,' stammered Lestrade. 'Do you think that there will be other explosions?'

'I am certain that other explosions are planned,' Holmes answered calmly. 'Whether they occur depends upon the acuity of those whose duty it is to prevent them. The cloakroom at Charing Cross station is directly beneath the hotel, where the consequences of an explosion are fearful to contemplate.'

Before Holmes had finished speaking, Lestrade, with an expression of the utmost dismay and apprehension upon his face, had dashed across to his cab, calling out as he reached it, 'Back to the Yard!'

'The undertaking will be a colossal one if they must examine the contents of every package deposited in the cloakrooms of London,' I remarked.

'It will certainly be a large operation if that is the way they choose to set about it,' replied Holmes. 'But the application of a modest quantum of mental power will considerably lighten their task. Since this cloakroom was closed at midnight, and the explosion did not occur until one hour later, some agency must have been at work during the intervening period. Almost certainly this was some form of clockwork, such as an ordinary alarm clock. It is for the ticking of that tell-tale clock that Lestrade's men must listen out.'

'But surely,' said I, 'the perpetrators of this terrible deed will endeavour to obscure the sound by enveloping the device in layers of thick material.'

'Very likely. Just as you are enveloped in five distinct layers of clothing. I do not hear the beating of your heart, but were I to put a stethoscope to the lapel of your ulster, I should learn that it still beats strong and true. Lestrade has borrowed enough of his better habits from me. Let him now consider the time-saving advantages of one of yours. But we will discuss the case no further, for I see that you are done in. Your hand is trembling violently.'

'It is nothing,' I answered. 'A nervous reaction. The fit will soon pass.'

'You look ready to drop. Here is a cab. No, say nothing more of dukes, or Dutchmen, or dynamite. The subjects are closed until after you have breakfasted tomorrow. I cannot afford to have my aide and confidant laid low.'

My right hand was now shaking violently, and no exertion of will had any effect upon it. I have no recollection of entering the cab. At one moment I was leaning against an iron column in the booking-hall hearing Holmes speak to me in a voice oddly distorted, as though coming from a great distance. The next I remember I was sitting beside him in a cab, rattling towards Baker Street.

'What can you think of me!' I exclaimed miserably. 'I have not suffered an attack like that since I left India.'

'The brain is a delicate instrument,' remarked my friend. 'Our proximity to the explosion has activated memories that are no longer useful to you, and which normally you are able to ignore. But the brain forgets nothing. If the proper stimulus is applied, the floodgate of memory opens, perhaps only a crack, but that is enough to inundate the mind.'

'It is true that the sight of that mound of debris was a shock to me.'

'That is the effect which the explosion was designed to have. But no more of that. A night's sleep will prove a sovereign remedy.'

But sleep was a long time coming to me that night. The different strands of the case kept arranging and rearranging themselves inside my brain, but no pattern held firm. Eventually I found myself drifting into slumber, but there I was disturbed by the alarums and excursions of an old war. I seemed to see again my valiant fellow-campaigners, Brown and Hayter,[46] brought down by the murderous Ghazi bullets. I struggled to move them into a place of safety, away from the mysterious blue flames that were flickering along the ground towards them, but their cries of pain were joined by the cries of countless others. I saw the Prince of Orange and the Duke of Albany half buried in the earth, stretching out their arms towards me with expressions on their faces of the most terrible despair. I must have shouted out in my sleep, because in the midst of the holocaust I heard the urgent voice of Holmes calling upon me to awake. I opened my eyes and found him at my bedside.

'Come down to the fire, old fellow,' said he, helping me into my dressing-gown and guiding me down the stairs to our room.

Here he coaxed the coals back into life and, fortified by a tumbler of brandy, I began to speak of deeds done upon a foreign field that I have breathed to no man, before or since. He listened gravely, and for the most part in silence and without moving, staring at the end of the poker where it glowed red in the fire. And when I had said my lengthy say, he helped me back to my bed, where now sleep came upon me swiftly, a deep and dreamless sleep like that dark current which shall one day bear each of us away.

I awoke the next morning refreshed in body and restored in mind. Holmes had concluded his breakfast before I put in an appearance, and was immersed in the newspapers, which lay scattered ankle-deep over the carpet.

'Last night's adventure occurred too late to make the morning papers,' he remarked, 'but the evenings are full of it. I hope that Lestrade reads them. I am afraid that the Anarchists do not rate a mention.'

He threw across the *Standard* and pointed to a long notice, which was headed in the boldest type, 'Fenian Outrage at London Station.' The concluding paragraph read as follows:

That these diabolical plots against English Society are hatched in the United States is as evident as the apathy of the American people at the terrible outrage they have caused. It seems incredible that no law can be put in force on the other side of the Atlantic to suppress a conspiracy that makes war upon humanity, and that the authorities of New York are unable to prevent public appeals for a so-called 'Emergency Fund', the avowed object of which is indiscriminately to kill innocent men, women and children.[47]

I glanced at the other papers. 'The *Globe* is another that nails the guilt at the doors of Irish insurrectionist lodges in Boston and New York,' I said.

'They are greatly to blame. Antagonism to England based on

ancient woes has combined with popular aspirations that have some ground in justice. But in pursuing their campaign of hatred they have allowed themselves to become the dupes of a dangerous friend. An adversary, Watson, with access to resources infinitely greater than the dollar contributions of a people in exile.'

'What can you mean?' I exclaimed. 'What adversary is it that would vent acts of war upon the innocent!'

Holmes rose from his chair and went to stand in our window, gazing intently at the dark grey clouds that moved heavily towards us across a leaden sky.

'The wind has shifted to the east,' he said, in a sombre voice.

'There will be snow by nightfall,' I agreed.

'And after the snow, what then, Watson?'

'I do not follow you.'

'Perhaps it is as well that you do not. I was forgetting that your brain is overtaxed.'

'I am fully recovered this morning,' I returned.

'I am glad to hear it, for I should welcome your customary sagacity. Here is a boy with a wire, and it may bring the news I am expecting. Ah, yes. What do you think of that, Watson?'

He tossed the telegram over to me. It ran as follows:

Portmanteau found at Charing Cross cloakroom. Come immediately.

                              Lestrade.

'I congratulate you, Holmes,' I said. 'This is what you foresaw. Do you wish to leave for the station immediately?'

'What is the time? Not ten o'clock. We should go now, for we dare not assume that the danger is past.'

When we arrived at Charing Cross, we found the dapper detective waiting for us outside the cloakroom. He greeted Holmes with a respectful deference very different from his cock-sure manner of the night before.

'I am glad that you were able to come, Mr Holmes,' said he. 'Acting upon your suggestion, I issued a general warning to all the London stations. Package No. 314 is our first fruit.'

'Have you left the portmanteau *in situ*?'

'No. The senior counter-clerk, who discovered the nature of its contents, and acting upon his own initiative, removed a metal box that was inside the portmanteau and carried it to the far end of the arrival platform, afterwards returning for the portmanteau itself. They can now be examined without the risk of an explosion demolishing the station buildings.'

Whilst Lestrade had been recounting these facts, he had led us across the station concourse, crowded with the usual press of travellers, and through a gate in the barrier that separated it from the platforms. A further barrier had been erected across the approach to the last platform, which was quite deserted except for the small knot of officials gathered around a porter's truck placed at the far end of the platform, where it runs out to Hungerford bridge. The men fell back as our party approached, enabling us to see, placed at opposite ends of the truck, a long black portmanteau and a small tin box.

'Apart from lifting out the box, the contents of the portmanteau have not been disturbed,' said Lestrade. He inserted his hand into one of the wells of the portmanteau and lifted out a small, flat object similar in shape and appearance to a cake of cheap soap, whitish-grey in colour and oily to the touch.

Holmes took the object from him, turned it over carefully in his hands, examining it closely, and held it for a moment to his nose.

'It is dynamite of American manufacture,' he said at last. 'Probably from Philadelphia, where it is known as Atlas Powder and is made by a process which substitutes wood-pulp for the more usual absorbent, kieselguhr. It looks innocuous, does it not, Watson? Yet the destructive force of dynamite is thirteen times greater than that of gunpowder.'

'A boon to engineers,' said I, 'but a barbarous weapon in the hands of reckless men.'

'You are right. How often, within the fruits of man's ingenuity, lie the seeds of his own destruction! At what time was the portmanteau handed in?'

'Mr Newnes, who is the senior counter-clerk, received it,' answered Lestrade, indicating a prim-faced man of about thirty years standing among the railway officials.

'I understand that it was you who removed the portmanteau to the platform. You are a brave man,' said Holmes, shaking his hand.

'Thank you, Sir. It was nothing, Sir. The portmanteau was handed to me yesterday afternoon, between seven o'clock and half past the hour.'

'You cannot be more definite?'

'Forty-two packages were received during the period in question. Number 314 was the seventh of them.'

'Seventh out of forty-two. Then it was almost certainly handed to you during the first half of the period.'

'That is so. The procedure followed in the cloakroom is to record the time of receipt for the first package received after each hour, and again for the first received after each half-hour. This saves the clerks' time when a sudden rush is on, and generally there is no need to be more precise.'

'Naturally not. Seven o'clock. That is fifteen hours ago. Can you describe the person who handed in this package?'

'He was above the middle height, shaved on the chin but with whiskers and a moustache, a sallow complexion, with a flattened nose, wearing a brown billycock and a black overcoat. This was of good quality, but at least one size too small for him.'

'I see that courage is not the limit of your qualities. You are certain of the detail concerning the overcoat?'

'I am.'

'Proceed.'

'He struck me as a man of impatient habit. He spoke with an American colour to his speech, and smoked short thick cigars of a brand which I know to be American.'

'You are a remarkable observer of detail, Mr Newnes. May I ask if you recall so precisely all the passengers who deposit their luggage at your cloakroom?'

'I retain an impression of them for a short time, Sir,' answered the clerk. 'Longer if the person strikes me as unusual. It is a hobby with me to estimate their circumstances and occupation.'

'And a most useful one. What conclusion did you reach in this case?'

'No definite conclusion, Sir. The person displayed the agitated manner of a man who is anxious to catch a train, and yet a furtive quality which put me in mind of an absconder. There was a distinct air of the vagabond about him.'

'Excellent. Lestrade, you must enrol this man into the Force at once! So, an anxious and furtive man wearing a coat too small for him hands in this portmanteau soon after seven o'clock. Have you seen him since?'

'Yes, Sir. He returned an hour later and took one of his packages away.'

'He deposited more than one?'

'This portmanteau, and a large green canvas bag. He was insistent that I should take particular care of the bag, and on no account was I to stack any other package upon it. I have to say that I did not follow his instructions. The canvas bag was uncommonly heavy, and I placed it upon the lower rack. Shortly afterwards I placed another package on top of it. When the American called again, after eight o'clock, he may have observed this, and for this reason withdrew it.'

'Did he complain of your treatment of the bag?'

'No.'

'So he may have returned with the preconceived intention of withdrawing it?'

'That is possible.'

'Lestrade, have you discovered what time the infernal machine was deposited at Victoria station?'

The Scotland Yard detective pulled out a dog-eared notebook and thumbed the pages. 'When the wreckage was cleared away from the cloakroom, several fragments of a dark blue portmanteau were found to be embedded in the splintered planks of the floor. No other parts of any luggage were found forced into the woodwork to such a depth, which suggests that the blue portmanteau contained the device.'

'Well reasoned,' said Holmes approvingly.

'A blue portmanteau was left at the cloakroom between half-past-seven and eight o'clock,' Lestrade continued. 'The clerk does not recall the appearance of the person who deposited it, because that period of the evening is exceptionally busy. The Continental Express departs at eight.'

'Our man may have taken that fact into consideration when planning his movements. Very well. Since the missing green canvas bag did not go to Victoria, it must have been taken somewhere else. Do not relax your vigilance, Lestrade, just because the danger of another explosion has receded.'

'Do you believe that it has?' asked Lestrade hopefully.

'I do. The simple mechanism which is used in these machines can be wound up to go for twenty-four hours. Sometimes more. But the alarum mechanism, which has to be separately wound, can only be set for twelve hours. The hand has then completed a full circle of the dial and can only repeat its traverse. More than twelve hours have now elapsed since the devices were placed in position, which means that the danger of an explosion from that cause has passed. We may even be able to estimate the time when the devices were prepared, because, as you can hear, the clockwork within this metal box has not yet run down.'

In the silence that followed this remark I distinctly heard a hard, measured ticking that issued from the tin box.

'Do not handle it roughly,' warned Holmes, as Lestrade reached out to take the box. 'It is the detonator and should have exploded already.'

10

A CAKE OF DYNAMITE

HOLMES'S OBSERVATION PRODUCED a strong tendency on the part of those gathered around the truck to move away from it. When I observed my friend bending forward to examine the detonating box, I began to share their disinclination to remain. Holmes, however, seemed unaware of our apprehensions, and evidently shared none of them, for he proceeded to study the exterior of the box as dispassionately as though it had been a shilling caddy of Mazawattee.

'What if the mechanism is set to detonate when the lid of the box is raised?' I asked anxiously.

'I have considered that possibility but discarded it,' answered Holmes. 'The purpose of these outrages is to strike terror into the heart of the populace by reason of their unpredictability as to time and place. There will be no element of surprise if we are blown to pieces while examining it. Black cobblers' wax has been used to seal the lid. Well, that is easy enough to obtain. And it will be easy to remove. However, our first task must be to convey the explosive contents of the portmanteau to a safe distance. Lestrade, if one of your men will bring the mail-basket which I see at the end of the platform, we may begin to empty the portmanteau of its lethal hoard.'

I am no stranger to danger, but the scene which followed, though short in duration, remains etched upon my mind as the most alarming episode of its kind that fate has ever called upon me to endure. One slip on the part of Holmes or Lestrade as they transferred the deadly cargo to the basket, and our deaths would have been certain and immediate. In our last mortal moments, we should see with sudden horror the oatmeal-coloured bar slip from the hand that held it, elude the other that sought to grasp it, and fall with a dreadful slowness to the moment of devastating impact with the ground.

My eyes never strayed from the two men's hands as they repeated the same simple movements, at a uniform and unhurried pace. Steadily the bars of dynamite in the portmanteau diminished in number and those in the basket increased. Eleven, twelve – each one of us was inwardly keeping the tally – twenty-five, twenty-six – the long seconds crawled past – forty-eight, forty-nine – now only one more bar remained in the portmanteau. Holmes lifted it with the same deliberate care that he had applied to its predecessors. He passed it to Lestrade who, in the increased tension of the moment, took it awkwardly, tried to catch it in his other hand, and succeeded only in knocking it to one side. Quick as lightning, Holmes's cupped hands were beneath the falling bar. They caught hold of it firmly, and pressed it a second time into the trembling hands of Lestrade. This time the detective made no mistake. Clasping it between both hands, he conveyed it, without further misadventure, to its place in the basket.

Each man present gave vent to a profound sigh of relief that seemed to well up from the very heart of his being. Lestrade's crimson face was shining with sweat, while even the normally impassive features of my friend were beaded with tiny drops of moisture.

Two constables wheeled the basket away along the platform, for eventual conveyance to Woolwich, and Holmes turned his attention upon the portmanteau.

'All the dynamite was packed into the left-hand well,' he said, 'resting upon what appears to be an old pair of trousers. Yes. Of American manufacture, I perceive. No English tailor would impose a pocket on the hip in that manner. It is exclusively an American styling. Attached to the trousers is an old pair of braces, mended with card.[48] Very good. In the pockets: nothing. That has emptied the left well. The right well contained the detonator. Beneath it is a crumpled newspaper – let me see – the *New York Sun*, dated February the 8th. That is three weeks ago. And at the bottom – dear me. What can this mean, Watson?'

He lifted out from the portmanteau the tweed overcoat which we had last seen upon the back of one of our pursuers of the previous day. There could be no mistaking the large buttons of imitation quartz which, as Holmes smoothed out the material, feebly caught the light, like wan diamonds.

'Curiouser and curiouser,' said Holmes. 'One of the buttons has been newly cut off. A knife has done it. See where the direction of force has dragged the cloth. The mutually opposed action of a pair of scissor-blades will never produce that effect. Well, what do you make of this mystery, Watson?'

'I am completely at a loss,' I exclaimed.

'The web is certainly complex. I think I may say that it is extraordinarily complex. Well, let us continue to advance into it. This metal box contains the detonating mechanism. I propose to open it. You have suggested that the box may be a snare. I consider the probability a slight one; nevertheless, it would be wise for everyone but myself to retire to a distance of thirty yards.'

'I shall remain here,' I answered promptly. 'If your body is to be distributed in pieces over the platform, then so shall mine.'

'I too am for staying,' echoed Lestrade.

'Very well,' agreed Holmes, 'but no more than the three of us shall remain. No purpose will be served by exposing family men to needless risk.'

When Lestrade's assistants and the railway officials had moved back along the platform, Holmes placed one hand firmly on the lid of the box, and with his pocket-knife chipped the black wax away from the four edges. When this was done, he hesitated for a moment.

'I do not believe that this will blow up in our faces, but if it should do so there will be no time then for *les bons adieux*.'

'Oh, open it, Holmes!' I cried. 'Nothing could be worse than this suspense.'

He knelt, so that his eye was at a level with the lid of the box. Then he prised open the lid very slowly, watching for any movement as the mechanism within the box became visible. At length the lid came away completely, and we were able to gaze into the wicked heart of the machine.

'The aspiring outrage-monger does not require much for his purposes,' Holmes mused. 'A pistol, a cheap alarum clock, a small cake of dynamite, and a handful of detonators. Add a few inches of wire and he is fully equipped as the agent of destruction.'

'Provided that his fingers are nimble,' said I. 'And even that does not guarantee the success of his foul venture.'

'Apparently not. Let us discover what went wrong.'

'You mean, how it went right!' exclaimed Lestrade. 'The failure of the detonator may have queered his plans, but it preserved the lives of several hundred innocents sleeping in the hotel.'

'They have undoubtedly been spared a rude awakening,' observed Holmes.

He spoke abstractedly. His thin, delicate fingers probed the intricacies of the mechanism, tracing the wires between clock and pistol, while his keen brain determined the course of events.

'The alarum winder on this Peep o' Day has been wired to the trigger of the pistol,' he said at last. 'The alarum was set for – let me see – one o'clock, at which time the alarum duly sounded, the winder moved and the hammer of the pistol went down.'

'Then why did it not explode?' I asked.

'Because the percussion fuse, which should have fired the detonator embedded in the cake of dynamite, has been placed half an inch out of position. The hammer of the pistol has struck just to one side of it.'

'And it is that half inch which has made the difference between life and death!'

'Ah, Doctor,' interposed Lestrade, 'you may take it from someone who has been in the business a good many years. Sooner or later every criminal makes the mistake that takes him to the gallows. It is the job of detectives like Mr Holmes and myself to make sure that those mistakes do not go unnoticed. Isn't that so, Mr Holmes?'

'Indeed it is,' remarked my friend. 'We are the masters of trifles.' There was a world of irony in his voice.

'This error will cost our dynamiter dear,' Lestrade continued. 'It has given us his coat, his trousers, and a foreign newspaper. Our discovery of his other failures will undoubtedly supply further information. By the end of the day we shall possess a complete picture of the man, and it will only remain to locate his whereabouts.'

'His appearance you already have,' said Holmes briskly. 'The cloakroom clerk's description tallies in every detail with the appearance of a man who travelled with Dr Watson and myself on a roundabout journey through the southern counties. His name is Harry Burton. As to his whereabouts, he has been staying at Cobbett's boarding-house in Langham Mews, though I doubt that he is fool enough to be found there now.'

'He may have left personal effects in his room,' said Lestrade, writing the address in his pocket-book. 'He must be a clumsy fellow to have misplaced the fuse by half an inch.'

'It is certainly a considerable margin. Well, well, the morning has proved a most instructive one. Pray keep me informed of the progress of your inquiries at the other London stations. You and I, Watson, can now return to Baker Street. We will take a four-wheeler. This one will do. Climb in.'

'Do you intend to take up someone else on the way?'

'No, we shall return directly to Baker Street.'

'Could we not have done so easily in a hansom?'

'As easily, and more comfortably, Watson. But the London growler has one advantage over the hansom cab. It is equipped with a rear window, through which we can follow the movements of the hansom which was waiting for us to leave the station and has been following us ever since. Will he merely accompany us to our door, or does he entertain thoughts of visiting us? I should certainly like to make his acquaintance.'

'Do you recognize him?'

'I have not caught sight of him. He is far too wily a bird for that. But there is no doubt in mind as to his identity.'

'Then who is he, friend or foe?'

'Is it possible that you do not know? Well, you will not have long to wait for your answer. Here is Baker Street. Do not look back at the hansom, which has slowed to a halt behind us. Now up to our rooms. Ha. The hansom has stopped outside our door. Excellent. I do not anticipate that our visitor will threaten violence, but it is as well to be prepared.'

He slipped a revolver into his pocket and moved his chair so that he sat facing the door. It was not long before we heard the faint sounds of feet moving cat-like along the passage. They paused outside the door and were followed by a crisp knock.

'Come in,' called Holmes.

The door opened and John Klee stepped into the room.

11

THE BLUE-BLOODED ROGUE

'Mr Holmes,' said our young visitor, coolly. 'I have come here to make you an offer.'

'Mr Klee,' replied my companion, in the identical tone. 'I reject it.'

'One moment, if you please. Permit me to tell you what my offer is.'

'I know what it is. You will drop your interest in the Prince of Orange, upon certain conditions, which will leave you free to continue your nefarious activities elsewhere. If that is the extent of what you have to say, you may take your leave.'

Without attempting to conceal his scorn, Holmes turned aside and occupied himself in lighting his briar pipe from the fire. I took the opportunity to study our youthful visitor, who stood in the doorway, thoughtfully biting his lip. He was a short, slim, dark-haired, clean-shaven man, well-groomed and fastidiously clad. He was no more than two-and-twenty, and his fresh, boyish complexion looked unmarked by the harsh experiences of life, save for the white scar at his temple. Yet this seeming innocence was belied by the expression of his eyes. These windows of his soul were the alert, appraising eyes of the adventurer.

'I was warned against you,' he said at last to my companion, who had leaned back in his chair and closed his eyes, seemingly oblivious to Klee's presence. 'I was told that if the Prince employed an agent it would certainly be Sherlock Holmes. As soon as I arrived in London I made my first task that of acquainting myself of your appearance and general habits.'

'You arrived from Paris,' Holmes remarked, without opening an eye.

For a moment Klee looked startled. 'I travelled from Paris, that is correct. I conduct my business in various parts of Europe.'

'Wherever there is an ill-guarded bank to rob, or a man to be set upon and knifed at no risk to yourself.'

Klee coloured as these gibes went home, but he swiftly regained his composure. 'I see that you are trying to get my dander up. I should have thought that was too old-fashioned a ploy for you to try. Or have the friends who warned me against you misjudged your style?'

'Which friends are those?' drawled Holmes. 'The Russian friends whom you betrayed to the Nihilists? Or your Nihilist friends whom you sold to the Russian police?'

'Ah, Mr Holmes, we shall get nowhere sparring like this. I have come to throw my hand in, though it galls me to do so, but you have fairly whip-sawed me in this business. Why could you not have been engaged upon some other little affair these past few weeks? The ingenious system of the marked cards at the Rue Royale, for example.[49] Now there is a puzzle right up your street, I'd have said, but no, Prince Orange calls and finds you at home, and that's my first stroke of bad luck.'

He pulled a chair towards him and, after twisting it around upon one of its legs until it faced him, sat down upon it, with his feet on either side and his hands lightly clasping the moulding along the back. Without the slightest acknowledgement of my presence he continued to address his remarks to Holmes.

'My second stroke of bad luck came when your doctor friend

caught sight of me upon the boat train. Now that really knocked me, for I was on my way back to Warsaw, do you see, and it looked as if you knew more about my business than I cared for. I couldn't figure out what La Sutherland was doing with him, but Paris is Paris, eh? Later I learned that while her hat and cloak might be on their way to Dover right enough, the lady herself was tucking into a mutton-chop at Claridge's. So at last I twigged the game. It was well-played. I must compliment you on your performance, Doctor. The way you hung upon your judy quite took me in. I could have sworn that you were really soft on her.'

There was mockery in his voice, although his features continued in their set mould of apparent candour and straight dealing.

'What is it you want here?' I demanded, gripping the arms of my chair.

'Not so fast, Doctor. I must lead at my own pace. My third stroke of bad fortune came when I chose those two bunglers to watch you on the Folkestone train. I don't know how you gave the slip to them, but I rewarded Burton by giving him the bags to place at the station. Pulled the coat off his back too, to make the bulk agree with the weight. The bag at Victoria went up a treat but not the others. I wonder if you asked yourself why that is, Mr Holmes?'

Holmes opened his eyes and regarded Klee languidly. 'At Charing Cross you deliberately placed the fuse out of position so as to persuade me that your subsequent offer will be made in good faith.'

'And so it will, so it will. This Dutch job should have been a quick one, and would have been if his Precious Highness hadn't called you in. But what's done is done, and what hasn't been done must stay the way it is. To the point, therefore. I can't reach the Prince unless you give him up. The question is, will you do that? No, you won't. So here's my offer. I'll call off the pack for ten thousand pounds. And bring a halt to the dynamiters for another five. Your cheque or the Dutchman's will do for the first, and I daresay that the British Government will cough up for the second.'

'You received my answer at the beginning,' said Holmes. 'It remains unchanged.'

Klee studied him with his sharp, calculating eyes. 'When it comes to explosive bombs,' he said deliberately, 'I am the expert. There isn't much that has gone up in smoke this past few years but I've had my hand in it, as this mark on my forehead testifies.'

'It is the mark of Cain!' I burst out.

'You may be right!' he laughed serenely. 'I'm sure I hope so, for, as I recollect, the patron saint of murder was well protected by his mark. But when I return to London, I shall not be placing my wares in railway stations. I've an idea that hotel cloakrooms will suit nicely for the next attack. The police will find the task of placing a man in every London hotel a sight beyond them, I fancy, and so will you, though you enlist the aid of every guttersnipe in London. So you see, lives are at stake, Mr Holmes, innocent lives; for whose sake fifteen thousand quid looks cheap, I'd have said.'

'You do not impress me, Klee,' drawled Holmes. 'If Klee is your name. If indeed you have a name to lay a true claim to.'

'Take care what you say!' snarled Klee in sudden anger.

'For all your fine airs you are as common at heart as the meanest cut-throat in Seven Dials. I believe I have never listened to a more dastardly proposal. You have no intention of giving up your persecution of the Prince of Orange, nor of curtailing the dynamite outrages. Yet you expect me to set you up in funds so that you can be paid double for your crimes. If you do not leave the room this instant I shall give myself the satisfaction of throwing you down the stairs.'

He had risen to his feet while speaking and took a step forward. There he stopped, and I saw his eyes fixed upon a small revolver that had appeared, as if magically, in Klee's hand.

'I will not shoot to kill, but I shall aim to wound,' said Klee. His face was drawn and white, as if emotions of extreme violence were being reined back by the exercise of an unusually powerful will. 'You have sneered at the memory of my father, a man who lies today in a pauper's grave beside the St Lawrence River because his just rights were not recognized.' There was an infinity of bitterness in his voice as he spoke these words, words that were as much puzzling as they were unexpected. 'I swore to be revenged,' he continued, 'but what I seek now is greater than revenge! It is recompense! Recompense for the years of suffering that an innocent man was forced to endure by the callous indifference of a woman who could have brought him happiness by the stroke of a pen. The lines of battle were drawn up long ago, Mr Holmes, and it is a fight to the finish.'

'So be it,' replied Holmes gravely.

Klee regarded him silently for a moment, and then returned the pistol to his pocket. 'It is a pity that you have not taken longer to consider my offer. I am not alone. The army which I command began as a crew of Irish malcontents, who would pick a quarrel with a street lamp sooner than keep their peace. For years they feuded amongst themselves, but I have welded them into a fighting unit. They hate England, with a bitterness that you will never comprehend, and they will go to any extremity to bring you to your knees. I shall leave the bombs in their hands, for I must be gone from here, as I told you. But while you could trust me to time the explosions for the small hours, when no one's about, can you trust them in the same way? The age-old reckoning of a bog-people is quantity before quality. But it is your decision, Mr Holmes. And so I take my leave.'

With this remark, he turned upon his heel in the haughtiest manner and departed, like a prince withdrawing at the close of an audience.

Holmes stepped to the window to look down at the street where Klee's hansom had been joined by a second, and two men waited opposite our door. When Klee emerged from the house, he conferred with them briefly, and waited while several travelling-cases were transferred from their cab to his own. He then stepped into his cab and was driven away, while the other turned and disappeared in the opposite direction.

When Holmes returned to the fire, he was shaking his head and chuckling uncontrollably. 'Well, what did you make of our visitor, Watson? A bold fellow, was he not?'

'Damned villain!' I answered. 'If he had not been armed, we two could have overpowered him and prevented much further mischief.'

'No doubt, no doubt. He is an interesting example, perhaps the most perfect example that I have observed, of the man of genius who permits a slight, real or imagined, to divert him from the right-hand path, and seek the left. What a scientist the world would have gained if he had pursued his studies in Paris! His work on isomerism might have taken him to the head of the field, and I need hardly remind you of the crucial *rôle* which that branch of science plays in the latest chemical theories. But if the world has lost a scientist, it has acquired a criminal possessed of a scientific mind: clear, tenacious, imaginative, yet animated by a grudge. Were it not for that crack in the marble, he might indeed become the invincible villain that he aspires to be.'

'But Holmes!' I cried. 'A moment ago you were comparing him to a common cut-throat! Now you set him up as some young Alexander of crime!'

'The Alexander of crime,' said he, musing. 'You have a distinct way with words, Watson, as I have frequently remarked. What features in Klee's proposition struck you as significant?'

'It was the performance of an impudent braggart,' said I, 'and I wish that I could have taken a strap to him.'

'His performance was nicely judged, but I think I had the better of him at the end.'

'Did he not threaten the murder of individuals by wholesale, if you did not buy him off?'

'Pooh. He knew that there was never the slightest possibility that I would bargain with him.'

'Then why did he make the offer?'

'To provide the stepping-stone for his real purpose.'

'I am still in the dark.'

'You heard him say that he intends to leave the country?'

'Yes. He mentioned it several times.'

'Five times, Watson. Directly or by allusion. Not to mention the conspicuous transfer of luggage into his cab beneath our window.'

'Is it possible that he wishes us to follow him?'

'He certainly intended us to notice his preparations.'

'Shall we go after him?'

'You are impetuous today, Watson. First ask yourself why Klee should wish to entice us from London at a time when the city is threatened as never before by dark and secret forces.'

I began to detect a glint of daylight beyond the walls of deceit. 'You mean that he intends us to leave England in pursuit of a man whom we suppose to be Klee, while the real Klee remains in London to direct his campaign of terror?'

'I believe that is how he expects us to reason.'

'So we shall remain in London?'

'By no means. We shall follow him to France.'

I struck my hand against my forehead. 'Holmes, I am quite bewildered. Not a moment ago you interpreted his words to mean that he will be staying in London!'

'That is why I remarked that I had the better of him at the end. Across the country of his mind, where nothing is what it seems, I followed him like a well-trained hound with my nose to his red herring. But at the last hulloo I looked up to see where the real quarry lay. It lies abroad, Watson, and thither we must go in quest of it.'

Holmes's remarkable powers of cerebration never failed to impress me, but I confess that I had sometimes felt that in his more daring speculations he would impute to lesser adversaries a subtlety of mind that was the equal of his own rare organ.

'It all seems needlessly complicated,' I protested. 'If Klee wished to conceal from us his intention to go abroad, why mention it at all?'

'Because you saw him on the boat train. That is the grit which his pearl of a plan is designed to conceal from our view. We were certain to suspect that he would try to leave the country again, and he hoped by constantly referring to his proposal to do so that he would excite our disbelief. We are dealing with a master of deception, Watson. But his real intentions are clear to my mind. He has business with the Duke of Albany, whom he had intended to meet upon the steamer or in Paris. Unless we can prevent him, I fear that he will inveigle the duke into a trap from which it may prove impossible to extricate His Royal Highness without a scandal.'

'But this is terrible! Can the danger be averted?'

'Well, let us set about the business of doing so. Pass me the *Bradshaw*. Hm. A steamer leaves St Katharine's Wharf for Boulogne at midnight. That is the slowest route to the Continent but the least conspicuous.'

'Can we afford the delay?'

'We cannot afford to be seen by any of Klee's men. They are certain to be watching all the principal railway stations, and the Prince of Orange will be accompanying us.'

'Holmes, is that wise? Surely it is a case of leading the kid to the tiger.'

'It is true that there is some element of risk. But there is no safety for the Prince in England once we are abroad, and his presence may prove to be of assistance. I will send a wire to the duchess, informing her of our intentions. Let me see. This should make the position clear.'

He scribbled a few lines on a sheet of paper and passed it to me to read. The message ran:

Albani can prepare *The Flying Dutchman* in time for Easter. Her departure for Saxony today keeps her at Dresden for eight nights.

As I glanced up from reading this unexpected message I saw Holmes chuckling at the expression on my face.

'You seem a little bewildered,' said he.

'I cannot see what conceivable purpose this message will serve. What can German opera and the engagements of Madame Albani have to do with the matter?'[50]

'You do not see the purpose, and perhaps a spy placed in the duchess's household will not see it either. But I assure you that Her Royal Highness will understand the matter perfectly. The Dutch prince will be waiting to leave with us at eight o'clock this evening. In the meantime a visit to Simpson's will not come amiss. Their Southdown mutton is unrivalled, and who can say when we shall taste its like again.'

He reached for his travelling cape and stood for a moment at the window, looking down into the street where the forked tongues of yellow fog had begun to lick at the gas lamps.

'The winter has been a long and disagreeable one, Watson. We are fortunate that this case will be taking us to a balmier clime. "Kennst du das Land, wo die Zitronen blühn." Goethe was never pithier.'

12

THE SALT BEACHES

At Esher, we found one of the Duke of Albany's carriages drawn up in the station yard, and at Claremont House the Prince of Orange stood waiting for us in the pillared entrance hall, as Holmes had predicted. When the Prince walked towards us, holding out his hand in greeting, I observed the glow of health in his complexion and a new resolution to his stride.

'I see that Your Royal Highness has found the air in this part of Surrey to be congenial,' Holmes remarked.

'Oh, my dear Sir!' replied the Prince. 'I cannot sufficiently thank you for selecting Claremont House as my place of refuge. There is a blessed presence here, a presiding angel, who has brought me peace and taught me values, such that I blush to recall my former ignorance. Ah, gentlemen, the Duke of Albany is in receipt of a happiness greater than is the common lot of princes. It is wrong of me, I know, to dwell upon such thoughts but had my life taken another course, I might have been the one to win a place at her side. Would it not have been strange for the father to wed one sister, and the son to wed the other! But hush! No more! She approaches; she is nigh!'

The double doors at the end of the room were thrown open

and the young duchess entered.

'Mr Holmes,' said she, bestowing upon him one of her grave and gentle smiles. 'You see that I have understood your cipher. The "Flying Dutchman" is prepared and the clock lacks but a minute to strike the eighth hour.'

'I never doubted that I could rely upon Your Royal Highness,' said Holmes, bending to kiss the hand she proffered.

'You will take a little refreshment before you go?' she asked, signing to a footman,

'No. We must depart immediately, or risk missing the night train to Liverpool.'

'Liverpool?' exclaimed the Prince, in some surprise. 'It is in Holland that my future lies. I see that clearly now.'

Holmes shook his head. 'Has Your Royal Highness ever visited Canada?'

'Never.'

'Like its great southern neighbour, it is a nation of youth and promise. The European traveller cannot fail to be impressed by the energy and easy informality of its people.'

The Prince pursed his lips, but then he shrugged, and said, with a sigh, 'Well, I have placed myself in your hands, so I must do as you advise.'

Holmes gazed thoughtfully at the Dutchman for a moment before turning his attention to the duchess. 'I understand that the Duke of Albany formed a highly favourable opinion of our transatlantic cousins.'

'The life led by the Canadian people struck him as greatly to be envied,' she replied. 'His heartfelt wish was to succeed his brother-in-law as Governor-General.'

'Do you know why he was passed over?'

'He was told that the reason was his poor health. But if the truth be told, Mr Holmes, it is the Queen who will not let him go. He is her Jonathan, and she has made him her private secretary, to keep him by her side. He is not strong, that is true, but he is obliged to exaggerate his weakness in order to obtain any respite at all from his treadmill. I myself shall not be in good health this year, but when my husband was presented with an occasion to leave England he had to seize it, rather than lose the opportunity of obtaining sorely-needed relief.'

The duchess's blue eyes brimmed with tears, which she dashed away with an angry shake of the head.

'Has he entirely abandoned hope of his appointment to Canada?' asked Holmes.

'I believed that he had done so, but recently he has begun to speak of it again.'

'Can you be more particular?'

'At first, it was only his manner which had changed. I had become used to seeing him grimace irritably when the subject of Canada was mentioned. Then I noticed that he was no longer doing so.'

'When was this?'

'It cannot be more than three weeks ago, because that was when we returned from a protracted stay with the Queen at Osborne.[51] Then, on the day that you visited him, he remarked, at breakfast, that Ottawa might not be lost after all.'

'Has he been visited recently by any of his Canadian acquaintances?'

'I cannot recall anyone, except young Mr Klee.'

'When did Klee call upon him?'

'He has done so on more than one occasion. He first presented himself upon the day following our return from Osborne. But surely he cannot have raised my husband's hopes? He is little more than a puppy. It will require the utmost skills of diplomacy to persuade the Queen to let my husband go.'

Holmes nodded, thoughtfully. 'Well, we must trespass on your kindness no longer,' he said.

The Prince took the duchess's slim, white hand, and kissed it tenderly. 'From the bottom of my heart I thank you for the peace which you have brought to my soul,' said he, in a trembling voice, while gazing into her eyes.

The duchess gently drew her hand away. 'I have taken good care of him, Mr Holmes,' she said. 'Do you likewise.'

'What a woman!' sighed the Prince, as we drove away from Claremont's terraced heights. 'I do believe she is a saint!'

'Whatever further devilment is afoot,' remarked Holmes, 'I think that she knows nothing of it.'

'Surely you never entertained suspicions of that noble creature?' exclaimed the Prince, colouring with anger and dismay.

'I exempt no one from suspicion,' answered Holmes coldly. 'The principle that a person is innocent until proved guilty is a cherished liberty of British justice. But to apply the same tolerance during an investigation would seriously restrict the process of inquiry. You will recall that I asked the duchess what had caused the revival of the duke's interest in Canada.'

'I was sure that you had a good reason for your question,' said I. 'Though I could not see what it was.'

'She pooh-poohed the importance of John Klee – of course, that proves nothing either way. But had she been privy to the encounter between them, she would never have dated Klee's visit so precisely to the recrudescence of her husband's hopes. Clearly, it does not occur to her that they could be associated. However, her scorn for the young man suggests that she is not entirely easy in her mind.'

'I am not surprised,' I exclaimed. 'I cannot conceive what mutual interest could unite the offspring of a Canadian pauper with a Prince of the Blood.'

'You do not see the connection? Well, perhaps it requires the specialized knowledge that I have taken pains to acquire. You are an assiduous reader of the society papers, Watson, but those journals merely record the froth upon the stream of life. To learn what dark, strange creatures move and prey beneath the surface we must turn to the gutter press. Nine tenths of what is written there is speculation and innuendo – but in that last tenth lies informa-tion which, when properly understood, could shake a dynasty.'

'But great heavens!' cried the Prince. 'If such dangers are press-ing about the duke in France, why are we travelling to Canada?'

Holmes shook his head. 'I have allowed Your Royal Highness to mistake our true destination. Throughout our conversation with the duchess, two footmen stood in attendance by the door. They will talk in the kitchens, and their talk may reach the ears of those who seek to ascertain your movements. If your adversaries catch the night train to Liverpool, they will have nothing but a walk by the Irish Sea to reward their enterprise. As for us – no, it is not to the land of the maple that we are bound, but to the home of the lemon tree; the rugged hills of Provence, land of your forefathers and mine.'

Two days later found us descending the fertile valley of the Rhône, passing Gevrey, Beaune, Meursault, and a score of other villages, nestling beside vineyards of no great size, yet dearer to the hearts of men than a thousand miles of featureless steppe.

'Hannibal trod this route,' Holmes observed. 'Caesar after him, and Abdur Rahman, captain of the Saracen host, whose ambitions once posed as terrible a threat to Europe as those of the Russian Czar today. Here is Orange, the Roman Arausio, cradle of Your Royal Highness's race.'

The Prince gazed through the window at the scant relics of that once mighty entrepôt. 'This was the richest city in Provencia,' he observed sombrely. 'Cities, like the nations which rise from them, wax and wane.'

I could not but reflect that a similar decline appeared to have come upon the royal house to which the city had given its name. At one time renowned throughout Europe for the enterprise and vigour of its princes, the family had dwindled to three uncertain members, a rake-hell king, a prince in fear for his life, and a four-year-old girl.

We broke our journey at Avignon, where, on a balcony above

the river, Holmes spoke once again of the dark matters which had brought us from the fogs and wintry winds of England to the warm and brilliant south.

'You will recollect that I have spoken of a multiplicity of threads in this case,' he began, 'unprecedented in my experience of crime. All the threads lead to John Klee but where do they stretch beyond him? Despite his fine ways, he has always been a hired man. Let us consider the threads in turn. The attempt to gain possession of Your Royal Highness was the first strand to present itself, and has proved the simplest to unravel.'

'My father has never concealed his hatred for me,' said the Prince bitterly.

'Well, we shall see. The second strand brought into view the desperate band of Irish dynamitards. Beyond Klee this thread leads to an American hand, moved by misguided hatred of the English people. But this thread also touches another, more shadowy hand. There are many nations which envy our ascendancy, and I have no doubt that Klee's malign humour is capable of drawing together two nations that lie on opposite sides of the world, and at opposite poles of civilization.'

'You do not name this other nation as Russia,' said I, 'but from the remarks that you have frequently let fall I suspect this to be the land, ambitious and tyrannical, that you mean. How will you frustrate its enmity?'

'I shall work to do so in Cannes, whither the third strand is leading us, to the encounter between Klee and the Duke of Albany.'

'Who is Klee's master there?'

'That is the question to which I have sought an answer since I first surmised that a liaison was being formed between them.'

'What conclusion have you reached?'

'I have found no evidence that in this matter he is working for anyone but himself. If this is so, his interests are more closely connected with its success than is customary with him. He will be more determined upon victory, and ruthless towards those who oppose him. We must therefore take every precaution not to alarm him until we are ready to pounce. For the three of us to arrive together in Cannes would be an act of the highest folly. I have made arrangements to proceed there alone.'

'Holmes, I forbid you!' I protested. 'If Klee is as desperate as you say, he will brook no interference in his vile plans.'

'I think that I have hit upon a ruse to approach the duke even under Klee's nose,' replied Holmes with a smile. 'Fifteen minutes alone with the duke will be sufficient for me to persuade him of the dangerous course he runs. Do not be apprehensive upon my account, but it is for your safety and that of His Royal Highness that I am concerned. Klee's attention will be firmly centred upon the duke, but the enemy is many-headed, and Avignon lies on the main route to the coast.'

'Can you suggest a more retired place?' inquired the Prince.

'Arles, where the Rhône divides at the head of its delta, is off the beaten track. To the south stretches the windswept and thinly-populated marshland of the Camargue.'

'There is no more to be said,' exclaimed the Prince, emptying his glass. 'For many years I have hoped to visit the lakes and islands of the Camargue, breeding ground for innumerable species of birds that are rare or unknown elsewhere in Europe. Dr Watson and I will take up residence in Arles tomorrow.'

'That is excellent. Letters will reach me at this address.' He scribbled a name upon a sheet of paper and passed it across the table. 'Keep me posted, Watson, of any events that strike you as unusual.

'I shall despatch a letter to you each evening,' I assured him.

So it was arranged, and thus we parted, Holmes travelling on to Cannes, and the Prince and I to the small provincial town of Arles. Once again the last of the Oranges had been placed in my care. I was determined not to fail Holmes a second time.

At breakfast next morning, the Prince expressed his eagerness to visit the eerie world of the Camargue. We engaged horses and a guide, and rode out from the city southwards along a stony track past lush farmland which, after a few miles, was succeeded by a landscape as wild, desolate and inhospitable as can be found anywhere on earth. For an account of the events of the next few days I am able to draw upon the letters that I composed during the afternoon hours of enforced idleness and posted upon our return to the hotel.

LA CAMARGUE, 24 March

My Dear Holmes,

This is an awful place. Since early morning, we have been encamped upon a slight eminence above one of the wide sheets of water that interpenetrate the arid plain. Though our position is no higher than a yard above sea level, so monotonously flat is the landscape that we are able to see for many miles in every direction. Acres of coarse grass and stunted prickly bushes stretch behind us and to either side, punctuated by the occasional tree bowed and broken before the relentless north-west wind.

The scant herbage provides sustenance for troops of wild black bulls and the white horses that roam freely across the dunes, watched over by peasants whose reed-hovels we have twice come upon, half-hidden in the marshes. The few fresh-water lakes prove, upon inspection, to be putrid and stinking, while those others formed by incursions of the sea are thickly encrusted with salt, and bordered by the grim skeletons of dead and dying tamarisk trees. Yet to an ornithologist as dedicated as Prince Alexander of Orange, this terrible land appears as desirable as the Elysian Fields. Wholly uninviting to man, it has provided safe harbour for an incalculable number of birds, which wade in their thousands in the brackish waters of the marshes, and fly in dense clouds above our heads.

The Prince stares intently at the birds for a considerable time, then he records an impression in his pocket-book – he is an accomplished water-colourist – annotating the sketch with details of the bird's habitat and behaviour. He is a true enthusiast.

But while for him the land that we have entered is a paradise on earth, a realm where he is content to remain an hour or more quite motionless lest he disturb the antics of a distant fowl, for me the Camargue presents a graver aspect. These stagnant tarns owe their curious outline to an archaic network of water channels that once brought to this place vessels and mariners from every corner of the ancient world. The ridges upon which we stand were then teeming wharves, well-stocked warehouses, and the dwelling places of rich merchants, echoing with cries and laughter in a score of tongues. All has vanished. The silt and the salt have claimed the land, and everything is ended as though it had never been....

25 March

I have discovered that we are not so isolated in these marshes as I had supposed. There are first of all the native inhabitants of the place, whose employment it is to corral the young bulls at certain seasons of the year, and to keep watch over the herds of horses that are owned commonly by the people. We sometimes see a troop of these creatures cantering in the distance, their long tails and manes streaming in the wind, and presenting a most brave spectacle. Our guide informs us that they are of a stock originally brought here by the Arabs in one of their frequent invasions of this region.

We had not been at the lake for more than an hour this morning when one of the *cabales*, as the riders of the white horses are known, galloped up to us. He was a tall, clean-shaven fellow, and stared down at us in a disdainful fashion and without a sign of deference. They are said to be a fiercely independent sort of people, hot-blooded yet living according to a harsh code of conduct which they scrupulously follow. The fellow exchanged a few words with our guide, in the *patois* which the natives use to communicate with one another, and after a further searching look at the Prince and myself, rode away along the dunes.

Then there are the bird-hunters, parties of citizens from Arles and further afield, who flock here each Sunday, and to a lesser degree on other days, intent to shoot and eat every bird unwise enough to fly within range of their guns. Their activities greatly distress the Prince, who would sooner kill a man, I think, than one of his beloved birds.

This morning we were approaching our camp when a small brown bird darted out from a tangle of dead trees ahead of us.

'It is surely Emberiza hortulana!' the Prince cried, and in an instant had whipped out his field-glasses and was following the darting flight of the pink-bellied bird along the reedy margin of the lake. 'Truly remarkable!' he exclaimed, turning to me once the bird had disappeared. 'The winter home of the Ortolan Bunting has never been ascertained, but it is assumed to lie somewhere in the northern regions of the African continent. Can it be in the safety of the Camargue that it sojourns during that season, before flying north to breed? If I can establish beyond doubt that these arid dunes are its winter home, I shall write a monograph about it for the *Bulletin*.'[52]

This discovery put him in high spirits. Indeed, you would be surprised at the great changes that this alfresco life have already wrought in him, in so short a time. Would I have prescribed persistent wind, the persecutions by insects, and proximity to a stinking marsh as the surest remedy for his condition? Yet such they may prove to be.

26 March

Today we saw no one on the marshes until our journey home in the evening. In the lea of a small group of trees bordering the road we encountered the first of the gipsies who, each spring, journey to this remote corner of the world from every part of Europe. They come to honour their gipsy saint, and for three days the fields around her shrine echo to the strange music and exotic stamping of this proud and secret people. The solitary gipsy whom we met today, vanguard of the army of many thousands that will shortly arrive here, was a young man, with the nut-brown skin of one who has passed the greater portion of his life beneath the open sky. His clothes were shabby and stained but he wore a bright, spotted handkerchief over his head, and below each ear dangled a gleaming ring of gold.

He had undoubtedly been keeping us under observation because, after addressing us in his incomprehensible lingo, he approached the Prince and, delving into his grubby shoulder-pack, brought out a brilliantly-plumaged teal, still alive but with its feet bound, which he endeavoured to press upon him.

The Prince declined the offering, until a sudden thought occurred to him. He took the bird and examined it carefully.

'This bird has not been limed. How was it trapped?'

As though he could sense the drift of the Prince's question, the gipsy gave a broad grin and pulled from his pocket a length of tough cord terminating at each end in a heavy wooden ball the size of a cob-nut.

'How does he use this?' asked the Prince, turning the unfamiliar object over in his hand.

'It is almost certainly thrown,' I answered. 'Like the weapon employed by the Hottentot in their pursuit of ostrich. The cord wraps itself around the legs of the bird and brings it down.'

'Unharmed?'

'If thrown by an expert.'

The Prince became intensely excited. 'But this will enable me to secure a live specimen of the Emberiza hortulana which we were fortunate enough to observe yesterday.' He rippled through the pages of his pocket-book to the sketch he had made of the winter visitor and, by using a mixture of hand-signs and French, reinforced by the offer of a dozen gold coins, he conveyed his meaning to the Romany, who, nodding vigorously, pointed to the Prince's drawing and then to his singular weapon.

'Alive,' insisted the Prince emphatically. 'It must be alive.'

The gipsy twisted his mouth and gave a skilful imitation of the lilting chirrup of the feathered treasure for which he was to seek. The Prince nodded approvingly, and pressed two coins into the man's hand.

'Tomorrow, at this place,' he said, pointing to a nearby clump of trees.

With a further unintelligible outburst and a last grin the gipsy stepped off the path for us to pass.

'What good fortune to come upon so fine a fellow!' the Prince declared as we rode on. 'This evening I will prepare copies of my sketches of those other species I require. I am really impatient to return with them to The Hague. When will Mr Holmes be done with this business at Cannes?'

I could not answer him, and there was still no letter awaiting us at the hotel, which I interpret to mean that your business with the duke has not yet reached a satisfactory conclusion. I have some misgivings about the proposed meeting tomorrow, but they are based upon nothing firmer than a feeling of unease, and you have often insisted that one must not place reliance upon feelings alone. Yet I could wish that the Prince had been less impulsive in his offer of money, which must always excite the cupidity of the gipsy race. The possibility of an ambush haunts my thoughts, but I can think of no argument strong enough to persuade the Prince to stay away from this rendezvous. Perhaps tomorrow's dawn may suggest a course for me. I pray that it can, and that we shall shortly have the pleasure of seeing you.

13

THE INGENUOUS CHUM

NEXT MORNING THE *mistral* was blowing. A yellowish haze obscured the pale disc of the sun, and clouds of dust, blown in from the surrounding hills, swirled down the narrow streets, coating every inch of space to which they could not penetrate with a fine, choking powder.

'The gipsy will not go abroad today,' I said to the Prince, over breakfast. 'No one ventures out in the *mistral* who can remain indoors.'

'You forget that for the *Romany* race there is no indoors,' the Prince answered with a smile. 'They are born and bred beneath the open sky. The *mistral* holds no terrors for them, nor shall it deter us.'

Further argument proving useless, I resigned myself to another day amidst the salt-marshes. We were the only travellers upon the road, and the land to either side appeared to be deserted, yet, as we rode southward, the conviction grew upon me that every inch of our progress was being watched by hidden eyes. In that wide, flat terrain our singular party was plainly visible over a distance of many miles; and the network of ditches and other irregularities of ground, though slight, was sufficient to conceal an observer from our view though he might lie no more than twenty paces from us. Our guide, hitherto the most phlegmatic of ciceroni, was plainly ill at ease, and glanced repeatedly over his shoulder, as though warned by the peasant's atavistic sense of the proximity of some unseen foe.

'Sire, let us go no farther!' I cried, after we had stopped to water the horses at a reed-girt canal. 'If this gipsy is an honest man, he will seek us out. Theirs is a brotherhood with a thousand eyes. If he comes to the hotel with his prize, you may reward him there, and handsomely. But suppose there is evil in his heart? We are alone in this place, and far from help, and known to be bearing gold. Can the reward be worth the risk?'

'You do not understand,' replied the Prince, staring at me sombrely. 'I am the Hereditary Prince of Orange, heir to the throne of the Netherlands and the Grand Duchy of Luxembourg. I have worn the Order of the Netherlands Lion since I was a child. If I become King, your Queen will send me the Garter. From Denmark will come the Order of the Elephant. From Prussia the Black Eagle, from Russia the White Eagle – but what true honour lies in possessing such toys!'

'Your Royal Highness is a scion of an ancient house.'

'Pah! When my name is no more than a passing reference in the history books, men will still talk of Przhevalsky's horse and Wilson's phalarope. My position debars me from crossing Siberia in search of unknown herds, and from penetrating the tangled waterways of the Amazon basin where, it is certain, strange discoveries await the intrepid explorer. I must be content with lesser finds. Yet even the least of these brings honour – a true honour – to its finder. I tell you, Doctor, that Emberiza hortulana *var.* Alexandrii will give me a greater satisfaction than all the lions and elephants and eagles from all the kingdoms of the world!'[53]

No words of mine could weigh against so passionate a declaration, and so we resumed our journey. We had almost reached the agreed rendezvous when we heard, from some distance behind us, faint yet clear, the call of a bugle. I cocked my revolver, and cast an anxious glance at the tussocky landscape that flanked the road, lest that warning sound should be the signal for an attack upon our small party. The rank grass dipped and rose, and the dark flame of a solitary cypress guttered in the wind like a devil's candle, yet of the presence of man in that wilderness there was no sign.

'Look there!' the Prince exclaimed, pointing a beringed finger at a small cloud of dust which had appeared upon the road from Arles. Again the note of a bugle sounded.

'It is the post-horn,' explained our guide, squinting into the wind. 'It will be young Pierre. Soon you will see him. There!'

The figure of a solitary horseman had become visible against the cloud of dust kicked up by the hooves of a horse that was galloping furiously towards us.

'What does it mean?' the Prince asked nervously. 'I am unarmed.'

'Place yourself behind me,' I said. 'They shall shoot me before they take you.'

The approaching horseman was now clearly visible. He was dressed in the baggy uniform of the French Telegraph Service, and a blue and gold tasselled bugle swung from his shoulders. From time to time he stood up in the stirrups and raised the bugle to his lips, and then the plaintive notes rang out upon the silent air. When at last he came up to us, and reined in his steaming mount, he plunged his hand into an inner pocket, from which he brought out a telegram, and handed it to the Prince with an extravagant flourish.

The Prince read the contents in silence, and in silence passed the flimsy across to me. The message read:

Danger is all around you. Return to Arles immediately, as you value your lives.
HOLMES.

'See yonder!' our guide shrieked, pointing to a nearby brake of trees, where, from the cover of their tangled growth, two gipsies had stepped forth. Seeing our horses at a standstill, they began to run towards the road.

'Ride!' I shouted. 'Ride like the wind!'

I fired my revolver into the air and our horses took off like Derby yearlings,[54] nor did they slacken their pace until the Rhône bridge was in sight. As we clattered over the cobbled streets of the old town a familiar figure sprang from a cab to seize my horse.

'Holmes, can it be you?' I cried.

'Thank heavens that you are both safe,' said Sherlock Holmes. 'There was a moment when I feared – but no, that is past. Yet we must be gone from Arles immediately. The hunt is up and our bird is at the souse.'

'What of the hotel bill?' I protested.

'Paid.'

'Our luggage?'

'Awaits you at the station. For one hour we have the advantage over them, and it may be our last opportunity.'

'Advantage over whom?' said the Prince, speaking for the first time. 'What danger surrounds us? You have called me from an ornithological discovery of the first importance, Mr Holmes. I trust your apprehensions are not mistaken.'

'I was never more certain of anything,' answered my friend. 'Here we are at the station, and the train from Tarascon is in. This compartment will suit us. Who else is boarding the train? Nobody of note. Ah, Watson, old friend,' he exclaimed, flinging himself down in a corner seat. 'Never did I suppose that your industrious pen was destined to do more than chronicle my modest achievements. Yet today that same inky instrument has served to frustrate a great crime.'

'You amaze me, Holmes. How is that?'

'I will tell you. First I must inform you that I have not yet found the opportunity to alert the Duke of Albany to the perils of his present situation.'

'Has the duke been unwell?' asked the Prince.

'He has been particularly active. But he never leaves the Villa Nevada, where he is residing, save in the company of his medical attendant, Dr Roylott, or, latterly, the most dangerous of his companions: John Klee.'

'Klee is staying at the Villa!' I exclaimed.

'He arrived in Cannes upon the train following mine.'

'But could you not have spoken to the duke on those occasions when he was with Dr Roylott?'

Holmes frowned. 'Dr Roylott is something of an enigma. He has served his royal master faithfully for many years, but his behaviour in Cannes does not reassure me. On my first morning in the town, a servant from the villa brought a letter to the Hotel des Pins, where Klee was dining. His companion was a certain Count Pobedonostsev.'

'The Czar's chief minister!' ejaculated the Prince.

'A devious counsellor and a pitiless man. He is the evil genius behind the present tyranny in Russia.[55] I was able to glance at the envelope as it was being taken to the dining room. The hand was Dr Roylott's, with which I took the opportunity to familiarize myself when we were last at Claremont.'

'If Roylott and Klee are conspiring, that is bad, very bad,' said I. 'But why could you not present yourself at the Villa and ask for a private interview with the duke?'

'If I had done what you suggest, my appearance would instantly have aroused the suspicion that you and His Royal Highness were in the vicinity.'

'Then what course of action did you pursue?'

Holmes smiled. 'Perhaps you noticed in the duke's sitting room the framed copy of the signatures to the Berlin Treaty?'

'I must confess that I did not notice it.'

'The duke is a collector of autograph signatures. Upon my arrival at Cannes I took rooms under the name and character of Monsieur Vernet an elderly and white-haired *bouquiniste* of Avignon.[56] I sent a note to the duke, offering, among other choice items, a letter from Mary, Queen of Scots, to her first husband, Lord Darnley, creating him Duke of Albany.'

'Does such a letter exist?'

Holmes waved his hands impatiently. 'That is immaterial. I anticipated that this relic of his unhappy forebear would arouse the present duke's interest, and was not surprised when a carriage drew up outside my rooms with a request to bring the letter to the Villa.'

'Brilliant!'

'Thank you, Watson. But even the best-laid plans "gang aft a-gley" as the Scottish Herrick reminds us. At the Villa I was shown into a small room on the ground floor, where I was shortly joined by a young man with a white scar upon his temple.'

'The devil! The man is everywhere!' the Prince broke in.

'He leaned against a marble table as though the place belonged to him,' continued Holmes. '"So, Monsieur Vernet," he said, puffing at his cigarette, "you have brought us an old billy-doo."

'"Monsieur," I replied, in my coldest tone, "I have been invited here by Monsieur-le-duc."

'"Not so, old cabbage," he answered gaily. "I took the liberty of opening your note, d'you see, and I'll make you an offer for the item in question."

'"Monsieur," said I, "it is more fitting that the Duc of Albany should be the owner of this family heirloom."

'"Oh, he will be, never fear. His birthday is next week, and I've a mind to present it to him." The situation was plainly one from which I had to extricate myself with some celerity. The document-case that I had taken with me contained nothing of consequence since, in the presence of the duke, I should have thrown off my wig and revealed myself, in my usual fashion.

'"So I am not to meet the duc?" I asked.

'"Fraid not, monsieur. So open your bag and let's have a

dekko." I bent down to open my valise, and as I did so uttered a loud cry, and clapped my hand to the small of my back.

'"Are you ill?" he asked, eyeing me suspiciously.

'"It is nothing. It will pass. Help me to this chair. Thank you. Here. Take these keys. Open the valise and bring the letter to me." As I anticipated, this offer dissipated any suspicion which he may have formed that I was shamming. He took the keys from me and tried them one after the other in the lock, but without success.

'"Give them to me," I told him, and peered at them, muttering to myself. I turned out all my pockets, searched in the lining of my hat, until finally, after expressing many apologies for my foolishness in leaving the key at my hotel, I was able to take my leave.'

'That was a stroke of luck!' I said.

'Luck be damned!' answered Holmes shortly. 'While he was assisting me to the chair, I was able to remove the necessary key from the ring.'

'Nevertheless, you were fortunate that he did not recognize you.'

'Ah. As to that, Watson, I greatly fear that some portion of my disguise, possibly the hairline above the collar, was applied with less than my usual attention to detail. In my struggle to locate the absent key I may inadvertently have drawn Klee's attention to this.'

'But this is alarming!' I exclaimed. 'What did he do?'

'I gave him no time to do anything. But as I climbed into the carriage, he was studying me curiously, and I had not been back in the town for half an hour when two ruffians took up a position across the road from my rooms to watch my window.'

'Did they observe you?'

'I had taken the precaution of changing my hotel.'

'Should you not have come away from Cannes at once?'

'And left my work unfinished? You know me better than that,

Watson. No. I had to continue my efforts to reach the duke. But for the remainder of the day, and again yesterday morning, Klee remained close to the duke on their drives through the suburbs of Cannes, where I took care not to be recognized a second time. Klee wore a striped white suit of the most expensive cut and his tie was secured with a topaz, but it was his ears which interested me.'

'His ears?' I asked, not certain that I had heard him correctly.

'They had been pierced.'

'What? Like a woman's!' I exclaimed.

'Exactly so. The carnival reaches its climax today with the Battle of the Flowers. It was possible that he wished to attend the festivities *en travestie*. His features are of a delicacy and pallor that would make such a personation an easy matter. However, during the garden party to which he accompanied the duke yesterday afternoon, Klee disappeared. Nor did he attend the Ball given last night at the Hotel Grand Fleuri. A few discreet inquiries among the servants at the Villa Nevada brought the information that he had temporarily quit Cannes altogether. The reason for his departure, at the very height of the carnival, remained unclear until this morning when your letter, Watson, provided me both with the explanation for his absence, and the purpose for which he had pierced his ears.'

'Did you really learn all that from my letter?' I asked in some astonishment.

'Certainly.'

'I am at a loss to understand how you could do so. I scarcely recall what I wrote. Some description of the salt marshes....'

'Vividly depicted, my dear Watson. I must congratulate you.'

'The teeming bird life. The gipsy that we met upon the road.'

'Ah, yes. The gipsy.'

'The gipsy,' the Prince said quietly.

'The gipsy, yes. What of him?' I asked.

'Is it not obvious?' the Prince continued. 'He was John Klee.'

'Impossible!'

The Prince turned his watery eyes upon Holmes. 'I believe I have made the correct deduction?' said he.

'Your Royal Highness has shrewdly understood the matter,' agreed my friend, though not without a touch of asperity, for his was a temperament that did not always relish the perceptions of others.

'But the gipsy stood some three inches taller than Klee,' I protested.

'Lifts in his heels.'

'His nose was hooked like an Egyptian.'

'Putty.'

'His face weather-beaten and browned by the sun.'

'Come, Watson, these are trifles.'

'He wore gold rings in his ears – ah! What a fool I have been!' I dashed my hand against my head.

'Once he had suspected my identity, it was inevitable that he should instruct his agents to search for you,' said Holmes. 'In so far as anything is widely known concerning Your Royal Highness, it is your sympathy with bird life. Where else, then, were you more likely to be found than within that paradise for ornithologists, the Camargue? Having located you by inquiring of the *cabales,* he set about preparing his trap with all the ingenuity and fiendish daring that we have learnt to expect of him.'

I said, 'Do you mean that it was in order to personate a gipsy that he has pierced his ears?'

'In several respects Klee is a man after my own heart,' Holmes replied. 'He has abundant energy. He possesses the mental brilliance which can retain control of several intricate and interlocking ventures. But in chief, he is a perfectionist. He knew that the gold earrings, which you particularly remarked upon in your letter, would convince you that you had encountered a true gipsy. Though I expect that he took care to pull his scarf lower over his forehead than is usual among that far-flung fraternity.'

'That is so,' I agreed. 'Ah – of course! To hide the acid scar.'

Holmes smiled gravely. 'I fear that if you had proceeded to your rendezvous this morning, the meeting can have had but one outcome, and that a violent one.'

'Mr Holmes,' asked the Prince, 'am I to understand that you deduced Klee's presence in the Camargue from your observation that he had pierced his ears?'

Holmes shook his head. 'That would have taxed even my powers beyond their limit,' he answered. 'Fortunately, Dr Watson provided me with another detail, and this, taken with the first enabled me to see the full nature of the threat to Your Royal Highness.'

'I am glad that I presented you with something useful,' said I.

'I should add that you entirely failed to grasp the significance of your information,' Holmes went on. 'It is certainly correct that every year many thousands of gipsies assemble in the Camargue village of Saintes-Marie where, in the vicinity of their ancient church, they conduct their hallowed ceremonies. A week before the pilgrimage commences no gipsy is to be found within the region of the Camargue, while after the climax they immediately disperse along the roads that will return them to the farthest corners of Europe.'

'Well, what of it?'

'It would have been a wise precaution to ascertain the date of this festival.'

'I see that my account would have been more complete if I had done so. I suppose that it falls on some day next week.'

'It is not for another two months,' replied Holmes. 'To be precise, upon the 24th of May.'

I groaned aloud. 'You mean ...'

'There can be no genuine gipsies today within a hundred miles of the Camargue. But do not blame yourself too severely,' he added, seeing my downcast countenance. 'By writing to me so fully you brought to my attention the facts from which I was able to make my deductions.'

A troubling thought occurred to me. 'Holmes,' I asked, 'when did you first suspect that Klee would search for us in the Camargue?'

'Dear me, this is St Raphael!' he exclaimed, glancing out of the window.[57] 'Cannes is the next station. We have one certain hour before Klee can reach us. That is the interval between the trains from Arles. When he discovers that you departed upon this train, he will know that we have out-manoeuvred him. Undoubtedly, he will follow us. He may telegraph one of his associates in Cannes, but time is still upon our side. The stage is set, gentlemen, for the final act of our drama. What boots it that one of the actors is absent! His presence would have introduced violent action, a fault against which Aristotle expressly warns us.'

14

GOLDEN BAYS

WITHIN A FEW moments of our arrival in Cannes we were in a cab rattling up the hilly lanes to the back of the town, where each turn of the road brought us a wider panorama of the coast below. Outspread before our eyes lay the great, tideless sea, protected by the high Alps from the rage of the *mistral*, and of that intense sapphire-blue which only the Mediterranean can assume. Grand hotels studded the length of the shore. Villas of every degree of size and shape nestled within banks of pine and eucalyptus trees in all the outlying portions of the town, and far into the hills. Everywhere flowers grew in profusion. Roses and other plants of summer, all in full bloom, clambered up the houses and cascaded from garden walls.

'You are about to pass a comment upon the physical attractions of this place,' said Holmes, looking at me sardonically.

'What man with half an eye could restrain himself from doing so!' I exclaimed.

'Perhaps your enthusiasm will be tempered when I tell you that more wickedness is gathered along this coast than can be found in any other spot upon the globe. Not London nor Paris nor Manaos contains more evils planned nor greater crimes committed than daily occur within this bower of roses.'

'Nevertheless, you will agree that the view is very fine.'

'The prettiest smile that I ever saw was upon the face of Lucy Hampton. I saw her the day before she was hanged, for poisoning four children for their insurance money. Her face radiated the demure charm of a Greuze.'

'Holmes, you are incorrigible. How far is the Duke of Albany's villa?'

'Another turn of the road and we are there. If the duke is alone, I can proceed at once with my warning. But it is more likely that Dr Roylott will be accompanying him. As my information is for the duke's ear alone, I will require your assistance, gentlemen.'

'We are at your disposal,' said the Prince.

'Your Royal Highness is very good. Are you up to the task of fainting to order?'

'I daresay that I could attempt something along that line. As a boy I took part in theatricals, although I fear that my performances were sadly wooden.'

'So much the better. Watch me closely, and when you observe me raise my hand – so – be so good as to faint.'

'I understand.'

'When you have seen the Prince measure his length upon the ground, Watson, you will hurry to him, examine him swiftly, and turn to me with an expression of anxiety upon your face. Utter the following words: "It has happened again. What am I to do?" Do you understand me?'

'Perfectly.'

'The rest you may leave to me. Here is the villa.'

Our carriage turned off the road between two modest gateposts and, after a short drive along a curving avenue of umbrella pines, stopped in front of a pretty little building set in a small and verdant garden overlooking the sea. A carriage was already drawn up outside the principal door of the villa, in which the dapper figure of the Duke of Albany had just taken his seat. He stared blankly in our direction, then bent his head to Dr Roylott, who was standing by the carriage steps. Dr Roylott murmured a few words in his ear, which had the effect of causing the duke to smile broadly and lift his hand in gracious welcome.

'Mr Holmes, this is an unexpected pleasure. Dr Watson. And – Cousin Alexander, can it be you? You must forgive my poor-sightedness. The sun is quite remarkably bright for the time of year.'

'I trust that Your Royal Highness has benefited from its restorative powers,' said Holmes. 'In England the weather is still exceptionally severe.'

'Ha. Do you hear that, Roylott? Perhaps we shall not return there yet after all. But the grindstone calls, Mr Holmes, there's no doubt about that, I'm afraid. Cousin, I am quite delighted to be able to welcome you to my home from home. Where are you staying? How long shall you be here?'

Leaning upon the arm of the ever-ready Dr Roylott, the duke descended from his carriage and eagerly plied the Prince of Orange with a succession of lively questions. Dr Roylott's eyes flickered from one to the other of us with an expression in which uneasiness appeared to struggle for mastery with curiosity. At a moment when the doctor's gaze was turned from him, Holmes raised his hand, and an instant later the duke gave a cry of alarm. I turned in time to see the Prince of Orange fall like a tree into the duke's swiftly outstretched arms.

'Help me, gentlemen!' the duke cried, and Holmes and I jumped to relieve him of the inert body of the Prince, and bore it carefully to the ground.

'He is stiff as a board,' I exclaimed, endeavouring to take his pulse. In obedience to Holmes's answering nod, I continued with the part assigned to me. 'It has happened again, Holmes. What can I do?'

'What is the matter with him?' asked the anxious duke.

'Are the symptoms as before, Watson?' Holmes asked.

I read the desired reply in the urgency of his expression. 'They are.'

'It is evidently a seizure of some sort,' said Holmes. 'I hesitate to call it epilepsy, for the Prince has assured me that he experienced no previous attacks of this nature prior to this year. The epileptic generally has a history of such attacks, dating back to childhood. That was Golgi's view, and Bertrand's after his Paduan studies. Is it wise to leave the Prince lying in the sun?'

'No, of course not,' said the duke immediately. 'Carry the poor fellow inside.'

'Watson,' Holmes said sharply, 'where is your bag? It is unlike you to be without it.'

Before I could protest that my bag was still in the carriage, the duke intervened. 'No matter. Roylott, have you something in your box of marvels that will serve the purpose?'

Dr Roylott tugged his beard doubtfully. He had said not a word in all this time, although he had followed my pretended examination of the Prince with a keen attention. What suspicions he may have formed he kept to himself. Two stablemen lifted the still rigid body and carried it into the cool interior of the villa, followed by the duke's doctor and myself. We had reached the door when the sound of carriage wheels caused us to look back, to discover that Holmes had by some means persuaded the duke back into the carriage, which was now being driven rapidly away up the avenue. Dr Roylott ran a few paces after the retreating carriage, and then returned to me.

'What is the meaning of this charade?' he demanded angrily.

I stared him fiercely in the eye. 'I must ask you, Sir, to choose your words with greater care.'

'I shall choose them as I damned well please!' was his heated reply. 'Who is that person whom the servants have taken inside?'

'The Prince of Orange.'

'It is truly the Prince of Orange?'

'Certainly.'

Dr Roylott hesitated for a moment before asking, in a more restrained tone. 'Is the duke in danger?'

'Not from Mr Holmes,' I replied.

'Then I suppose there is nothing to be done but await their return.'

He led the way into a shaded room, where the Prince had been laid upon a day-bed, and stood gazing down at him, torn, so it seemed to me, between his suspicion that the Prince was shamming, and his respect for the person of the shammer.

Now that the purpose of the ruse had been accomplished, and Holmes was at last alone with the duke, I judged it permissible to release the Prince from his role. 'I think I see his eyelids flutter,' I said, and obediently the Prince fluttered his eyelids. 'I believe that he is trying to speak.'

'Water,' the Prince murmured, hoarsely.

'Bring the Prince of Orange a glass of water,' Dr Roylott told a servant.

A painful half-hour ensued, during which Dr Roylott asked the Prince, with much show of solicitude, but with an ironic smile upon his face, questions as to the Prince's general health, the frequency of his fainting attacks, and the sensations which accompanied them. At length I had to intervene, pleading the Prince's general weakness, whereupon Dr Roylott, after lighting a cigar, took up a position by a window that commanded a view of the avenue. Here he remained until the duke and Holmes returned, both wearing expressions of the uttermost gravity, and the duke's face, in addition, being a deathly pale.

Upon entering the villa the duke issued orders for every door and window upon the ground floor to be secured. 'On no account is Mr Klee to be admitted,' he emphasized. 'Cousin – gentlemen – be so good as to accompany me to my room.'

We followed him up to a large, airy chamber that opened onto a balcony overlooking the town. For some minutes the duke paced the floor restlessly and in silence. At length he composed himself and addressed us as follows:

'Gentlemen. Mr Sherlock Holmes is the bearer of most unwelcome tidings.' He cast an anguished look at Holmes and then at Dr Roylott before resuming. 'John Klee came to me with the highest recommendation as a man of unimpeachable reticence and honour. Lord Borrowmere spoke of him with high approval, and Sir Richard Curtoys was enthusiastic in his favour. I now have reason to believe that those who introduced him to me had been laid under some vile and intolerable compulsion to do so. That is to say, blackmail.'

The duke hesitated, and in a moment Dr Roylott was at his side. 'Your Royal Highness might prefer to rest now and speak about this matter later.'

The duke gazed sorrowfully at his doctor and shook his head. 'I prefer to speak now, although I confess that the news has shaken me. As you know, Klee swiftly found the way into my confidence. I opened my heart to him and spoke of my longing for an active command. For Canada! He already knew of my thwarted hopes – as who did not – and persuaded me that he could devise a strategy to remove the obstacles that lay between me and my goal. In the desperate state to which I had been reduced, I believed him, I trusted him, never guessing at the terrible means that he would seek to employ.'

His voice tailed away. He appeared to have become the victim of an emotion too powerful to express in words.

'Murder, gentlemen. And such a murder as has not been seen in England these five hundred years. The assassination of Her Majesty the Queen.'

As these fearful words escaped his lips, the duke swayed, and he flung out an arm as though to ward off the assault of some primordial beast. Holmes sprang forward to assist him to a chair. Dr Roylott hurried to a locked cupboard, where he poured some dark liquid into a glass and pressed it into the duke's hand. The duke held the glass but did not drink from it.

'Mr Holmes tells me that this would not have been Klee's first experience of murder,' he continued. 'Responsibility for the dynamite explosions in London can be placed at his door. You, Cousin, are another of his intended victims. Oh, Arnold!' he cried out, suddenly turning to his doctor, and clinging to his lapels. 'You were not convinced that he could help me, and I persuaded you against your better judgement. It's my cursed ambition, which blinds me to the dictates of reason.' Slumping back into his chair, he seemed to shrink in stature. He had become a youth, a child, stricken by the sudden knowledge of the evil which is in the world.

'There is still time to repair any damage that has been done,' said his loyal doctor, gently. 'His appointment as Extra Secretary has not been gazetted.'

'I took him into my household yesterday, Mr Holmes. Thank God that you came when you did.'

I could remain silent no longer. 'In heaven's name,' I burst out, 'why should he attack the Queen?'

The duke hid his face in his hands.

'Her Majesty would never have consented to the Canadian appointment,' said Holmes. 'But if the Prince of Wales became King he would do so, to oblige his brother.'

The duke shuddered. 'What shall I say to Klee when he comes? He will come. I know it.'

'He will be most ill-advised to try,' said Holmes. 'I took the precaution of alerting the French police, who are particularly anxious to interview him in connection with the Besançon murder.'

'No, he will come,' insisted the duke. 'I have a presentiment. He is a man of steel. I recognized this quality in him from the first. I knew that in my service he would be invaluable. He is a man of purpose. Once he spoke to me of his father, who died in penury, broken by a woman's cruel whim. He was determined to right this wrong, so as to lift his head proudly once more in the world of men. He was so resolute. I assured him that I would give him all the help that lay in my command. I would have done so, Mr Holmes, but his passion should have warned me. I no longer know what kind of friend he would have made.'

'An exceedingly dangerous one,' said Holmes.

'I daresay you are right. I do know that he will prove a determined enemy. Perhaps it is not wise to venture into the town today.'

'Your Royal Highness had planned to do so?'

'Yes. To watch the Battle of Flowers from the Club. Perhaps I should have taken part. I have a suit of violet silk decorated with white and violet bows which I had intended to use.'

'Then I should wear it,' Holmes declared. 'With Klee in the hands of the police, you have nothing further to fear from that quarter.'

'Nor you, Cousin, either,' the duke remarked to the Prince of Orange. 'You may return to your country, and I to mine; you to prepare for the day when you are king, I to resume the same old grind, eh, Roylott? For a time it looked as though the New World beckoned. It was always too good a prospect to be true. Well, then, gentlemen, let us to battle – though it be only with botanical weapons. I invite all of you to the Cercle Nautique as my guests.'

After a light repast, during which we digested the fearful news that the duke had broadcast, we drove into the town, and took up our places on the balcony of the Cercle. The premier club in Cannes, like every other building in the town, from the most imposing to the meanest, was dressed with flowers and coloured calico. Windows were draped, banners were everywhere fluttering, and long before the procession was expected to move, the streets and promenades were choked with citizenry, colourfully habited. Circlets of flowers hung about their necks, and in their hats, and in many cases were worn instead of hats, for parties of young girls and not a few young men wore elaborate headpieces fashioned entirely of roses and other flowers of the locality.

When the procession came into sight we were able to observe that the odd devices upon the cars put flowers to even more ingenious use.[58] A myriad daffodil went to form a golden crown; a white boat upon a sea of blue was decked with many-coloured flags and all was done with flowers. Anchors, gigantic lobsters, sea monsters, giants' heads, and many other wonderful representations were greeted with rapturous cheers from the raucous mob.

Alone of our party on the balcony Holmes held himself aloof from the enthusiasm that greeted each new marvel.

'I should have heard from the Sûreté,' he complained. 'I left instructions that I was to be informed as soon as Klee was taken. Is it possible that there is some factor which I have overlooked? It will be a serious blow if he escapes our net. Keep an eye upon the windows of the houses opposite, and I will scan the crowd below.'

'Our task may be an impossible one,' said I. 'With the whole town dressed en fête and many in costume, how are we to distinguish one man among so many?'

'By observing his actions, Watson, rather than his appearance. Certainly his scar will be covered with a mask, and his pierced ears enveloped beneath one of those monstrous hats that so many of the populace are affecting. But his eyes will not be upon the parade but upon us. Ah. Who is that? Do not turn your head until I have looked away. Now. Behind the lemon-seller – do you see him? The man with the fez?'

'I see no one.'

'Has he gone already? Yes. He is running down the alley beside the building opposite us.'

'Can he enter it through a door at the rear?'

'Perhaps. I should feel easier in my mind if we left the balcony.'

At that moment the duke expressed a wish to take part in the procession, and our party retired.

The next events occurred swiftly, within a matter of a few

seconds and yet, though months have passed since that terrible day, the scene still holds the fateful clarity of a dream. I waited with Dr Roylott and some officials of the club behind the Prince of Orange, who stood between Holmes and the duke at the foot of the stairway leading up to private rooms. I heard a curious, rustling sigh in the air. As it grew louder, Holmes shot out his arm and pulled the Prince back from the stairs. Two white roses, dislodged, so I thought, from one of the festoons above us, floated past my face and struck the wall. The duke stumbled against the first step and fell to the ground.

He uttered a sharp cry of pain and, in the instant, Dr Roylott was beside his prostrate master, to ascertain the gravity of his injury. Holmes jumped away from us in pursuit of a slim figure dressed as Harlequin whom I glimpsed disappearing through a narrow door across the hall. A few moments later, Holmes returned, greatly crestfallen, and shook his head.

'Who was he?' faintly inquired the duke, as Dr Roylott and one of the officials prepared to raise him from the floor. 'Was it Klee?'

Holmes nodded.

'You see?' said the duke, with a thin smile. 'He has done for me after all.'

15

THE GRAVE RITUAL

No words of mine can express the horror and despair of the scenes that next ensued. From the moment that the duke fell to the floor we entered a nightmare world, where familiar landmarks seemed to take on a fearful aspect, aloof where not hostile, and where all events conspired against us, to proclaim that man's attempts to mould destiny to his will are ever doomed to disappointment.

The duke was carried from the stairway to the saloon of the club, where Dr Roylott examined his leg, which he had bruised in his fall, and dressed the knee.

'There is no external bleeding,' the good doctor informed us in a low voice, while the duke wrote a telegram of reassurance to his wife. 'But in His Royal Highness's special case, an internal injury presents the greater threat.'

'Is there evidence of such an injury?' asked Holmes.

'Some time elapses before the presence of internal bleeding manifests itself. For the moment I can do nothing but wait, and watch. And fear, Mr Holmes. I do not need to tell you that it is precisely against such an injury of this sort that we have always endeavoured to guard His Royal Highness.'

'I blame myself,' exclaimed the Prince of Orange, holding his head in his hands. 'It was I who knocked him off his balance. Oh, Mr Holmes, it would have been better to allow the falling garland to strike me. It would not have delivered more than a glancing blow.'

'A deathly glance,' replied Holmes grimly. 'Here is the garland in question, which I picked up from the stairs after the duke was carried here.' He carefully lifted the disordered remains of the festoon of white roses from the table where he had placed it upon entering the saloon. 'The garland has the appearance of an ordinary wreath, composed of two small bouquets connected by a longer portion of loosely bound stems. But a glance at the underside reveals a structure significantly different from the usual framework of bent wire and pegs of wood. Concealed beneath each bouquet lies a wooden ball, two inches in diameter, and the connecting stems are secured to a leather thong.'

'But, Holmes!' I cried.

'Yes, Watson. The essence of the structure is identical to the gipsy weapon that felled the bird in the Camargue. In itself it is a weapon unlikely to inflict severe damage upon a man, but if I am not mistaken Klee has introduced a devilish refinement.' He bent his hawk-like features over the garland and carefully sniffed the stalks. 'As I thought. When the garland passed me on its aerial flight I detected a sour odour which had nothing to do with roses.' He cut a thorn from one of the stalks and placed it in a small envelope. 'The stalks of the roses that are selected for the Battle of Flowers are stripped of their thorns. Not one thorn has been removed from these stems, although they are exceptionally long and recurved. A considerable number present a mottled appearance, and have been daubed with a sticky fluid which I am confident will prove to be the same poison that did for Vanderbanck in The Hague. One scratch would be fatal.'

'But any one of us might have picked up the garland!' I cried.

'Klee's attacks are becoming desperate. That is all to the good.

A wild criminal is a foolish criminal.'

'Excuse me,' muttered the Prince of Orange, in a strained voice. 'Excuse me, I am faint.' Clutching the back of a chair, he lowered himself into the seat, and rested the side of his face against the antimacassar.

'If we are not careful we shall have two royal invalids upon our hands,' said Dr Roylott. 'The duke must be taken back to the Villa Nevada as soon as possible. It would be advisable for the Prince of Orange to accompany us.'

Within a few minutes, our carriages were nosing their slow passage through the crowds that were still filling the streets all the way to the outskirts of the town. Their merriment presented a counterpoint of piquant irony to the sombre measure of our thoughts.

We were a mournful party at dinner that evening. The duke ate a little food and chatted with us all, but his conversation was depressed and melancholy. As if convinced that his end was approaching, he talked of his own funeral, and of the royal tombs at Windsor. The Prince of Orange, haggard around the eyes, seemed sunk in despondency so deep that nothing would draw him forth. Only when the duke's remarks turned to the afterlife did the downcast Prince contribute a few words.

'Mr Holmes,' the duke began, 'do you believe in dreams, and ghosts?'

'It is certain that dreams exist,' replied Holmes.

'And are you visited by dreams?'

'I believe that all men are. Few of us can look back upon a life entirely untainted by regret.'

'Ah!' the duke remarked. 'I see that you belong to the school that maintains that the dream is caused by the dreamer.'

'I would place some responsibility upon certain German cheeses,' Holmes answered drily.

The Prince of Orange impatiently pushed aside his glass. 'Have you seen a ghost?' he asked the duke.

The duke bowed his head. 'I believe I have, and it was last night,' he replied. 'My sister Alice visited me; she married the Grand Duke of Hesse. Ten years ago her youngest boy Frittie fell from a window onto the terrace below. Like me he was hae-mophiliac, and though the doctors did all they could to stop the bleeding, their efforts were in vain. Frittie was not four years old, and had the smile of an angel, but I wrote to Alice saying that she was not to mourn. I could not wish upon any child, I told her, the futile life that I have had to endure, tainted by my mother's poisoned gift. My broken-hearted sister died soon afterwards, but last night she came to me. She smiled tenderly, as if she expected me to see her again, very soon.'[59]

'Come, Sir, these are melancholy thoughts,' Dr Roylott broke in.

'Would you prefer us to play tiddlywinks?' the Prince of Orange cried out, in a shrill voice. 'Or hunt-the-slipper, eh? Or leap-frog, now there's a merry game!' He tipped his chair over and leapt across it, and then back again, before resuming his seat at the table before our astonished eyes. 'All too soon we shall not speak at all,' he said, with an abrupt return to his former melancholy. 'Why waste our breath upon trifles.'

The duke retired early, complaining of a headache, and the Prince of Orange announced his intention to do likewise. Before he quitted the room he took Holmes and myself aside.

'I wish to speak of a private matter. I shall not wish to do so when the duke has died.'

'*If* the duke dies,' I corrected him. 'Dr Roylott has examined him repeatedly, and can find no evidence of bleeding.'

'I am not a fool,' the Prince answered. 'We have come through enough dangers together for you to treat me honestly. The duke's doctor can find no evidence because the injury lies too deep. Every hour that passes makes the duke's prospect for recovery worse not better. Dr Roylott knows this well enough. There have been tears in his eyes all evening. Kindly be honest with me, Mr

Holmes. I want no mealy answer. Did Klee aim that poisoned garland at the duke, or at me?'

'I believe that it was aimed at Your Royal Highness,' replied Holmes, with an expression of the most solemn gravity.

'So that in saving my life, we have brought about the death of the Duke of Albany?'

'If His Royal Highness should die as a consequence of his fall, we cannot escape that responsibility. The accident is one that I profoundly regret, but in the particular circumstance I do not believe that it could have been avoided.'

'There was a time, and only recently, when I should not have regretted it at all,' muttered the Dutchman hoarsely. The blood had drained from his face and there was a feverish glitter to his eyes, so that his features had returned to the haggardness which they displayed upon his first visit to our rooms in Baker Street. 'While I was staying at Claremont House I hoped that he would suffer an accident. Yes, it is true. He is not strong and will never be strong. I was not strong but I gained strength with every passing day. The duchess – ah, *la belle Hélène* – if an accident should befall the duke, the duchess in a foreign land. What would become of her? You follow my drift?'

'Perhaps Your Royal Highness should speak no more of this,' said I, for I had begun to understand the sense of his words, and did not wish him to regret his openness in the morning.

'No, I must speak of it, once and for all. But you have guessed, I think, and Mr Holmes too, I daresay. After a decent interval I should have asked the young duchess to be my wife. She has protected me against my enemies. Now it would be my turn to protect her. My father will not live for ever, and then my wife would follow her sister as Queen of Holland. That was my gallant scheme, Mr Holmes, and nothing can ever come of it now. I have killed my Uriah. Do you think that we shall sleep well tonight?'

With this curious remark the Prince left us, and soon afterwards Holmes and I retired to the rooms that had been prepared for us. I rested in a chair beside the fire, for anxiety had driven sleep far from my thoughts, while Holmes stood at the window staring out at the darkened garden and beyond, to where the lights of the city glimmered far below us like a cloud of stars.

'Klee is still there, I am sure of it,' said my friend. 'He knows that he has failed to injure the Prince. Now that he has forfeited the patronage of the duke, the Prince's death offers him his only chance of rich reward. I should be down there, at the Hotel des Pins, for Klee will certainly try to communicate with his pay-master. It is from Count Pobedonostsev that he takes his orders to foment rebellion in Ireland. The opponent of all change in his own land, the Count is not averse to buying sedition abroad. Yes, I should be there now! Here I can do nothing.'

We had relapsed into an uneasy silence when there came to our ears a sudden cry from a room at the front of the house. In an instant Holmes was through the door, and I had risen from my chair to follow him. The upper passage was brightly lit, and the door to the duke's room stood wide open, framing a scene that tore at my heart. The stricken duke lay outstretched upon his simple bed, with Dr Roylett upon his knees beside him, press-ing his master's hands to his lips. I took my place at the bedside, and gazed down at the royal duke, from whose frail body a noble spirit had just breathed its last *adieux*. The face that we had seen so often contract with pain, knew peace at last.

The sound of a terrible weeping broke in upon my sombre thoughts. The Prince of Orange had joined us, his face white as his shirt. I moved to support him, but he shook my hand free and, without uttering a word, reeled from the room.

'The end came swiftly,' Dr Roylott told us, in an unsteady voice. 'When I was roused by the sound of a low cough from His Royal Highness's bed, I hurried to his side, and raised his head to facilitate the breathing. He smiled his thanks and said, "This is it, Roylott." Then came one last cough and he was gone.' The doctor turned his head away and a shudder passed over his strong shoulders. 'I will be obliged,' he continued, with no alteration in his tone, 'if you two gentlemen and the Prince of Orange leave the villa as soon as possible tomorrow. Your presence here can only invite speculation, and there must be no breath of scandal surrounding the duke's death.'

Holmes bowed. 'I will acquaint the Prince with your request,' said he. 'He may wish to leave directly.'

'So much the better. I will order the carriage.' He pulled the bell and faced Holmes again. A dark light that I had not previously observed burned in his eyes, and the brows were drawn tightly together. 'I have little doubt that your reputation for recovering jewels mislaid by foolish women is well-deserved,' said he. 'I think that you also make it your business to contrive the escape of young heiresses from their rapacious guardians. There is a place for all such works of piety. What there is no place for, Mr Holmes, is meddlers. Particularly is there no place for meddlers in affairs of state, where ill-informed interference can tear the fabric of history. My own sorrow is of little account. But you must know that by your antics, Mr Holmes, you have left a grieving mother and a stricken wife, a fatherless child, and another shortly due who will never know his father.[60] You have given us to understand that you place little credence in the afterlife, but I strongly advise you to pray to whatever you hold sacred that Her Royal Highness may safely bear her child, despite the despair into which your reckless prying must now cast her. Good night.'

We filed past the door, which was closed upon us. Back in our room I observed that Holmes's sallow features were unusually flushed but his spirits seemed in no way downcast.

'You look dismayed, old friend,' said he. 'Do you believe that I deserve to be given so harsh a character?'

I lowered my eyes. 'You are the finest man that I have ever known,' I answered.

'Ha. Then you do believe that I merit the doctor's lash. You are right. The death of the duke is a blunder that hurts my pride.

And if there is to be no scandal then I must swallow it. But if Dr Roylott had not been in such a hurry to be rid of us, I should have addressed some pertinent questions to him. He might have found himself hard-pressed to justify his intimate association with John Klee. The dubious game that he has played with his master's trust might have provoked the scandal which he now seeks to conceal.'

'But it was he who counselled the duke against heeding Klee's importunities. The duke told us so himself.'

'Can you think of a shrewder concealment for the doctor's real intent than an ardent opposition to the creature that he was secretly serving?'

'Then you consider that he and Klee are associates after all?'

'I have never doubted it. I do not say that the doctor was privy to the plot to assassinate the Queen. After all, he is an Englishman. Nor is Klee likely to have confided his intentions concerning the Prince of Orange. But the man is not blind. He can not have remained ignorant of the calibre of Klee's associates.'

'But what was Dr Roylott's interest in pursuing the association?'

'Misguided loyalty to his master, Watson. The haemophiliac must pursue a life of gentle stimulation or risk perturbation of the blood. Abrupt excitement is harmful, but so are the effects of prolonged frustration. Dr Roylott believed that the duke's health could be improved by the Canadian appointment. He trusted Klee and has paid dearly for it. I am ready to leave. If you will rouse the Prince we can be on our way to the Hotel des Pins.'

The Prince's room was next to ours, but my knocks went unanswered.

'Have you tried the handle?' asked Holmes.

'Surely the Prince will have locked his door!'

'Evidently not, for see! It opens.'

I burst into the room and cast a frantic look around it. The chamber was empty.

'He has been taken!' I cried. 'Oh, Holmes, to fail again, so soon!'

'Come, come, Watson. You are not yourself. Why assume that the Prince has been abducted before we look for evidence that he has left of his own accord. I daresay that this letter propped against the flask will throw some light upon the matter. In the Prince's own hand too. Let us see what it tells us. Ha. As I expected.'

He passed the sheet of paper across to me. The words scrawled upon it were ill-formed, and had evidently been composed at speed, but I had no difficulty in deciphering the brief message.

DEAR MR HOLMES,

The time has come for me to return to my native land. There lies my destiny. Since I have no wish to endanger further lives, I will go alone. Please do not attempt to follow me.

ALEXANDER.

Beneath the signature he had added, as a touching after-thought, '*De vergeten Kroonprins.*'

'Will you follow him?' I asked.

'You see that he does not wish it. If he succeeds in making his own way home he will thereby acquire a confidence in his own skills that will prove invaluable to him in the difficult months ahead.'

'But suppose that Klee follows him?'

'He will undoubtedly try to do so, unless we can show that the Prince is still in Cannes.'

'I do not follow you.'

'First I must take my leave of Dr Roylott. Remain here in the Prince's room until I rejoin you. Do not be alarmed if I reappear by way of the window. I see that the trellis on the wall extends to the sills of the first floor. It is strongly attached and will bear my weight. I shall not keep you waiting long.'

A few moments after he left the room I could hear his voice in the hall, and Dr Roylott's deeper bass speaking in answer.

'The Prince and Dr Watson will take the carriage,' Holmes replied. 'I have a mind to walk down to the town. The night air is conducive to thought, and I have much to reflect upon.'

The remainder of the conversation was blotted out by the sounds of hurrying servants along the passage. The life of the house was adapting itself to the presence of death in its midst, and soon there came the muffled sounds of necessary tasks swiftly but silently performed. Around the harsher contours of death, the mundane balms of life were being spread like the nacreous layers of a black pearl.

A moment later there was a rustling below the window and Holmes climbed onto the sill.[61]

'The egregious Doctor is now convinced that I have gone,' said he. 'Next to show him that you and the Prince have followed. His Royal Highness wisely left his coat and hat behind. Either of those articles would have identified him immediately. Help me into the coat. Now bring me the small case from our room. Thank you. I call it my box of tricks. Some yellow at the nose. Darker eyes. The Prince's beard is growing again, but remains patchy along the cheeks. This false hair should serve the purpose. There.'

He turned to face me and I gasped aloud, for I was gazing into the very features of the Prince of Orange: the sunken eyes, the wispy beard, the expression of refined melancholy that I had come to know so well.

'It is brilliant!' I cried. 'It is Prince Alexander to the life!'

Holmes bowed, with an awkward, jerking movement of his limbs that were the Prince's own.

'Then let us make our exit,' said he. 'We shall not pass unobserved. Open the door. These stairs are steep. Watson, my good English friend, let me lean upon your arm.'

16

THE BLUE UNCLE

WITH HOLMES'S ARM resting upon mine, we made our way slowly through the hall of the Villa Nevada and out towards the waiting carriage. Here Holmes hesitated for a moment. Then he took a few halting steps back, as if he had remembered some article that he had left behind in his room. At the steps of the villa he hesitated again, and became the very picture of indecision, with his hand tapping his protruding lower lip and then his bearded cheeks, before he turned once more and resumed his careful walk to the carriage.

Once inside he lounged into his seat and said, with a satisfied chuckle, 'Take a squint, Watson, at the second window from the left.'

I did as he directed and saw the tall and brooding figure of Dr Roylott, standing in the shadow of a curtain, and gazing down upon us.

'He is making certain that Dr Watson and the Dutch prince are leaving,' said Holmes. 'Did you observe that I turned about so that the light from the porch shone directly onto my face?'

'I did.'

'Dr Roylott will hardly mistake me for that meddler Holmes.

When Klee arrived in Cannes, a servant of the villa conveyed Dr Roylott's letters to him. I fully expect the doctor to send a letter now, in which he will report, with perfect confidence, that the meddler has left on foot, and that you and the Prince of Orange have left in a carriage. Driver, stop in the shadow of those trees. We will remain here, Watson, until the messenger has overtaken us. Here he comes. Yes, it is the same fellow. Wait until he has disappeared around that curve in the road. Now drive on. The news of the duke's death will provoke Klee to even greater efforts to retrieve his fortunes by securing the person of the Prince of Orange. We do not know where Klee is lodging now. But when he learns that the Prince is at the Hotel des Pins, he will not be slow to make his presence felt. Here is the hotel. Your arm again, Watson.'

Once more clinging to me for support, Holmes resumed his halting gait as we descended from the carriage and climbed the steps to the grand hotel. He darted suspicious eyes from side to side, and kept up a continuous stream of question and complaint, which was far from resembling the habitual conversation of the Prince, but captured the tone of the querulous invalid that he was popularly supposed to be.

'Ah, these steps are an effort,' he wailed. 'Take me to that chair. You will have to inspect the rooms for me, my English friend. They must be on the first floor, and overlook the islands. Do not pay the top price.[62] I am not a rich man. My father is stingy and a miser. Is that the dining room? It looks very crowded. Take me there. More steps. It is an hotel built for athletes. Who is that desiccated clerk seated in the corner? I know the face. Surely it is Count Pobedonostsev? One glance from him and our wine will turn. The fat fellow with him does not appear to be troubled by such niceties. What a contrast! The Beanpole and the Beerbarrel. Are they not like the two giants in the story? Well, well. I fear that their proximity would not be conducive to good digestion. Let us sit over there. What has happened? Did I overturn that ice-bucket? It is the fault of the management. The tables are too close. This will do for us.'

For my part I was glad to sit down. I felt sure that Holmes pursued a definite purpose in boldly drawing attention to himself, but the numerous pillars and doorways in the public rooms were a constant reminder of the dangers of attack. The two persons whose physical features he had so ably characterized stared curiously at my companion, and I had little doubt that theirs was the interest which he had sought to arouse.

The bloodless face of the Russian minister, fastidiously sipping a small glass of wine, was familiar to me from his photographs. His pale eyes glittered behind the rimless pince-nez upon his beak-like nose. A bright red tongue flickered perpetually across his thin lips, like that of a loathsome snake. This was the Czar's evil genius, the Russian Torquemada, who held his own nation in chains, and sought by every means to enslave others. From such a man did Klee take his orders, and his rich reward in gold, and in exchange armed the malcontents of Ireland against the English people.

The identity of his companion was unknown to me, but the impression that he gave me was scarcely more agreeable. He was a man of advanced years, exceedingly corpulent, with a round, red face, an abundant walrus moustache, and two deep grey eyes, which gleamed brightly from behind broad, gold-rimmed glasses. There was something of Mr Pickwick's benevolence in his appearance, marred only by the cold glitter of those restless and penetrating eyes.[63] After subjecting us to a long and hard scrutiny, he rose from his seat and lumbered heavily towards us.

'What is happening?' croaked Holmes beside me. 'The Beer-barrel is rolling in our direction. It opens its mouth. This is positively alarming. Why, Cousin Adolphe of Nassau, can it be you?'

I viewed with consternation the arrival of a true prince – and yet I need not have feared, for Holmes's mastery of each part that he assumed enabled him to personate a prince as ably as a potman. I consoled myself with the reflection that, since the Duke of Nassau was the uncle of the present Queen of Holland, he must be personally unacquainted with the Prince of Orange, who would have nothing to do with the Queen or her family. Duke Adolphe took Holmes to be the Prince of Orange without a trace of hesitation.'

'Alex, my young fellow,' he boomed, placing a pair of massive paws upon Holmes's shoulders and gazing eagerly into his face. 'What has brought you from your bed in the far north, hey? Upon my soul, you don't look well. You should go about more, visit your family, travel.'

'This is what I am doing,' replied Holmes, extricating himself from the bear's clasp. 'As a consequence, my health is notably improved. I may outlive you after all.'

The old Duke started back at this remark, but he recovered himself instantly and said, with a laugh. 'Why should you not outlive me! I am older than your father. Outlive me? I should think you would outlive me! 'Pon my soul, though, you mustn't overdo it. Are you staying long in Cannes?'

'As to that,' Holmes answered in an airy manner. 'I may and I mayn't. I have plans to visit Rome, but I scarcely want the fever to carry me off.'

'Ah, yes, the fever.'

'Then again, it is many years since I have taken a sea voyage.'

'Excellent for the health, a sea voyage.'

'But suppose the ship were to sink? The mountain air might serve as well.'

'I would recommend the sea voyage.'

'Well, there is no urgency.'

At this moment one of that diminutive race of boy, which inhabits the marble courts of hotels, approached the Duke with a letter upon a silver tray. The old man opened it, gazed at the contents with astonishment, and cried out, 'The Duke of Albany is dead!'

'I was at his bedside an hour since,' Holmes remarked.

'But this is fearful news! Hélène's husband. How can such a tragedy have occurred!'

'Does your Highness truly wish to know?'

The Duke stared at him, in the wildest consternation. 'What are you saying?' he gasped. 'Why do you ask that?'

'Because I am Sherlock Holmes,' replied my friend in his usual voice. 'A name that should be tolerably familiar to you. I daresay that it occurs in that letter, which I see from the hand was written by John Klee.'

The old Duke's face assumed a ghastly hue, of livid purple blotched with white, and he clutched at his heart like a man with an arrow in his chest.

'Possibly your Highness would welcome the comfort of a chair,' continued Holmes imperturbably. 'The smoking room is empty. Let us proceed there. Watson, be so good as to remain at the door to see that we are not disturbed. A few moments with the Duke of Nassau may bring this case to an unexpectedly swift conclusion.'

With a supreme effort of self-command the Duke gripped the back of a chair and remained so, head bowed, until the normal colour returned to his face. When he had recovered, but without another word, he marched into the smoking room, followed by Holmes, while I took a seat at the table by the door.

I was too distant to distinguish the words that passed between them, but several times the Duke raised his voice in anger, before a few words spoken in Holmes's level tone caused him to fall silent.

From the table in the corner Count Pobedonostsev had watched these proceedings without giving evidence of more than passing interest. He drank the last of his wine, neatly folded his napkin, and rose to his feet. A servant hurried towards him offering a nosegay, which the Count accepted and, placing it in his lapel, walked slowly towards me.

'Dr Watson, I daresay,' he remarked, in an accent which was unnaturally perfect and precise. 'But where is Mr Sherlock Holmes?'

I kept my seat and made no answer.

'I was much impressed by your companion's physical resilience,' he continued, with an ironic smile. 'He entered the room requiring your arm for support, but has stepped into the smoking room without any indication of disability. Indeed, his upright carriage and bearing put me in mind of the descriptions I have been given of Mr Holmes himself.'

Again I said nothing.

'Are you an Irishman, Dr Watson?'

'No, Sir,' I replied warmly. 'And nor are you, Sir, though I understand that you interest yourself in Irish affairs.'

The Count's smile became even more disdainful, upon his mean lips. 'Will you try a Russian cigarette, Dr Watson, and we can join them in the smoking room.'

'I prefer to remain outside.'

'Then you will excuse me if I enjoy a cigarette in your absence.'

He stepped towards the smoking room. I stood up, but with only the crudest idea of how to prevent him interrupting Holmes. Two other diners also approached the door, and I saw no alternative but that we must all go in. The Count led the way.

'I see that we have the place to ourselves after all,' he said, looking around at the Moorish niches and carved tables with which the room was oppressively furnished. Of Holmes and the Duke of Nassau there was no sign. 'I suppose that there is another door. Yes, this one. It opens onto one of the main corridors of the hotel. I do not think that I will follow them. A little brandy suits my mood. Will you join me in a glass? Then good day to you.'

He picked his way back to his table and sat there, licking his brandy, without another glance in my direction. A further ten minutes passed before Holmes and the Duke returned to the dining room. The Duke was scowling and crimson in the face as he lurched past me to his table. Holmes seemed in high spirits.

'It has been an excellent evening's work,' said he, packing a letter away in his pocket. 'This letter has been written by the Duke, at my dictation. It contains an order to Klee to call off the hunt of the Prince of Orange, and I shall give myself the satisfaction of delivering it to him personally.'

'But what has the Duke of Nassau to do with the Prince of Orange?'

'He has everything to do with him. Wait. Look who has entered the room! Well. I shall take the opportunity of delivering the letter before the Duke's eyes.'

It was indeed John Klee, wearing an immaculate pale suit, but with his hair rippled, who had entered the dining room and was making his way to the corner table.

'Mr Klee,' said Holmes.

Klee quickly turned his head, looked at us in a strange and puzzled manner, and glanced quickly again at the Russian minister and the Duke of Nassau, who, for their part, gazed studiously into their brandy glasses.

'A word before you leave us,' Holmes said, pulling the false hair from his cheeks until he stood before the astonished Klee as his own self. 'I have a letter from the Duke of Nassau. You see that it is addressed to you.'

Klee snatched the letter and tore it open. His eyes quickly devoured its contents, and the blood drained from his face. When he had done, he turned a whitened mask to the corner table, as if seeking a confirmation or denial of the letter's contents. As before, the eyes of the Duke and the Count never left their glasses.

'You will pay for this, Holmes,' Klee hissed between clenched teeth.

'To whom should I make out my cheque?' Holmes inquired blandly. 'To John Klee, is it, or Clay? Or will it be a number, addressed to Devil's Island? I think the latter – unless a serious complaint of the neck carries you off first.'

Klee drew himself back and stared at Holmes with a return to his old arrogance. 'You – Englishman!' he spat, and walked from the room.

'Do you suppose that he intends that as an insult?' Holmes mused, cocking his eyebrows, when Klee was gone. 'I think that I will take it as a compliment. What do you say, Watson?'

'No Englishman could do otherwise,' I replied.

17

THE INITIAL PROBLEM

Early the following morning Holmes and I left Cannes for England. This lovely city, placed in a setting of incomparable beauty, would henceforth strike only a melancholy chord in my heart. For the first part of our journey, Holmes studied a bundle of the local papers, which he had purchased at the station. At length he rolled them up into a large ball and pushed it to the far corner of the seat.

'Dr Roylott has managed to keep our names out of the reports of the death of the Duke of Albany,' he said. 'Nor is the Prince of Orange mentioned. If the Prince takes the direct route he will be at The Hague by nightfall.'

'Do you believe that it is safe for him to return there?'

'It is as safe as human skill can make it.'

'What of his father's enmity?'

'There was never any danger from that quarter.'

'You greatly surprise me. The Prince repeatedly told us that his father regarded him with contempt.'

Holmes leaned back, and his gaze took on a reflective cast. 'It is a common phenomenon among men of a nervous disposition to suppose that their fathers harbour feelings of animosity towards them. I do not say that such destructive impulses never occur. Peter the Great killed his son with his own hands, and so did Ivan the Terrible. But these are extreme cases, and Russian to boot.[64] Sensations of antagonism between the generations are the common experience of mankind. They are inevitable. They are a fact of human life. We cannot doubt that they were expressed in substantially the same form in the hillside caves of Neanderthal. A man's belief that his father plots his death is an extreme manifestation of this impulse, commonly associated with a peculiar devotion to the mother. The Prince of Orange was especially, one might go so far as to say excessively, attached to his mother, the late Queen Sophie. His gesture at her funeral, when he stepped down into her grave to kiss the coffin, is an indication of the unusual intensity of his regard.'

'But have you forgotten the mocking letters that he received from his father?' I protested. 'They were penned by no natural parent.'

'Indeed not, and I confess I was suspicious of them from the start.'

'Upon what grounds?'

'Let me refresh your memory of the affair, as the Prince of Orange related the details to us. First, he received a deputation of Luxemburgers, who urged him to marry, in order to reserve the grand-ducal crown for the senior branch of Orange-Nassau. This was followed immediately by the receipt of two hostile letters emanating from the King's palace.'

'I remember.'

'These were not written by the King himself but by a secretary, and were signed with the King's initial. After the ensuing charade, in which the Prince announced his engagement to the lady whom he supposed to be his cousin, a third letter was received. Again the Prince's matrimonial projects were the subject, but this letter was undoubtedly written by the King himself, and signed by him. Do you recall the details of this letter?'

'The King began by alluding to his own first marriage, which, like his son's proposed marriage, was made against the wishes of his parents, and concluded with a remark in poor taste.'

'Your memory is exemplary, as far as it goes. But the tone, Watson? The letter was brusque, but did it strike you as unsympathetic?'

'Now that you draw my attention to it, I would describe the tone as one that a man might use in addressing a younger member of his club.'

'Exactly. As one man to another. But not to another whom he despised.'

'I should say not.'

'Below his signature the King added the word "Papa", which the Prince considered as the expression of his father's wish to thrust him back into the nursery. But another interpretation is possible, in which the word may be seen as a touching attempt to heal the rift between them, by recalling an earlier period when trust and amiability prevailed.'

'I think that interpretation is very possible.'

'Very well. In the abusive tone of the first two letters I believe we can trace the hand of the Prince's equerry, the treacherous Vanderbanck. This is confirmed by the reluctance of the forger to sign the King's full name, which is technically a capital offence in Holland.[65] The letter "W" was as far as he dared to go. I think that disposes of the letters. Whatever the nature of the King's true feelings for his last surviving son, we have no evidence that contempt and hatred are amongst them.

'When I considered the elaborate hoax that had been perpetrated upon the Prince, it was evident that the intention of the deception was to discourage him from thoughts of matrimony. Two persons stood to gain from his celibacy. One was of course the King's young daughter, Wilhelmina, who would inherit the throne of Holland. But the Prince of Orange's antagonism towards his father prevented him from considering the second, and more suggestive, possibility. This is the Duke Adolphe of Nassau who, though a very remote cousin of the King, is – after the Prince of Orange – his closest male relative.[66] You will recall that in Luxembourg the Salic Law prevails and no woman can be sovereign there. If Princess Wilhelmina becomes Queen of Holland, the Duke of Nassau becomes the Grand Duke of Luxembourg.'

'I begin to understand.'

'My suspicions of this worthy were confirmed when I learned that he was also, through a different line, the uncle of the present Queen, and incidentally of the Duchess of Albany. He therefore possessed both the interest to devise the personation and the authority to implement it. It was an easy matter for him to play upon the young Queen Emma's yearning for a romantic attachment. You must remember that the King of Holland is forty years her senior and a man of little refinement. Forced into marriage by an ambitious mother, her equally ambitious uncle was able to exploit her natural disappointment. Possibly the two combined forces; they would have made a formidable partnership.'

'I know nothing of the Duke of Nassau. What is his character?'

'He is a bitter and frustrated man. Born sixty years ago in the small Rhineland duchy of Nassau, he ruled there from an early age until he had the misfortune to back the losing side in the war of '66. Expelled from his duchy by the victorious Prussians, but compensated with the payment of one and a quarter million pounds in gold, he retired to Vienna where he has spent the past eighteen years, enjoying the life of a wealthy aristocrat and indulging his taste for actresses. There he might have remained until his death, a warning example of the fate of princes, if the remarkable series of male deaths in the House of Orange had not presented him with the possibility of a grander destiny. If he had limited his intervention to the events of last summer he might have secured his object without arousing suspicion. But he is a man of advanced years, impatient for his destiny. The Prince of Orange is barely thirty, and likely to live many years yet. So the

Duke made his fateful compact with John Klee, who undertook to clear the obstacle from the Duke's path.'

'Has the Duke admitted all this?' I asked.

'He shows no remorse for his crimes,' answered Holmes. 'Nor horror at the loathsome death of Vanderbanck, which was intended to be the Prince's fate. He refused point blank to acknowledge his share in the responsibility for these foul deeds. I could persuade him to write the letter to Klee only by insisting that I would not hesitate to make his association with John Klee known to certain exalted ears. He would be barred from all the decent courts of Europe. Klee's responsibility for the death of the Duke of Albany was my trump card, and when I played it he threw in his hand.[67] But I do not envy the lot of the Luxemburgers should he ever become their prince. Well, it is up to us to see that he does not. We know that the Prince of Orange is not unimpressed with the charms of the Duchess of Albany. She is now a widow. These are early days, but perhaps in a year or two.... Hymen's garden can be reached by many paths. When one is closed, another opens.'

Upon our arrival in England, Holmes lost no time in calling upon the duchess at Claremont House. She received us in her boudoir, attired in deepest mourning, and accompanied by a slightly older woman strikingly similar to her in appearance. This was the youthful Queen Emma of Holland, come to offer comfort to her bereaved sister. I saw a courageous spirit in her clear, blue eyes, and recognized the nobility of a woman for whom the sufferings of others are as her own.

Like her elder sister, the duchess entertained, in the midst of her afflictions, the tenderest thought for others. One of her first requests was for news of the Prince of Orange, and Holmes, who had recently received a telegram from The Hague, was able to inform her that the Prince had once again taken up his residence in the Kneuterdijk.

'My sister has informed me,' said the Queen of Holland, 'that you have guessed that it was I who played a cruel trick upon him. Believe me, Mr Holmes, there is no place in my heart for cruelty to anyone, and our little drama was commenced in all innocence.'

'Your Majesty's gentle nature is well known,' said Holmes. 'I do believe that you played an innocent *rôle*, although the play was carefully planned with cruelty as the prime element. Was it your Uncle Adolphe who encouraged you?'

'He used to praise my play-acting when I was a child,' faltered the Queen, with a nervous glance at her sister.

'Perhaps your mother played a significant *rôle*?' continued Holmes. 'Anxious for her brother's future as for her daughter's?'

'I cannot tell you,' murmured the Queen. 'That is to say, it is too painful for me to tell you. Let it be sufficient that the Prince of Orange has returned home, I hope refreshed in spirits, and with a long future ahead of him.'

'As Your Majesty pleases,' replied Holmes, evidently satisfied by the Queen's statement.

The young duchess was greatly astonished to learn that we had visited Cannes, and had attended her husband on his last day.

'Dr Roylott said nothing of this in his wire,' said she, with a frown.

'The telegraph is an excellent instrument, but its privacy cannot be trusted,' said Holmes, in a reassuring tone. 'Dr Roylott is anxious that there should be no hint of irregularity, which my presence unfortunately can sometimes suggest.'

The duchess was silent for a while. At length she asked, 'Were you in Cannes because of John Klee?'

Holmes bowed his assent.

'I knew that he was a wrong one!' she cried, with a passionate gesture of the hand. Dr Roylott warned my husband, and I warned him, yet he would not listen to us. Once, when Klee was waiting in an anteroom, unaware that I could observe him through a half-opened door, he darted a glance of the utmost malignancy at a photograph of the Prince of Wales. He professed a deep devotion to our family, but I do not believe him. Did my husband retain his faith in him until the end?'

Holmes shook his head. 'I took it upon myself to alert him to the dangers, and he believed me.'

After expressing her heartfelt thanks, the duchess, with that refinement of spirit for which she is renowned, opened the door to the room that had been her husband's sitting room and the scene of our first encounter. She pressed Holmes to accept some memento of the duke, but in turn he declined an amethyst ring, a gold snuffbox, and a Kaffir jawala bowl.[68]

'Your Royal Highness has something which I should value even more highly,' said he.

'You have but to name it.'

Holmes stepped forward and picked up a large button of imitation quartz which was lying among the pens upon the duke's desk.

The duchess stared at him in amazement.

'Certainly, if you wish it. Though I cannot understand what it is doing there. I am certain that the duke never wore a jacket fitted with buttons of that sort.'

'Nevertheless, it would give me the greatest satisfaction to take it with me.'

'Very well. And Dr Watson?'

'Nothing for me, Ma'am,' said I, 'although I should esteem it a privilege to examine more closely the Jezail rifle which hangs yonder by the window. Just such a weapon as that left me with a bullet in my shoulder at Maiwand.'

The duchess graciously invited me to lift the ominous weapon down; and it was with an awesome sense of the resurgent past that I lifted the rifle from its hooks and weighed it in my hands. A wealth of memories flooded through me, recalling unspeakable deeds performed in the heat of battle by men more valorous, less fortunate than myself. With a sudden and overwhelming sensation of repugnance I thrust the instrument of death from me, and in a moment of mental abstraction for which I never can forgive myself, I cocked the gun with one hand and pressed the trigger with the other. A fearful report ensued, and a bullet issued from the barrel, which I had omitted to examine, and plunged into my thigh.

Holmes rushed to my side.

'It is nothing!' I shrieked. 'A graze, merely!'

I relapsed into a chair, where Holmes tore at my garments to examine the wound. The duchess and her royal sister, resolute and undeterred by the sight of blood, called for water and bandages. The Queen of Holland herself drew the scissors from her chatelaine to cut the singed cloth from around the wound.

'The bullet has passed across the femur, without touching the patella,' observed Holmes. 'The blood will soon cease to flow. There. Now try to place your foot upon the ground.'

The pain was considerable, but it was far outweighed by my mortification at having ignored the foremost rule of weaponry. But there was nothing to be done about that, and as soon as I was able to convince Holmes that I could walk we took our leave.

'Good old Watson,' said he, as our carriage bore us away from that house of grief. 'I can always depend upon you to end a scene with a flourish.[69]

18

THE *JULIE GUELPH*

BACK IN BAKER Street Holmes placed the button of imitation quartz upon the table and sat gazing at it for a considerable time, his brows rapt in deepest thought. At last he picked up the button, opened a drawer in his desk, and dropped it inside.

'My mind is made up, Watson,' said he shutting the drawer with a slam. 'If I tell Lestrade of this, it will confuse him, and may distract his men from the hunt for Klee's gang.'

'How did it come to be upon the duke's table?' I asked.

'It was deliberately placed there. I suspected the existence of a contingency plan after the discovery at Charing Cross of the portmanteau which so obligingly failed to explode, and allowed us to examine its contents.'

'You must give Lestrade his due for recognizing the significance of the missing button.'

'He recognized nothing! For him it was a button accidentally torn from its jacket. I gave him a helping hand by showing that it had been cut, but his mind was closed to the implications.'

'And what are they?'

'Think, man. To connect His Royal Highness with the explosion.'

'You mean blackmail?'

'Klee was prepared to go to any lengths to secure his objectives. If the duke proved to be resistant, he was ready to use threats. An anonymous wire to the Yard to examine the duke's desk, and His Royal Highness would be in Queer Street.'

I shuddered. 'The scandal would have been appalling.'

'Well, we have shielded his memory from that slur. As for Klee's men, Lestrade has all the information he needs to arrest the small fry, and I think the pike will steer clear of our waters for a while.'

My leg had begun to throb painfully, and I retired to bed early. But Afghanistan casts a long shadow, and on the following morning the entire left side of my body burned as though it were on fire. Holmes himself extracted the bullet, but several weeks were to pass before I was able to rest my weight upon that leg with any ease.

As Holmes had foreseen, Klee's gang were duly caught, some in Birmingham, some trying to board the Irish Mail at Birkenhead.[70] Lestrade brought us the news, and sat in our best chair, grinning all over his face, and repeatedly slapping his knee.

'You won't find the force sleeping on the job,' he declared, in his most smug and self-congratulatory manner.

'And what of John Klee?' inquired Holmes. 'Their leader, who is more dangerous than all the rest pressed together.'

'Never fear,' the detective assured us, without losing a shade of his complacency. 'Allow us time, Mr Holmes, and he'll be in the bag along with the rest of them.'

Lestrade's confidence was somewhat shaken when, upon the following day, an explosion occurred in an alley adjoining Scotland Yard itself.[71] The blast broke open a gap nearly twenty feet high in the brickwork, and caused severe damage to four rooms on that side of the building.

'Klee has a sense of humour that does not chime with Lestrade's.' said Holmes, after returning from the scene. 'The fact of it is that the explosion has destroyed the very rooms which the Yard has set apart for investigating these explosions. All their documents are so much confetti. And yet,' he added grimly, 'it is no laughing matter.'

'Does this new outrage mean that Klee has returned to England?'

'The crime certainly bears his signature. But surely he is too wily to leave the continent, where he knows that he is safe. Here is the boy with a wire. Hm. This is grave news. It is from Inspector Vandermast in The Hague, whom I asked to keep me informed of the health of the Prince of Orange. The message is in code, but a simple one.'

He tossed the flimsy note across to me, and I read the message that it contained:

Pip sinking. Come immediately.—VANDERMAST.

'Is this Klee's handiwork?' I asked.

'I cannot say.'

'You will go, of course.'

'I hope that you will accompany me. Is your leg recovered?'

'It will do well enough,' I answered.

So once again we set forth from England's shores for the greater world beyond. The following afternoon found us driving through the tree-lined streets and time-honoured squares of the capital city of the Netherlands. A watery sun shone down upon us from a sky bustling with clouds as we stopped outside the venerable façade of the Prince's residence on the Kneuterdijk.

The heavy door swung open and we entered a sombrely furnished hall, panelled from floor to ceiling with ornately-carved wood, blackened with age. The effect was overwhelmingly depressing, and was not relieved by the hanging cloth of faded brocade that occupied the lower section of the wall, nor by the pictures above, so browned with age that little could be discerned of their subjects. Here the yellow crescent of a ruff suggested an antique portrait, there a horizontal band paler than that below it hinted at a seascape in the manner of the old school. There hung in the air a dankness and a chill in starkest contrast to the busy sunlit scene from which we had stepped but a moment before.

We were escorted up a richly carved staircase, and then up a steeper staircase ill-lit by a single candle set in a candelabrum designed to hold a dozen.

'A dismal enough place to call your home,' remarked Holmes. 'Do you wonder that the Prince blossomed in the warm South.'

The room into which we were shown was a large chamber lit along one wall by high windows that stood open to let the sunlight stream in.

'This is not the Prince's own bedroom,' explained the white-haired doctor who received us. 'That is a smaller room, where he is closely surrounded by his pet birds and animals. But when his condition worsened I insisted that his bed be brought to this place, to give him the benefits of the air.'

'Quite so,' said Holmes. 'How grave is his situation?'

'I fear it is very bad. We have sent word to His Majesty, who is in Carlsbad, taking the cure.'

'What is the Prince's malady?'

'We are at a loss to say. He has the symptoms of typhus, but without the dilated pupils.'

'Poison?'

'Why, dear me. It had never occurred to us, but no, I do not think so. No, I am certain of it. In truth, there does not seem anything ascertainably wrong with His Royal Highness. But he lies motionless in his bed, refusing food, and only after the greatest efforts of persuasion will he allow a little watered brandy to pass his lips.'

'I will tell you where the malady lies,' said I. 'In the heart. He is sick of a broken heart.'

'Has the Queen been sent for?' asked Holmes.

'Why, no.' The doctor coughed awkwardly. 'Perhaps you do not know that relations between them have never....'

'Send for the Queen,' said Holmes.

'Do you really think that wise?'

'It is the only hope we have. I would send for the Duchess of Albany,' he explained to me, 'but for her to make the journey at such a time would be impossible. Dear me, what an untoward development.'

We made our way to the simple iron bed upon which lay the still body of the Prince who had become our friend. His eyes were closed, his cheeks unshaven, and his face deathly pale. Only the fingers that played restlessly upon the sheet testified that life still glowed in that stricken body.

'Your Royal Highness,' said Holmes, leaning over the bed. 'It is I, Sherlock Holmes. Dr Watson and I have come to bring you the strength and the hope to live.'

There was a faint fluttering of the eyelids, and after a further moment the eyes opened and bent a watery stare upon us.

'Good of you to come, gentlemen. Disappointing journey, I fear. No hope.' The eyes closed once more.

'Holmes,' I muttered. 'What are we to do?'

'We can do nothing,' he replied. 'I fear that your diagnosis is correct. It is a sickness that no doctor can cure, nor any friend alleviate. Time alone can heal this wound, and that is an agent that the Prince is doing his utmost to outwit. I should have foreseen the impression that the young Duchess of Albany, so like her royal sister, would create upon his disordered senses. It is my fault. I freely admit it.'

At this moment there came the sound of a woman's upraised voice at the door. 'Let me in! You shall let me in!' The door opened to reveal the figure of a veiled woman, and several servants, who were endeavouring to restrain her. When their efforts appeared to be succeeding, she lifted the veil with a proud gesture and said, in a voice that compelled obedience, 'Stand back! I am the Queen!'

With a sudden movement the servants fell back and the Queen of Holland entered the room. Yet it was a very different figure from the dignified and self-possessed young woman whom we had seen tenderly holding her sister's hand at Claremont House. She wore tinted glasses, which concealed her pale, blue eyes, and her cheeks were flushed with recent weeping.

'I came as soon as I heard the news,' she told us. 'The King sent me a wire from Carlsbad. Oh, Alex, you must not die. You must live! You must live!'

'Who is it?' murmured the Prince, opening his eyes once again. He stared at the young Queen, and it seemed as if a cloud passed across his face while his memory sought to identify the face that bent over him. 'Is it Elsi...?' he asked, in a quavering voice. 'Hélène...?'

The Queen flung off her glasses. 'My name does not matter!' she cried. 'It is our love that matters! Be strong! Be well! Love will find a way!'

A smile spread over the Prince's face, sweetening those ravaged features. 'Can it really be that you love me?' he asked in a trembling voice.

'Oh, Alex, Alex, you know the answer!'

Seeing that answer in her stricken face, he said, 'Then I need nothing more,' and, gazing up at her, the life went out from him.

'So the death of the Prince of Orange is not to be placed at Klee's door,' I remarked to Holmes, as the steamer bore us out from Rotterdam bound for England.

'There may be no direct connection,' replied Holmes, 'yet he is morally responsible, as is a man with a gun who drives a rabbit into a lake, where it drowns.'

'And when the King of Holland dies, Duke Adolphe of Nassau will become Grand Duke of Luxembourg.'

'Villainy triumphs. The architects of evil see their schemes prosper. We live in a dark age, Watson, and I fear that the shadows are closing.'

'The news from Egypt is good,' said I. 'General Gordon is marching to Khartoum.'

'Tush. The country is whistling in the dark. What will be said when he and his army lie dead in the sandy wastes of the Soudan!'

'Perhaps it will spur us on to greater things,' I ventured.

'Well, you may be right, although I do not have great confidence in your views.'

'There is much about the activities of John Klee that I do not understand,' I said, to turn the conversation into easier channels. 'I believe I follow his intentions concerning the Prince of Orange, but I am puzzled by his wish to attach himself to the Duke of Albany.'

'Then I shall endeavour to elucidate the matter for you. But let us not miss the prospect of the coast as it recedes from us. Vandevelde would have revelled in those chopping waves. That cutter has almost overtaken us. It is the latest design. Why, what the devil!'

The small cutter, which had approached unnoticed in the press of craft about the harbour mouth, now came abreast of us, and one of her crew flung a square package across the narrow gap that separated the two vessels. She then drew swiftly away but continued upon a parallel course. A few moments later a seaman presented himself before my friend.

'Mr Sherlock Holmes?' he inquired, and upon receiving an affirmative reply, handed the package to him. It was addressed to 'Mr Sherlock Holmes, *en route* for England.'

Holmes tore open the outer layer of paper, within which he found a second package, and within that a third, and then a fourth. When this in turn had been unwrapped, a sheet of paper fell out. It was of the most expensive vellum, and bore the British coat of arms at its head. The message was brief: 'Dear me, Mr

Holmes! Dear me!'

'What does this mean!' I cried.

'Give me your glasses, Watson, and I will tell you!' He clapped my field-glasses to his eyes and stared intently at the cutter. 'Yes, it is he. There. You may see him for yourself.'

I focused upon the small boat, which was now turning abaft from us, and saw upon the deck the jaunty figure of John Klee, in naval dress, waving mockingly in our direction.

'Really, it is too much!' I exclaimed. 'Can we not pursue him?'

'If we could, what would you have us do? Snatch him from his own boat?'

'How do you know that it is his?'

'Do you not read her name?'

I stared through the glasses again, and read, with some difficulty, for the boat had now considerably receded from us, the name *Julie Guelph*.

'A curious name, is it not?' said Holmes.

'Surely Guelph is the name recently borne by our own royal family?' I observed.[72]

'Well done, Watson. But who is Julie, eh? Know that and you penetrate the mystery of John Klee. His passion, his ambition, and now his downfall.'

'As to the last, I hope you are right.'

'Oh, he will continue his life as a hired murderer and thief, and perhaps England will be troubled by him again. But gone is the dream that he would topple the Queen of England from her throne, and place himself there in her stead.'

'Good God, Holmes, is the man a lunatic!'

'He is very sane. Therein lay his great danger.'

'This Julie Guelph. Who is she?'

'Who was she, Watson. She has been dead nearly forty years. Born Julie de St Laurent de Montgenet in the small Norman town of Calvados, she was raised among the family's sugar plantations in Martinique, where a fellow pupil was the future Empress

200

Josephine. Back in France she married her cousin, the Baron de Fortisson, and fled to Geneva to escape the revolution. It was there that she met the young Englishman with whom she was to live, in England, France and Canada, for the next twenty-seven years.'

'And who was he?'

'Edward, the Duke of Kent, fourth son of His Majesty King George III, and father of our present Queen.'

'Edward Guelph! I begin to understand. Were they married?'

'Undoubtedly.'

'But then, several sons of George III went through a form of marriage with women who had been their mistresses.'

'A form of marriage, yes, for the Royal Marriage Act forbade any prince to marry without the King's consent. Offspring from such a marriage are always debarred from the succession.'

'I take it that John Klee is a descendant of the marriage between the Duke of Kent and Julie de St. Laurent?'

'The grandson. The son was a minister in the Canadian church who vainly tried to have his descent officially recognized. John Klee is his only child. The Duke of Albany was his half-cousin. So is the Prince of Wales. I fear that he has a better claim to the throne than either of them. Better than the Queen herself.'[73]

'Holmes, what are you saying!'

'The Duke of Kent left his faithful Julie to marry the Princess of Saxe-Coburg, and in due course fathered the princess who is now our Queen. But his marriage was bigamous. His previous marriage to Julie de St Laurent had received the approval and blessing of George III, but later the King became incurably insane, and was in no condition to object to the Saxe-Coburg match.'

'So Her Majesty is illegitimate,' I whispered. 'And John Klee our true sovereign.'

'King John the Second. Yes.'

'What is to be done?'

'Nothing is to be done. A grave wrong has been committed, it is true, and if Klee had shown himself to be a man of a different stamp, then perhaps another course might have prevailed. But he was evidently set to equal the monstrous doings of the first King John. *Festina lente*, Watson. It is our best and only course.'

'But how did he hope to press his claim? And why befriend the Duke of Albany?'

'He knew that the papers proving his right to the throne are kept in the Royal Archives in Windsor. The duke, as private secretary to the Queen, had access to the archives. It was Klee's intention to become the duke's assistant and search in the archives at his leisure. Once the papers were found, his claim to the Crown would have to be seriously considered. The constitutional crisis would have been unimaginable.'

'Well, at least we are spared that.'

'At the cost, perhaps, of a greater ill. It is natural that he holds a grudge against the Queen, and all the members of the House of Saxe-Coburg. It was inevitable that he should espouse the cause of Ireland against that of England. Klee, the very name that he chose for himself, the shamrock, is the national emblem of that divided and unhappy land. Her present troubles excite the sympathies of members of her race dispersed across the Atlantic, who will support any conspiracy against England that is decked out in the catchy tapes of Irish liberty. Anything that can damage England excites the covetous interest of Russia. Every dollar which the Americans contribute to the so-called Emergency Fund, the avowed object of which is indiscriminately to kill innocent men, women and children, is the equivalent of twenty Russian roubles. Klee has fished well in this murky water. The Americans do not understand that in scheming against England they are playing Russia's game; that Irish murderers are trained by Russian assassins and that if England falls, the strongest bulwark that protects their own liberty has been swept away.'

'Your words depress me, Holmes,' I said, when at last my friend was silent.

'I trust not,' he replied. 'The fight is not lost. The fight will go on, till every dynamitard is behind bars and every wrong is righted. England's rule in Erin's land has not been noted for its wisdom. Nor for compassion. There is much to do, and when this boat reaches England we must set to doing it. First, John Klee. Every port shall be alerted, from Cadiz to Murmansk. I shall devise such a charge that no country will dare to halt his arrest.'

But this was not to be. There is ever a flaw in the best-intended human plan, and John Klee has yet to be brought before a court of law. Holmes circulated all the ports of Europe with details of the *Julie Guelph* but before the week was out news arrived to show that the young villain had anticipated Holmes's action and contrived to outwit him. Once his cutter had passed from our sight she had evidently turned about and returned to Rotterdam where her crew was discharged and Klee, after some legal business was concluded, disappeared. Holmes took the news with an ill grace, and when a report came that the fellow had been sighted in Vienna, he struck the flat of his hand against the table and, unlike himself, let out an angry oath.

'It is too bad!' he exclaimed. 'He will be safe there. Can it be that he is attempting a *rapprochement* with Duke Adolphe, claiming the death of Prince Alexander to have been at his hands?'

In the following weeks further sightings were reported, in Warsaw, St Petersburg, and then, after a month's silence, Montreal.

'What the devil is he doing there?' I exclaimed when Holmes informed me of his appearance in the land of his birth.

'I do not think that it is sentiment calls him back,' said he. 'There is much mischief to be made there among those who chafe against British rule, descendants of the French settlers as well as among the indigenous Indians.'

At home, however, the terrible outrages that had shattered the normal calm of London in that summer of 1884 gradually petered out. Daley, Burton, and the other members of Klee's gang were tried in the absence of their head, and all were sentenced to long terms of imprisonment.[74] Latterly, wiser counsels have come to be in the ascendant in dealings with 'John Bull's other island', and all good men must hope that these counsels will prevail.

Shortly after our return to England, the young Duchess of Albany became the mother of a baby boy, who inherited the title of duke from the moment of his birth – an event unprecedented in the history of England. At the royal christening, which was celebrated in the quaint old church at Esher, and to which Holmes and I had the great honour to be invited, my friend remarked: 'Upon the shoulders of such babes grown to manhood will rest the burdens of a different world. Who can pierce the veil which hides what lies ahead? We can only hope, and work towards that better time. Shall we live to see it, Watson?'

I do not know. Perhaps such men as Holmes, who exist to free the world of ignorance and evil, will not be needed in that 'brave new world' which lies ahead. Yet even as I write, the mocking face of John Klee as I last saw him rises before my eyes, and I am as certain as I am of anything that, however this dear world changes, there will always be wicked and scheming men upon it, for whom murder and extortion give a zest to their lives, and whose ambition is to exert tyranny over other men's souls. Against them the fight must never slacken.

Would that Sherlock Holmes were immortal! That can never be. Yet his spirit is immortal, and I pray that in time of danger there will always be others like Holmes, ten thousand others, to carry on the ceaseless fight for liberty, and truth, and England.

EDITOR'S AFTERWORD

HERE WATSON'S NARRATIVE ends.

Six years later, the King of Holland – properly styled King of the Netherlands – died and the 10-year-old Princess Wilhelmina became Queen, reigning until her abdication in 1948. Duke Adolphe of Nassau became Grand Duke of Luxembourg, and reigned there till his death fifteen years later at the age of eighty-eight. Fate, which usually gives short shrift to fallen princes, spared Adolphe and raised him up greater than before. Ironically, his son Guillaume (William) IV was the father of six daughters but no son, and eighteen months into his reign the law debarring females from inheriting the throne was abolished. The present Grand Duke of Luxembourg is the grandson of one of these daughters

As for the little Duke of Albany, Holmes's hopes were doomed to disappointment. In 1897 the reigning Duke of Saxe-Coburg (Queen Victoria's brother-in-law) died without legitimate issue, and within a couple of years the title passed to the 14-year-old duke. From an evidently happy life at Eton he was transported to Germany and educated with the children of the Kaiser. Not surprisingly, he came to identify himself with his adopted country. He fought with a German regiment during the First World War (which cost him his English dukedom) and later attached himself enthusiastically to the Nazi cause. He died rather miserably in 1955.

As for the 'Irish Question', dare one hope that the answer has been found? The counsels of the mid-1880s were wiser than those of their predecessors but could not, in the context of their times, be wise enough. Much of Ireland became a free state in 1921 but the six counties of Ulster were excluded from it. A century after American fundraisers had aided Burton and Daley, a new generation was arming their successors. American dollars again paid for Russian guns. The irony would have been comic had it not been cruel. Since that time wiser counsels have indeed come to be in the ascendant, and relations between 'John Bull's other island', as Dr Watson – so much a man of his time – called it and John Bull's homeland would seem to have become pacific at last.

APPENDIX A : IRELAND

ANGLO-IRISH RELATIONS IN the nineteenth century are not easy to summarize. Resistance to British rule several times erupted into armed conflict, and in the wake of Irish emigration to the United States various organizations were set up to finance the campaign. Chief of these was the Fenian Brotherhood, known in Ireland as the Irish Republican Brotherhood. Two military raids into Canada ended in failure. In England, an attack upon the police in Manchester and the dynamiting of the Clerkenwell Prison resulted in a number of deaths, and the elevation of the killers to the status of 'martyrs'.

From discontented elements in the Fenians arose the Irish Invincibles, who committed the Phoenix Park murders in 1882, and the Clan na Gael. The manifesto of this organization proposed the blowing up of public buildings in England and elsewhere, describing this as 'inaugurating scientific warfare'. In 1877, the Clan na Gael sent a deputation to the Russian ambassador in Washington to present proposals for an expedition to Ireland.

Throughout the 1880s, the British Parliament rejected Gladstone's proposals for Home Rule for Ireland, but local land reforms were gradually introduced until by the end of the century Irish affairs – somewhat surprisingly – ceased to be seen as a pressing matter. Violence in Ireland remained negligible until the eve of the First World War.

APPENDIX B : HAEMOPHILIA

SUFFERERS OF WHAT Queen Victoria called 'this awful disease, the worst I know' are by no means restricted to royal personages, but since they are the best-known victims haemophilia has sometimes been called the 'Royal Disease.'

As the Duke of Albany reminded Dr Watson, the blood of a haemophiliac does not coagulate, or does so only slowly. Any injury can be fatal, the slightest knock can cause an internal haemorrhage and lead to death.

A curious feature of the disease is that its symptoms only appear in males but it can be inherited and passed on by females. Not every male child need inherit it. Victoria's eldest son (later King Edward VII) did not, and the disease is absent from the present Queen's immediate family. 'Not until a woman has children will it be known whether or not she is a carrier; not until a son first bleeds will it be known whether or not he has haemophilia.' Theo Aronson, *Grandmama of Europe*.

The disease does not seem to have been present in Victoria's known ancestors, nor in those of her husband, Prince Albert. It has long been assumed to have originated in Victoria herself, by a mutation in her genes. Three of her nine children were affected by it: Prince Leopold (the Duke of Albany) and the Princesses Alice and Beatrice. Beatrice married Prince Henry of Battenberg: two of her sons were haemophiliac, and her daughter Ena married Alfonso XIII and carried the disease into the Spanish royal family.

Alice married the Grand Duke of Hesse. The death of her young son Fritz spread alarm through the entire family as the facts of female inheritance became apparent. Her daughter Irene married the Kaiser's brother and two of their sons were haemophiliac. Alice's daughter Alexandra married Czar Nicholas II of Russia, where the haemophilia of their only son, the Czarevich, had serious political consequences and led to the ascendancy of Rasputin.

Leopold's daughter Alice (Countess of Athlone) was presumably a carrier. Her only son died of internal bleeding after an accident at the age of twenty.

Although the Duke of Albany speaks of the disease spreading throughout Europe, at the time of his death it had spread only to the Hessian family. The marriages into the royal families of Prussia, Russia and Spain lay some years ahead. But perhaps the Duke, as his mother's private secretary, was privy to her dynastic plans.

APPENDIX C : QUEEN VICTORIA'S FATHER

THE SUGGESTION THAT the Duke of Kent may have fathered other children while living in Canada was whispered freely at the end of Victoria's reign. There are stories of the Queen and her mother burning bundles of the Duke's letters which contained proofs of his guilty secret. Although Holmes's biographical sketch of Julie de St Laurent contains several major errors of fact, the information he gives accords with what was known at the time. She and the Duke did live together for twenty-seven remarkably happy years, and he left her only because the childlessness of his elder brothers had made him heir to the throne.

At least seven children have been attributed to the Duke and Madame de St Laurent, and two of them, Robert Wood and Jean de Mestre, are still accepted as such in the *Oxford Companion to Canadian History and Literature*. In addition, the father of Constance Kent, whose conviction for murdering her young brother was a scandal of the 1860s, was also said to be a son of the Duke.

There is no way of telling which, if any of the above was the father of John Klee – or Clay, as he sometimes spelled it. Mollie Gillen's deeply researched book *The Prince and his Lady* (1970) disposes of all the claims except that of Constance Kent's father. She does not mention Klee.[75]

NOTES

1 (p16)   The remarkable sun-glows were caused by the enormous mass of dust ejected into the atmosphere by the eruption of Krakatoa the previous August. The memory of their brilliance persisted through the lifetime of those who witnessed them, and halfway into the twentieth century elderly people could be heard to contrast modern sunsets unfavourably with those of their youth.

2 (p17)   The need to ensure that a pro-British Amir ruled in Afghanistan became increasingly important as Russian expansion 'absorbed' the independent khanates of Central Asia. The submission at Merv enabled the Russians to claim that their 'natural' boundary was the frontier with Afghanistan. The significance of the event did not pass entirely unnoticed in the British press, as Holmes alleges, although it is true that the major preoccupation of the day was the imbroglio in the Soudan.

3 (p18)   The appointment of General Charles Gordon to relieve the military garrison (chiefly made up of Egyptian soldiers) was on the whole enthusiastically received. However, the oddly named *Court Journal* printed a phrenologist's opinion of Gordon which closely accords with Holmes's critical analysis. Within a month of Gordon's arrival in Khartoum the city was surrounded by Arab forces under their charismatic leader, the Mahdi. After a siege of ten months the city was stormed and captured, with frightful slaughter. Gordon was speared to death and his head hacked off.

4 (p18)   It is interesting to learn how there came to be a picture of Gordon in the sitting room of 221B. By the time Watson mentions it again (in *The Resident Patient*) the print had acquired a frame, possibly to give permanence to Holmes's warning.

5 (p22)   The Prince of Orange presided over the conference held at The Hague in 1877 to celebrate the 200th anniversary of the birth of the Dutch-Jewish philosopher Spinoza. His eloquent address was said to be remarkable for its learning, breadth of thought, etc.

6 (p24)   Emma, daughter of the Prince of Waldeck-Pyrmont, a small principality between Westphalia and Hesse with a population of (1880) 55,000.

7 (p24)   The Salic Laws were a codification of the tribal customs of the Salian Franks, who conquered Gaul in the fifth century. They contained a section declaring that daughters cannot inherit land, and this was interpreted by French monarchs in the fourteenth century to restrict the crown to descendants in the male line. This action precipitated the Hundred Years War between France and England. Nassau, Luxembourg and other principalities in the Lower Rhine (including Hanover), where the Salian Franks originated, applied the Law to their own dynasties. When Queen Victoria ascended the British throne in 1837 she was debarred from also becoming the sovereign of Hanover, a title borne by her immediate (and male) predecessors. The Duke of Cumberland, her dead father's younger brother and the nearest male heir, thus became King of Hanover.

8 (p26)   The announcement appeared in *The Times* on 25 June 1883.

9 (p27)   Watson records a very similar trick in *A Case of Identity*, which may be an altered version of the Dutch case. It is significant that the villain in that short story bears the curious name of Windibank. This is so un-English a name that it is not to be found in any directory I have consulted. On the other hand, it bears a close similarity to the familiar Dutch name of Van der Banck.

10 (p29)   An ominous name. The Tapanuli fever and the black

Formosan corruption are two of the dread diseases mentioned by Holmes in *The Dying Detective*.

11 (p30) These symptoms are much the same as those described by Balzac at the end of his novel *Cousin Bette* where Valérie is poisoned by her South American lover. The only reference to Balzac in the recorded cases of Sherlock Holmes occurs in *A Case of Identity*, in a letter from the obnoxious Windibank.

12 (p34) The Prince proved luckier than Holmes's client in *The Five Orange Pips*, casually sent to his death on the steps of Waterloo Bridge.

13 (p36) 'All knowledge, except heraldry, has some use,' said by Robert Lowe (1811-1892), wit, albino and sometime Chancellor of the Exchequer.

14 (p36) '... no man may bear the same arms as any other.' Holmes means as any other living man. A coat of arms can be passed down unchanged through the generations but at any one time only the head of the family may display it undifferenced. Holmes' account of armorial descent is not as helpful as it could be. Despite his protestations, clarity and exactitude never marked his own references to heraldry (e.g. in *The Noble Bachelor*).

15 (p39) Holmes calls the Prince of Orange young but other evidence suggests that they are the same age: thirty-three.

16 (p41) It is surprising that Watson does not mention the white elephant, which arrived from Burma earlier that year and disappointed many visitors by proving to be not white at all but the usual elephant-colour with some pink patches on face, neck and chest. The editor of the *Illustrated London News* dismissed it as a 'piebald brute'.

17 (p44) Presumably The Keeper of Manuscripts, who at this time was Mr (later Sir Edward) Maude Thompson, later Principal Librarian and Director of the Museum.

18 (p45) Nor does Watson mention that he has heard the name when Holmes describes John Clay in much the same way in *The Red-Headed League*.

19 (p45)   Czar Alexander II ruled from 1855 to 1881. Colonel Soudekin was himself assassinated in 1883, and Degazeff, a pardoned Nihilist, was accused of the crime.

20 (p50)   Built in the 1770s by Launcelot 'Capability' Brown, Claremont's first owner, Clive of India, committed suicide. The house passed through several hands before being given to Princess Charlotte, the daughter of George IV, who died in childbirth there in 1817. The wife of its previous owner had died in the same manner. Jane Austen, visiting the house about this time, wrote that it seemed 'never to have prospered'. Louis-Philippe, King of the French, died in exile there in 1850. The building is now a school.

21 (p50)   The Duke's dress accords closely with the outfit he wore in Chicago four years earlier, as described in the American press at the time, and quoted in *The Life of the Duke of Albany, the Scholar Prince*. Even the necktie is the same. It was evidently a favourite outfit.

22 (p51)   See the opening chapter of *A Study in Scarlet*, where Watson states that his shoulder was struck by a Jezail bullet during the second Afghan War. Students of the life of Dr Watson have wondered why all subsequent references to his injury place it in his leg. Some have accused him of not knowing where his own wounds were – an unfortunate lacuna for a medical man. Others have charitably suggested that the confusion stems from Watson's innate delicacy of mind, and that his wound was in a more embarrassing location. But see Note 69.

23 (p55)   Not to all her children. See Appendix B.

24 (p55)   The Marquess of Lorne, afterwards tenth Duke of Argyll. He married Queen Victoria's one-eared daughter Louise, but the union was not a success. She was the only one of Victoria's large family to have no children. Lord Lorne was Governor-General of Canada from 1878 to 1883.

25 (p59)   Adolphe, born 1817, reigning Duke of Nassau from 1839 to 1866. Died 1905.

26 (p60)   In *A Case of Identity*, where the Andover parallel is also

mentioned, Watson significantly reports Holmes as adding 'there was something of the sort at The Hague last year'.

27 (p65) Fenians, Invincibles and Irish dynamite: see Appendix A.

28 (p75) But when Watson came to write *A Case of Identity* he gave the heroine a preposterous hat, a vacuous face and the name Mary Sutherland.

Maida Vale, a northern district of London, off the beaten track but easily reached, had become popular at this time as a convenient place for setting up a discreet love-nest, second home or other irregular household. The poet Swinburne visited a flagellation brothel there.

29 (p76) Possibly an elder brother of the street-Arab who worked for Holmes in *The Crooked Man*.

30 (p78) Horace. *Odes*. Book III.6. 'Our parents were feebler than our grand-parents, we are feebler still.' The conclusion is 'our offspring will be even worse than us'. Horace is the only Latin poet from whom Holmes and Watson ever quote.

31 (p78) Or the left eye.

32 (p79) The incident of the man dressed as a woman may strike the contemporary reader as far-fetched, but the principal elements of the scene – even down to the words spoken by the guard – later appeared in an account by A. Conan Doyle of the so-called Rugby Mystery, published in the *Strand Magazine* in July 1898 as 'The Story of the Man with the Watches'. Holmes does not figure in it by name, although 'a well-known criminal investigator' suggests an explanation of the crime. Nineteenth century authors wrote of men dressed as women with an artlessness impossible for their successors.

33 (p81) Popular author of *Carrots, Herr Baby* and other attractive stories for children; of Scottish parentage but born in Rotterdam.

34 (p83) The name of the Duke's medical attendant was Royle not Roylott. Dr Royle served in India in the 1860s and joined the Duke's household in 1875. Later he became a local

government medical inspector, dying at an advanced age in 1919. Roylott is the name of the violent doctor of Stoke Moran (not far from Esher) who was horribly destroyed by his own speckled band. Why Watson altered Royle's name is uncertain, although the exchange that marred their last encounter can hardly have disposed Watson to regard him favourably.

35 (p85)   An early use of the word to mean what I take it to mean. In 1884 *queer* meant peculiar or false, and *queers* could only mean counterfeit notes, e.g. 'I passed him a couple of queers.' The word did not take on its modern association until after 1915, and then only as an adjective. This suggests that Holmes read the manuscript and added the chapter titles some time after that date. Unless it was somebody else.

36 (p86)   King William III and his eldest son, William of Orange – known because of his jaundiced complexion, as 'Citron' – at one time shared the same mistress in Paris.

37 (p88)   Such places of resort as the Golden Lion were not uncommon in mid-Victorian times, although they had virtually disappeared by the end of the century. Whether Watson appreciated precisely where he was is a matter that readers must decide for themselves.

38 (p89)   In the preamble to *The Engineer's Thumb* Watson explains that it was one of only two cases which he was the means of introducing to Holmes's notice, the other being 'that of Colonel Warburton's madness'. As he gives no details of the case, the information contained here is particularly valuable and suggestive.

39 (p94)   A patent boot, advertised as combining a comfortable fit with elegant shape, to be purchased ('CASH ONLY') from an address in Haymarket, London SW.

40 (p95)   At about the same time the Duke of Albany was using very similar words to describe himself. The day after his arrival in Cannes a boat in which he was sailing met with an accident and was wrecked. 'My usual fate,' he observed. 'Disaster to friends as well as to myself.'

41 (p95)   Holmes was right. Upon the death of King William III his daughter Wilhelmina succeeded him as Queen of Holland, and Prince Alexander became a figure irrelevant to history. When Fred J. Lammers came to write the first biography of the Prince in 1979, he was able to use Holmes's own words for the title, *Alexander – De vergeten Kroonprins.*

42 (p100) The only Cartwright mentioned in the published cases is the boy who brought food and messages to Holmes in his Dartmoor hide during the Baskerville Case. He was a London messenger-boy, not a Baker Street ragamuffin. If he was related to Doyle's cabman it suggests that the regular work and improved circumstances of a cabby made it possible to shift a young relative up a rung in the social ladder.

43 (p102) This time they entered the park from the Guildford Road. Many of the hundred-year-old chestnuts survive, and the gatehouse still shows the entwined letters L and H.

44 (p103) Where, indeed!

45 (p106) The explosion occurred at one o'clock on the morning of Tuesday, 26 February. Watson's description of the damage is confirmed by the reports in *The Times* and the *Illustrated London News*. I am unable to reconcile this date with the Leap Year celebration enjoyed by Watson and the Prince of Orange two days previously.

46 (p110) Colonel Hayter, who had come under Watson's professional care in Afghanistan, was responsible for introducing Holmes to the case of 'The Reigate Squires'.

It is tempting to identify Brown with Captain George Ulick Browne of the 12th Bengal Cavalry, who served in Afghanistan from 1879 to 1880, winning a medal and clasp. In 1903 his father succeeded as fifth Marquess of Sligo, and Captain Browne received the courtesy title of Earl of Altamont – the name adopted by Holmes for his secret work in Ireland prior to 1914. Altamont is not a common Irish name, though it was the middle name of Sir Arthur Conan Doyle's father, Charles Altamont Doyle.

47 (p111) It has not proved possible to locate this editorial in the

Standard, although the phraseology certainly captures that newspaper's high Conservative tone. It is remarkably similar to that of a leader published in the *Illustrated London News* after the explosions that wrecked houses in St James's Square later in the year.

48 (p120) Readers of *The Sign of Four* have often been puzzled that Holmes should ask for a bit of card to be tied round his neck, from which he hung a bull's-eye lantern, and clambered up to the roof of Pondicherry Lodge. Hitherto, the consensus of opinion has been that the word is a printer's error – like the Head Llama Holmes claimed to have visited in Tibet. It is now evident that a kind of card must have existed in the nineteenth century that was flexible enough to go round a man's neck and support a lantern while being sufficiently tough to tie together a pair of braces.

49 (p125) Accusations of cheating in this celebrated Paris club became publicly known by the beginning of February.

50 (p132) Dame Emma Albani (1847-1930), born Emma Lajeunesse at Chambly, near Montreal. When this famous soprano made her debut in Milan in 1870 she adopted the name Albani. The choice is thought to relate to her family's removal to Albany, NY, in 1864, where she became a soloist at St Joseph's Church, and the Bishop of Albany advised her to adopt a musical career.

51 (p135) Queen Victoria's residence on the Isle of Wight.

52 (p142) This must be the first recorded sighting of the Ortolan Bunting in the Camargue. 'Its winter home is supposed to be Northern and North-Eastern Africa, but little is really known about it.' Sharpe's *British Birds*, 1896. The Prince's monograph was never written and the winter whereabouts of this attractive bird remained unknown until the publication of G. K. Yeates: *Bird Life in Two Deltas* (1946) settled the matter.

53 (p147) The Prince's foreign orders were carried at his funeral procession. They numbered seventeen (five of them Russian) and included the Elephant, the Black Eagle, the Red Eagle, as well as more recherché honours such as the Nichan El Dem

of Tunis and the Kalakaua of Hawaii. He never received the Garter.

54 (p149) In fact the Derby is a race for 3-year-olds. Watson's knowledge of the Turf was always patchy, even though he betted frequently and regularly lost half his wound pension on futile wagers. Such lack of success is not surprising if his curious ideas concerning racecourse procedure are anything to go by. In *Silver Blaze* odds were apparently quoted at fifteen to five.

55 (p150) Konstantin Pobedonostsev (1827-1907), Alexander III's most reactionary minister. His resistance to change in any form made certain that the revolution when it did come would be all the more savage for the long repression of the most elementary human aspirations.

56 (p151) An apt name for Holmes to adopt. In *The Greek Interpreter*, disclosing a rare detail of family history, he tells Watson that his grandmother was 'the sister of Vernet, the French artist'. He presumably meant Émile Jean Horace Vernet (1789-1863), the painter whose legendary ability to recall the features of a subject after a single glance was a trait he shared with his great-nephew. Many of Vernet's paintings are at Versailles.

57 (p156) As Watson appears to have suspected, and Holmes's evasive answer surely confirms, the Prince of Orange was lucky to emerge safely from the Camargue. It seems all too likely that Holmes made use of the Prince to draw Klee away from the Duke of Albany.

58 (p165) Not motor-cars, of course, in 1884 but wheeled vehicles drawn by horses or men.

59 (p170) Watson's record of the topics of conversation on this evening broadly agrees with other reports, e.g. article by F.H. Myers in the *Fortnightly Review*, May 1884; *Life & Speeches of HRH Prince Leopold, Duke of Albany*, ed. J. R. Ware [not Warre, as printed in the *Dictionary of National Biography*]. Little Prince Frederick ('Frittie') was the first of Queen Victoria's descendants to be killed by his haemophilia. His death plunged the entire family into grief and apprehension.

60 (p173) Alice, later to become Countess of Athlone, born the previous year, and died ninety-eight years later, in 1981. And
Charles, second Duke of Albany and sometime ruling Duke
of Saxe-Coburg, born 1884, died 1955.

61 (p176) The *Illustrated London News* of 5 April 1884 gives a sketch of
the Villa Nevada. The trellis looks insubstantial but Watson
somewhere describes Holmes as 'cat-like' and he evidently
found the ascent within his powers.

62 (p178) According to a contemporary Baedeker, prices for rooms
at the Hotel des Pins, one of the most expensive in Cannes,
ranged between 3 francs and 12 francs. At that time 1fr 25c
was equivalent to 1 shilling (5p). Dinner at the hotel could
be obtained for 5 fr (20p).

63 (p179) Not only does Watson's description of the Duke of Nassau
resemble the villainous Charles Augustus Milverton in
the story of that title, but the Duke's names were Adolphe
William Charles Augustus. It is hard to accept this as
coincidence.

64 (p186) In fairness to Ivan's memory, he struck his son with an iron-
tipped staff in a fit of temper and was overcome with grief
at the effect. On the other hand Peter certainly attended and
may have assisted in the protracted torture of the Czarevich
Alexis.

65 (p187) This is not so.

66 (p188) Holmes means closest in male line of descent. The rela-
tionship was an exceptionally remote one, even for royal
families, King William being seventeenth in descent from
Otto I of Nassau-Dillenburg, and Adolphe eighteenth in
descent from Otto's brother Walram II of Nassau-Weilburg,
who died in 1276.

67 (p189) While Holmes evidently believed in the guilt of the Duke of
Nassau, it should be noted that the Duke admitted nothing
and wrote his letter to Klee under the threat of what smacks
unpleasantly of blackmail. It is suggestive that Watson
places himself at the periphery of the encounter in the
smoking room: close enough to know that something was

going on but not so close that he must admit to knowing what it is.

68 (p191)   The bowl was still at Claremont when Mary Spencer-Warren visited it for the *Strand Magazine*. Her article (January 1895) incudes photographs of the rooms, as they then were, and a portrait of the duchess with her children.

69 (p192)   This scene should also end the long debate as to the location of Watson's Jezail wound (see Note 22). There were *two wounds*, in his shoulder *and* in his leg, the first inflicted at the fatal battle of Maiwand and the second self-inflicted at Claremont. He most frequently mentions the latter injury, which is understandable since it occurred at a time when he was helping Holmes on many of his cases. In time the effects passed away. By the time the two of them set off after the *Hound of the Baskervilles*, Watson was able to say that he was 'reckoned fleet of foot'.

70 (p194)   Daley, alias Denman, was found to have upon him the mechanism of five infernal machines. Burton, who placed the dynamite at Victoria and Charing Cross, was arrested the following January, after further explosions at the House of Commons and the Tower of London.

71 (p194)   On 30 May.

72 (p200)   From 1714 when the Elector of Hanover succeeded his cousin, Queen Anne, to become King George I, until 1840, when the young Queen Victoria married Prince Albert of Saxe-Coburg-Gotha.

73 (p201)   After the revelation in Greville's *Diary* (published 1875) that Victoria's father and his mistress had lived openly together for a quarter of a century there was much speculation that their union had been blessed with issue. See Appendix C.

74 (p204)   Burton, presumably in the absence of Klee, was held to be the director of the dynamiters, and sentenced to penal servitude for life. Daley, conducting his own defence, 'criticized the conduct of the detectives and the little boys who were employed to watch and follow him, describing the boys as being trained up in the vile profession of a police detective'.

Evidently the lesson of the Baker Street Irregulars was being learned by the police.

75 (p210)   Only very recently has any serious attention been given to what would be considered, in a less exalted family, the likely explanation of the presence of the haemophilia gene in Queen Victoria, when none of her royal ancestors had suffered from this disease. She may not have been the child of the man acknowledged to be her father, and therefore had no claim to the throne. In 1819, with the death in child-birth of the future King George IV's only child, Charlotte, it became apparent that the crown would eventually pass to one of his six brothers, none of whom had sired legiti-mate issue, or to one of his five sisters, none of whom was to bear any issue at all. There followed what a hostile press called 'the Scramble to Marry'. The Dukes of Clarence (later King William IV), Kent and Cambridge married German princesses within a year, and each sired a royal babe. After the death of the Clarence daughter in infancy, Princess Victoria of Kent became heir presumptive, and eventually succeeded. Although her mother, also named Victoria, was later supposed to have enjoyed improper relations with the head of her household, there is no reason to infer from this that she did not remain faithful to her husband during his life. The future Queen Victoria was born twelve months after her parents' marriage – which lasted until the Duke of Kent's death the following winter – and her remains have not been examined in order to establish a genetic connec-tion with him. If this were ever to be done, and evidence discovered to be absent, the constitutional implications would indeed be daunting.